A STILL AND AWFUL RED

MICHAEL HOWARTH

TREPIDATIO PUBLISHING

This is a work of fiction. All of the characters, names, incidents, organizations, and dialogue in this novel are either the products of the author's imagination or are used fictitiously.

The views expressed in this work are solely those of the authors and do not necessarily reflect the views of the publisher, and the publisher hereby disclaims any responsibility for them.

ISBN: 978-1-950305-79-7 (sc)
ISBN: 978-1-950305-80-3 (ebook)
Library of Congress Control Number: 2021932660

First printing edition: April 23, 2021
Published by Trepidatio Publishing in the United States of America.
Cover Design and Layout: Mikio Murakami
Edited by Sean Leonard
Proofreading and Interior Layout by Scarlett R. Algee

Trepidatio Publishing, an imprint of JournalStone Publishing
3205 Sassafras Trail
Carbondale, Illinois 62901

Trepidatio books may be ordered through booksellers or by contacting:
JournalStone | www.journalstone.com

For Debra, my mother.

A STILL AND AWFUL RED

HUNGARY
1609

PROLOGUE

I WAS CHOPPING VEGETABLES when they arrived. Had we expected visitors, I would have worn my green woolen dress and clean stockings. I would have washed my face and hands, and brushed the thick knots out of my long black hair. Instead, I wore a dark gray dress that was full of seams and ripped at the bottom of the hemline. There was dirt under my fingernails, and I smelled of wood smoke from the fire. My clogs were covered with carrot shavings, my apron stained red from radishes and rhubarbs.

It was a mid-morning in early March, the fog not yet lifted from the marshes. Above the whistling wind, I heard hooves crunching through the ice and stone as horses descended into the glen. Jumping up from my seat near the fire, I overturned a clay bowl full of vegetables, which hit the earthen floor and shattered. When I knelt down to collect the jagged pieces, I sliced open the top of my thumb. Within seconds, the cut began to throb and bleed.

Cursing my foolishness, I washed my finger in a bucket of cold water and wrapped it tight in a piece of cheesecloth. Then I hurried to the front window and peered through the foggy glass. Two women rounded the bend on chestnut horses. They sat upright, reins clenched in both hands as snowflakes swirled around them in frosty gusts. They did not smile. One woman looked to be about sixty with an angular face and deep wrinkles in her forehead. The other, following directly behind, was a servant girl of no more than eighteen; she was thin and pale, and her eyes were ringed with dark circles. Both women wore red coats and white bonnets, their hands hidden inside thick black mittens.

The horses drew nearer, and soon my skin began to tingle and my stomach began to churn. I moved away from the window, dragging my footsteps as I called for my mother. A sour taste rose up in my mouth.

We did not often receive visitors, especially ones dressed in expensive clothes, and their presence was like a black storm cloud that reveals itself in a bright blue sky.

My mother was down in the root cellar, storing bacon and salted cabbage. She climbed up from the rickety ladder, swept the broken shards into a far corner, and opened the door just as the women were hitching their horses to the ramshackle fence that encircled our cottage. She welcomed them inside and offered them each a cup of hot cider. They refused. The servant girl closed the door and stood silent, glancing down at the cut-up vegetables still strewn across the floor.

The older woman removed her mittens and handed them to the servant girl, then took off her bonnet and laid it on the table. Her hair was snow white, knotted and disheveled, and though she seemed somewhat frail—as evidenced by the heavy limp that shuffled her into the cottage—her face shone with power and determination. Her eyes roamed over the birch shelves that my father had built, past the cast-iron pots and pans hanging on the walls, until they came to rest on the tiny straw mattress I shared with my mother.

"What a charming little shack." She tried to sound warm and proper, like a stranger come in from the cold, but I could detect the disgust that was hidden in her brittle voice. "Almost like something out of a fairy tale," she said.

I bit my lower lip and crossed my arms, then stared down at the floor. Fairy tales were for people who were privileged enough to have hopes and dreams, but I was not even allowed to go to school. Whenever I went into the village to trade eggs and cheese for muslin, I would curse the library and university, angry that their sturdy oak doors would not yield to a hardworking peasant girl. I could read and write better than most landowners, but I was denied an education because I lived in a thatched cottage, smelled like tallow wax, and wore splintered wooden clogs.

In my world, there were no elegant dances and ballroom feasts, only droughts and famines. Heroic deeds were replaced with cruelties, and instead of magical spells and enchantments, I witnessed peasants succumb to cholera and consumption. Each year ended not with riches and true love, but with the nobles raising our taxes and pushing us deeper into the cracked earth.

The old woman approached me. "You are Maria?"

I glanced over at my mother, who nodded.

"Yes," I told her.

"My name is Anna Darvolia. I have ridden a long way to meet with you."

I curtsied in one quick movement, my knees knocking together.

"You should be more polite when receiving special guests." She took a long look around the room. "Though I expect you don't get many, do you?"

I blushed. "I'm sorry, miss."

"How old are you?" she asked.

"Sixteen."

Anna took my chin in her bony hand and turned my head to the side, stroking my cheek with a thick, callused finger. "I've heard rumors that you are quite fetching, and it seems they are not at all false. Soft skin, no marks or blemishes, a healthy complexion." She surveyed me from top to bottom. "You are quite the specimen."

"Thank you, miss."

She grabbed a hank of my hair and smelled it. "Do you bathe regularly?"

"Yes, miss."

"Fleas or lice?"

"No, never."

She glanced around the room. "And where is your father?"

"Dead."

"Of what?"

"Heart sickness."

"Ah, of course." She tapped a long, yellow fingernail against the center of my chest. "Peasants rely too much on a heavy heart. It pumps them full of misguided dreams...convinces them to kneel in the dirt so they can fantasize about silk robes and full bellies. And then they have the gall to be surprised when all of those dreams fester like a runny sore, when their hearts burst open and they collapse in a pile of filthy straw, their eyes staring at nothing, which is exactly what they've been their entire lives."

I forced a smile. "My mother and I are quite happy here. We do not want for anything."

Anna's face tightened and then, for the first time since entering the cottage, she looked directly into my eyes. "You are a seamstress, yes?"

I nodded, remembering that cold, gray morning when my father took my hand and said, "You are smart, Maria, but they do not want you to be smart. They want you to be productive. So you must learn a trade. Or master a particular skill." We were walking through the village, watching a young girl beg for food. She was barefoot, her knees and elbows caked with mud, and her long blonde hair hung over her thin shoulders like frayed string. Papa hugged me and said, "If you are not skilled, then you are not useful. And if you are not useful, then you will not survive."

Anna snapped her fingers, just inches from my nose. "Pay attention, lazybones. I did not travel all this way to have my time wasted by a skinny lout."

"I'm sorry, miss."

"Stop being sorry," she told me. "Instead, be courteous and obliging, like a well-mannered farm girl."

I nodded, uncertain what I should say, or even how I should say it. I looked toward my mother for guidance, but she stood silent in the corner.

"What fabrics have you worked with?" Anna asked.

"Cotton, wool, velvet, linen…"

"Silk?"

I nodded again.

"Show me something you've made."

I walked over to a trunk in the corner, opened it, and removed a blue wool dress I had sewn the previous spring. Anna took it in her hands and inspected the seams and stitching, paying careful attention to the bodice and pleats. She held it up by the firelight, mumbling to herself as she gazed at the fabric and rubbed it between her fingers.

"Your skills are acceptable," she said.

"Thank you, miss."

She handed the dress to my mother, who folded it up and returned it to the trunk.

"How long have you been a seamstress?" Anna asked me.

"About six years."

"How often do you sew?"

"Every day, miss. Usually in the afternoons after I finish my chores."

"Do you know how to trim and backstitch and embroider?"

"As well as a blacksmith knows his anvil," I said.

Anna glanced down at the bloody cheesecloth wrapped around my thumb. "Running with scissors, perhaps?"

I felt my face flush. "It was an accident. With a knife."

She frowned. "I hope you are not as clumsy threading a needle."

"No, miss."

"Peasants are always spilling their blood." She said this to no one in particular, but laughed anyway, as though she had told a clever joke. "Wherever they go, they leave a trail of red filth behind them."

I cleared my throat. "Perhaps they bleed to feel more alive."

"They bleed," she said, "because they are too stubborn to accept their God-given position. Instead of cultivating pastures, they cultivate childish revolts."

I bit the inside of my cheek as drops of sweat collected on my forehead. "Some say they fight for noble causes."

Her eyes narrowed. "I hope you sew with as much passion as you speak."

My mother shushed me.

Anna stepped closer until she was inches from my face. "How, pray tell, is it possible to fight for a noble cause, to fulfill a higher purpose, when you're writhing on the ground and bleeding out like a stuck pig?"

I said nothing. This was a battle that had raged for centuries, debated and defended in churches and cottages and castles, and the silence in-between was constantly filled with mass graves and broken families. To the nobles, we peasants were nothing more than thin shadows, unappreciative children who, if left unsupervised, were sure to offend God and wreak havoc on the countryside.

"You are a simple girl," Anna said with a dismissive wave of her hand, "who is simply making excuses for a life she does not understand. No matter how many dresses you stitch together, my little Maria, you will never dig your way out of this shack."

She was right, of course. My condition was inherited, passed down from generation to generation like an ancient curse, a symptom of lack and neglect. Here, in the village of Trenčín, at the base of the Little Carpathians, there was always the threat of war and famine and disease. Peasants had to claw out a living from year to year, in constant fear of losing a child to starvation, or waking up in debtor's prison. They lived in cruck houses made of mud and straw and manure, the flimsy walls bursting with typhoid and plague; they worked every day, except for Sundays and holy days, their bodies pocked with scars, their bones dented with arthritis while they harvested corn and threshed the grains; they asked for medicine and died of smallpox; they clamored for land reform and saw their crops torched; they prayed to Heaven and wound up stabbed in a shallow ditch by the side of the road; and those who were brave enough to incite rebellion had their tongues ripped out with metal tongs.

My mother stepped forward and spoke, her voice ringing with pride. "My Maria can spin a skein of French silk into a beautiful ball gown in only three days' time."

"I've no doubt." Anna looked down at the floor and kicked at a dusty piece of carrot. "Fresh vegetables are so difficult to obtain during the winter months, especially for your kind."

"If you wish," my mother said, "you can make inquiries in the village."

"Inquiries have already been made," Anna said. "I do not travel this far from Čachtice Castle on a mere hunch."

I must have looked startled, for she smiled.

"You are familiar with Čachtice Castle?"

I nodded. Though I had never seen it, the castle was an elaborate royal residence, a grand display of towers and turrets that sat high on a hill in the nearby village of Čachtice.

"Then you must know that I am here on behalf of the Countess?"

"Yes, miss." I knew little about Elizabeth Báthory except that her family was one of the wealthiest and most powerful in all of Hungary. She had inherited the castle—and seventeen villages, including Trenčín—when she married Francis Nádasdy, a national war hero.

"I have traveled here today," Anna said, "to offer you good pay for steady work."

My lips parted as the tension within me unspooled in a sudden rush, like air being released from a bellows. This visit, then, was not so surprising. Local peasants, especially young ones such as myself, often provided for their families—whether they wanted to or not—by undertaking well-paid work for royalty.

"A seamstress?" I asked.

"The Countess requests that you design a series of gowns appropriate for a woman of her esteem. You will have all the materials and equipment you desire. Do you understand?"

"Yes," I said.

"Good." Anna took her bonnet off the table. "The Countess has, shall we say, unique tastes, so you may suggest ideas, but she is the one who will approve them. Is that clear?"

"Yes," I said again.

She looked at my dirty dress. "The Countess will provide you with more suitable clothes, but you may pack a few personal belongings, if you wish."

"Pack, miss? But…where am I going?"

She glared at me. "Her Ladyship's castle, of course."

I opened my mouth to speak, but the words slid back down my throat. In my entire life, I had never traveled more than an hour away from our cottage. I had dreamed about it often enough—my stomach fluttering as I bounded out the door to journey down unfamiliar roads—but the idea had always seemed distant and fantastic, like being granted three wishes in some exotic fairy tale.

"You should be more gracious," Anna said. "One does not often migrate from a shack to a castle." She shrugged. "Still, if you prefer to continue grubbing in the mud, then I can certainly oblige you…"

"No, of course not. It's just…" I looked at Mama, my amazement changing to apprehension. "But…who will take care of you? Who will tend to the animals and…"

"I will be fine, Maria."

"Yes, but…"

"My bones may be old, but they haven't yet cracked. I can feed the animals and watch over the cottage, and if I require help then I will ask someone in the village." She put her arm around me. "Your talents have reached wider and more important circles, and this is a fortunate opportunity you should not squander."

"The Countess is currently in Vienna, but she will return to the castle in three weeks' time," Anna said. "At which point she will send a guide to escort you to the castle. Once you arrive, she will meet with you in private to discuss her expectations in further detail." She turned to my mother. "The Countess is willing to pay you three gold pieces, one piece per gown, as well as one forint per month for the girl's services."

I leaned against the wall, my heart racing as I wondered about life at the castle. Would I have my own bedroom, or would I share it with other servants? Would the Countess give me fine dresses and shoes? Would she permit me to explore the gardens and grounds?

"Maria!" My mother gave me a stern look and motioned toward Anna, who stood in front of me, glowering.

"Apologies," I mumbled.

Anna reached out and took hold of my bloody thumb. She squeezed it, hard, and I cried out. "I pray the girl does not drift off and lose focus, especially when she is being paid to embroider and stitch, and to cut such expensive fabric."

I jerked my thumb away. "I won't, miss."

"Good," she said, smiling. "Because the Countess does not tolerate mistakes."

"I understand."

Anna stared down at her own finger, now smeared with my blood. "You would do well to remember that, my dear. You see, there are far worse inflictions than a nasty cut."

CHAPTER I

THE NIGHT BEFORE I left for Čachtice Castle, I sat with my mother in front of the fireplace. She was resting in her rocking chair, humming an old folk song while I knelt on the floor with my head in her lap, my face turned toward the window. I was nervous and sweaty, and a thin nightgown clung to my skin. I stared outside, watching clouds float past the full moon, listening to pieces of wood pop in the fire.

"Do you think the Countess will like me?" I asked.

"You are not royalty, Maria. Which means, at best, the Countess will merely tolerate you. She will not dote on you, or ask your opinion. In fact, I would be surprised if she looks you in the eye while speaking to you."

"Then I will kill her with kindness," I said.

"Please do. The way you greet her will determine how she welcomes you. Remember, royalty demands respect and hard work, and as long as you provide the Countess with both, she won't object to your presence."

"But what if the work is too difficult?"

Mama patted my hand. "You are obsessing, my child. It is fine to be nervous, but don't paint the devil onto the wall."

I nestled my cheek into her wool blanket, grinning as I imagined how the villagers would react when they learned that the Countess had chosen me as her personal seamstress. I stood up and studied each of my fingers, as if recognizing for the first time their true value. "What kind of gowns do you think she'll want me to sew?"

"Something grand and expensive, most likely. Either for her, or for her children."

"I'll leave you my pins and needles," I told her. "And there's extra thread and fabric in the cupboard. I have a few projects still unfinished, but..."

"I'll attend to them," she said, coughing. "I am fully capable of sewing in your absence, though I don't pretend to be quite as skilled."

She smiled at her concession, and I nodded my appreciation. Mama was a fine seamstress herself, and garnered much respect from the village folk—the nobles included—but when I was ten years old it soon became apparent that I possessed a special talent for weaving and sewing, my fingers gliding across satin and silk without pause or hesitation, never so much as a pinprick or a torn stitch. My patchwork was flawless, my seam lines were always centered, and I could thread a needle in two seconds.

Ever since Papa died, I had been supporting Mama by making dresses and gowns, shirts and breeches, and curtains and quilts. I worked hard, sometimes seven days a week, my fingers sore and my thumbs callused. Though we were not poor—Papa had left us enough money for our basic necessities—I felt an obligation to provide for Mama, and I strove to ensure that the two of us always had clean clothes and that we would never starve.

I glanced around our cottage, amazed that so much had changed in just a few short years—and was still changing. I remembered Papa leaving his parchments to stretch on large wooden racks; I remembered him rising early each morning to soak the calfskins in water—to remove all the blood and grime—and how he'd lime them and scrape them with his curved knife before bringing them back inside to dry. Even though paper was becoming cheaper and more fashionable, many nobles had continued to order Papa's parchment for their notes and important documents, and the priest in Trenčín had commissioned him to create devotional pictures and communion cards to sell to the parishioners.

I had grown up surrounded by vellum decorated with angels and flowers, books bound with stiffened leather, and scrolls tied with strings piled high on shelves and tables. When I wasn't sewing or caring for the animals, I was reading fantastic stories about brave princes fighting ogres and giants; treasure chests filled with gold and silver; children lost in enchanted forests; and far-away kingdoms filled with genies and tricksters and magical creatures.

Content with reading and sewing, and taking care of Mama when she allowed me to, I had never considered living a different life, much less one that existed beyond our ramshackle fence. But tomorrow, for the first time ever, I would leave home all by myself, and the overwhelming sense of freedom I felt was both exhilarating and terrifying.

My mother coughed again, and I wrapped the blanket around her shoulders. "Promise me that you'll take care of yourself while I'm away," I said.

She bowed her head. "Your wish is my command."

"And if you have any aches or pains, then go to the village and buy some herbs, or make yourself a poultice."

"I'll be fine," she told me. "Now go and pack. It's late, and you need to sleep. You don't want to meet the Countess with dark circles under your eyes."

Staring into the fire, I remembered a story I'd heard once in the village—whispered in the shadows by a young boy—about a servant girl who had stolen a coin during her first week at the castle. As punishment, the coin was heated under a flame and the girl was forced to clutch it in the palm of her hand until she fainted from the blistering pain.

I knelt down and took my mother's hand. "Do you think it's true that the Countess is a cruel woman?"

Mama stroked my long, black hair. "I think she is a lonely woman. Her husband died a few years ago, just like Papa. That kind of emptiness leaves a deep hole that can sometimes be covered, but it can never be filled."

"I'll return home as soon as I finish sewing the gowns," I told her. "And I'll try to write you whenever time allows."

"Don't return home just for me," she said. "Return home so you can settle down and prepare a future that involves more than simply sitting in a dark corner and sewing...or worrying about your poor mother."

"How cruel," I said, winking. "You make me sound like an old spinster."

She laughed again. "You are far too beautiful to be hobbling around in a forgetful haze. You should be courting and preparing for marriage."

"If I were royalty...like the Countess...then I would already be married, perhaps with a child."

"Then be happy you were born a peasant and not a noble," she said. "It means you can marry for love instead of strategy."

I was silent for a moment. "Do you think Papa would approve of me going to Čachtice?"

She kissed the top of my head. "You are a woman now, and he would want you to make your own decisions."

Somehow, that comforted me, but when I thought again about leaving our tiny cottage I had to fight back tears. I stood up and hugged my mother. "Everything seems both wonderful and terrible at the same time."

"Stop feeling guilty," she said. "You are not abandoning me."

I thought of my father and how I might have been able to save him if I'd acted sooner, if I hadn't let the fear weigh me down until I stumbled home in a daze and called for my mother. The memory of that day was a poison infecting my mind, a deep bruise pulsing with heat, and I winced in pain whenever I remembered how much confusion I had felt when faced with the daunting task of making such an important decision all by myself.

Though years had passed since Mama and I buried him on the small hill overlooking our cottage, the wound was still as fresh as ever, and perhaps always would be. Now, all I could do was close my eyes and remember how the wood chips clung to his cotton shirt in autumn when he returned from the forest at sundown, cradling a pile of wood in one hand and his axe in the other, or how the roughness of his beard scratched my cheek whenever he kissed me goodnight.

Nervous, I lit a candle and walked across the room to my small trunk, which sat beside our bed. The latch was broken, and the warped lid no longer closed completely shut. A gray frock spilled over the rusted metal edge like a pale tongue poking out of a gaping mouth. I grabbed a handful of clothes and tossed them onto the bed. I didn't know which clothes I should bring to Čachtice Castle, but none seemed pretty enough. Most of my dresses had patches where I had stitched up the rips and tears, and my stockings were frayed beyond repair.

After staring for several minutes, I selected the blue woolen dress I had shown to Anna Darvolia and draped it over a chair in the corner. I would wear it tomorrow when I met with the Countess. I balled up the rest of my clothes and shoved them into the trunk. After digging out a pair of cracked sheepskin sandals, which were comelier than my clunky wooden clogs, I rummaged around the bottom of the trunk, my fingers skimming over bonnets and tunics, until I found a small pine box.

Inside was a pendant my father had given to me on my tenth birthday, a Celtic love knot. I removed it from the box and held it up, admiring how the firelight reflected off the braided chain. It was the prettiest thing I owned, supposedly made from Irish silver mined on the outskirts of Killarney, and I thought the Countess might be impressed by such finery. I shut the trunk and placed the love knot around my neck, smiling as the cold metal rested against my warm skin. With my blue woolen dress and a pair of sandals, perhaps I might not embarrass myself when I arrived at the castle.

I walked across the room and knelt below the front window, admiring my father's trunk, which was a rich chestnut brown, the dome top covered in embossed tin. I opened it and inhaled the musty smell of his books, all seven of them lined up side by side, each one bound in leather with its title presented on the spine in gold stamping. These were the only books we owned, and we read them over and over again, night after night, until I had memorized entire passages. I wanted so much to take them with me to Čachtice, or perhaps just one that I could read by candlelight if I ever became homesick, but I feared they might be lost or stolen.

My eyes roamed over the titles: *The Odyssey*; *The Epic of Gilgamesh*; *Beowulf*; Dante's *Inferno*; Aristotle's *Poetics*; and *The Decameron* by Boccaccio. Each book had been given to my father by a nobleman who had commissioned him to bind particular works, and who had been pleased with the results. Often, these nobles desired new copies of books they already owned, and my father was asked to create decorative bindings that included gold and silver, pieces of ivory, or various jewels set into the cover to enhance the stitching.

I skimmed my fingers over each book, then whispered a goodbye and closed the lid. Papa had been proud of those books, honored with all the praises showered upon him by those who were not obligated in the least to commend his work, and I hoped that my time with the Countess would produce those same feelings of pleasure and fulfillment.

The fire was dying down, so I stoked the coals and added another log. Outside, the wind blew hard, rattling the windows.

My mother continued to rock in her chair. She glanced over at the dress and sandals I had chosen for tomorrow's journey. "You travel light, Maria. Except for your heart, which is so heavy it drags along the floor whenever you take a step."

"I don't want to burden myself," I told her, raising my voice. "Ms. Darvolia said the Countess will provide me with clothes."

She looked at me with a face as worn as leather. "You can't change out of your own skin. No matter how many luxuries the Countess provides, you will always be a servant girl from Trenčín."

"You don't think I'm worthy of such luxuries?" I asked, stung by her candor.

"You are capable and deserving, yes," she said. "But there are certain privileges a peasant can never hope to receive, no matter how many stars she wishes upon."

I bent down and kissed her cheek. "I'm tired, Mama. Goodnight."

She stood up and handed me the blanket, then reached out to touch my pendant, feeling its weight in the palm of her hand. "At least your father will be close by."

I crawled into bed and pulled the covers up to my chin, staring outside at the half moon above me. Scattered clouds drifted past, and thin branches scratched the sky with jagged swipes. Papa once told me that if a person makes a wish on a silver moonbeam, she will have a long and prosperous life, and at that moment I thought about the future that lay ahead of me on a road full of twists and turns. I thought about the Countess and the rigid demands she might make, and if all her cronies were as cruel as Anna Darvolia. I thought about knitting and stitching and becoming a revered seamstress, of living in a great house with Mama, our bellies always full and a carriage ready to carry us back and forth across a busy city where people knew my name and greeted me with respect.

Sometimes, the constant hope of wanting to survive is so heavy that a person's dreams cannot lift her into the clouds, but for the first time in my life I felt like I had been handed a magic carpet that could take me anywhere. I didn't know how long I could hold onto it, or even where it might bring me, but I intended to ride it into the heavens and never look back.

My mother blew out the candles and lay down beside me. The cottage was quiet and dark save for the flickering firelight that cast deep shadows on the empty walls. Closing my eyes, I breathed in the familiar scents of peat and dried meat and fresh baked bread, hoping that the same moon now shining outside my dirty window would look bigger and brighter the next time I gazed at it from my room inside Čachtice Castle.

CHAPTER II

I AWOKE JUST BEFORE dawn. Not wanting to incur bad luck, I stepped out of bed with my right foot first and patted the impression I'd left in the straw mattress. I threw on an old brown dress and a sheepskin cloak, ate some deer jerky, and stepped outside to fetch a bucket of water and collect rushes for kindling. Upon returning home, I built a fire and took a long hot bath, making sure to wash my face and hands and under my arms, scrubbing especially hard behind my ears and on the soles of my feet.

I put on my blue woolen dress, smoothing it out as best I could, then brushed my hair and slipped into my sandals. When Mama woke up, we sat together by the fire, neither of us speaking, just watching the embers glow red as the flames hissed and crackled. Daylight crept into the room, the sun rising over the mountains, and while Mama hummed her folk songs I leaned against the window and watched the narrow path outside, waiting to see who would come around the bend on horseback.

That someone was Benedict Deseo, who arrived in the late morning as gusts of wind roared through the valley to sweep thin swirls of snow into the chilly air. He seemed like a giant, over six feet tall, and when he rode into view his presence cast a shadow over everything around him, like a dark cloud blocking out the sun. Behind him trotted a second horse, much smaller than his own, and tethered to his red saddle.

I opened the door before he could knock, and curtsied. "Good morning, sir."

He took off a black fur hat and stepped inside the cottage, crouching down so his head wouldn't hit the top of the door. He introduced himself as the court master for Countess Báthory, in charge of all estates surrounding Čachtice Castle. He looked to be around thirty-five, with thin eyebrows, a hawk-like nose, and two brown moles on his right cheek.

Thick black hair hung down to his shoulders, and a scruffy beard wrapped around the lower half of his face, jutting out from the end of his chin in a long, sharp point.

But what unsettled me most were the two scars on his face. The smaller one extended across his forehead like a thin piece of white thread. The longer one slashed across his entire face; it began above his left ear and ran in a diagonal line across his cheek where it cut into his upper lip and disappeared into the tuft of his beard. It looked as if his face had been smashed into pieces and then reassembled.

My mother asked Benedict if he wanted something to eat or drink, but he waved her away.

"The Countess expects us by late afternoon," he said. "We mustn't keep her waiting."

I stood between the two of them, hands folded in front of me as I stared down at the floor, waiting for a handful of words to fill up the silence. For the past three weeks all I'd thought about was saying goodbye and leaving home; I'd thought about the long journey to Čachtice, of meeting the Countess and being accepted into her circle like an old friend come to visit.

But now that the time had finally come to step outside and close the door, I couldn't seem to put one foot in front of the other.

Mama spun me around and threw her arms around my waist. She held me tight and tried not to cry.

Benedict stood in the entryway, tapping his boot against the floor, his gray watery eyes unmoved by our separation.

I kissed her cheek and pulled away. "I will write when I can," I told her. "There should be enough firewood to last until the thaw. There are jarred apples and pears in the root cellar, and there are extra blankets in my trunk if you get cold."

"Stop worrying," she said, taking my hand. "I'm not your responsibility."

"Do you have any belongings?" Benedict asked me.

I blushed. "Only what I have on me."

He motioned toward my dress. "Wear a coat. The wind is frigid." He smiled, but it was crooked and tight, as if it might slide off his face.

I nodded, and suddenly felt very much like a lowly peasant girl. He wore a hefty red coat, the collar lined with otter fur, while I had the sheepskin cloak and a pair of mittens that were riddled with holes and tears.

Mama rummaged through her trunk and brought out a thick, gray coat. She shook it out, and a cloud of dust floated across the room.

Sticking out of the left pocket was an old white handkerchief, the edges threadbare. One corner was stained with blood from when Mama had sliced open her thumb while preparing goulash with sweet paprika.

She pressed the handkerchief into my hands. "Here is a piece of me. To keep you safe from evil spirits."

I smiled and tucked the handkerchief into my bosom, close to my heart so as to indulge her superstitious beliefs.

"And don't look back when you ride away," she said, "or you'll leave all your good luck at home."

Smiling, I took off my cloak and tossed it onto the bed. Mama wrapped the gray coat around my shoulders and buttoned it up, her face streaked with tears.

Benedict sighed and folded his arms. "The Countess."

"Wait." Mama reached into the trunk and pulled out a faded green hood, which she pressed into my mittened hands.

I slipped the hood over my head and fastened it around my neck. "Thank you."

"Be mindful of the Countess," Mama whispered into my ear. "And keep your tongue still."

I kissed her one last time and together we followed Benedict outside into the blinding sunshine. I climbed onto my horse and waved goodbye, my face buried in the hood to protect it from the cold. Then, with Benedict leading the way, I gripped the reins tight, squeezed my calves against the horse's sides, and rode away from the only place I had ever called home.

For the first hour we traveled in silence. The trail led up and over a series of low wooded hills, the rocks still slippery with broad patches of ice. In the warming sunshine, the melting snow flowed off in trickles, running across the ground in tiny brown rivers. Soon, they became enormous mud puddles, and the horses splashed through them as the trail became less rocky, strewn with crunching leaves and yellowed pine needles.

Later, when the sun was high in the sky, we wove through a long valley of rolling meadows. In the distance, small ponds lay nestled against the base of the Little Carpathians, their tops still crusted over with thin layers of ice, some of which were beginning to crack and split open. Low stone walls lined the country path, and red-necked grebes flew overhead in flashes of color, wailing into the gusting wind.

Rounding a wide bend, we passed cottages with thatched roofs and thick, white smoke pouring out of the chimneys. Brown cows grazed in the fields while farmers fed their chickens and goats, and mended their fences; they smoked clay pipes and dug into the hard earth with rusted shovels. A small girl played in the dirt with a stick, stabbing at patches of ice while a dog ran around her in circles. Farther on down the road, two young boys sat atop a fence and peeled potatoes that they dropped into a small bucket at their feet.

Most folks did not look up as we rode by, though some of the older ones made the sign of the cross and pointed two fingers toward us. An emaciated woman wearing a ratty shawl scowled at us from across the trail. A few goats wandered around at her feet, and a scraggly cat meowed from the front door where the woman stood half-hidden, sweeping out a thick brown cloud of dust. She picked up the hem of her dress, which was ripped and covered in mud, and hurried inside the cottage, slamming the splintered door behind her.

Benedict reined in his horse and pulled up alongside me. "Pay them no attention. They are a naïve breed. They fear ghouls and goblins, and believe there are demons hiding in the trees. They fear the Nachtkrapp will steal their children if they wander too far from home."

The Nachtkrapp was a giant raven-like bird with thick black feathers and a wingspan wider than the average man. My father told me that it lived deep in the forest and left its nest at night to scavenge the countryside for small children. Once its prey had been carried back to its nest, which was constructed out of skins and bones, the Nachtkrapp would strip away the soft flesh and devour the child limb by limb until finally pecking out its still-beating heart.

"But what is it that frightens them now?" I asked.

He raised one eyebrow.

"Me? But...why?"

"You are a pale, beautiful creature that has stepped out of the dark woods. You might be a witch, or even the devil's mistress." He stared straight ahead, his lips curving into a smile. "Who knows what curses you might bestow with such an innocent gaze?"

"I am no demon," I said, raising my voice. "My weapons of choice are needle and thread, not hellish chants."

"But I've been told you can read and write. To some, those are magical powers, indeed."

"Magical, no," I said. "Necessary, yes."

He frowned. "A peasant's daily meanderings should not require the use of parchment and quill."

"Only because they haven't been taught their respected value. My father believed that being educated makes people fit company for themselves."

"In that case, you may find the company at Čachtice a tad lacking," he said. "Though you will find the Countess to be quite learned. Even more so than King Matthias. She is trained in the classics, mathematics, and botany. And she can read and write in Hungarian, Greek, Latin, and German."

"Her Ladyship must be an exceptional woman," I said.

Benedict grunted, which I took as acknowledgement. "Was it your father who taught you to read and write?"

I nodded.

"What was his trade?"

"Parchment maker," I said.

"Ah, of course. A man who creates paper must be a lover of words. A blank sheet of paper is like a body without a soul."

"Papa didn't own many books," I said. "Mostly chapbooks and sonnet collections. His most prized possession was a hardbound copy of *The Odyssey*. It was given to him by an archduke who admired his craftsmanship."

"You have read *The Odyssey*?"

"Yes, several times." I felt bolder and sat a bit straighter, my voice growing louder. "Sometimes, after supper, Papa would read parts of it aloud. After a while he taught me how to write letters and build sentences. I would copy down poems and passages using spare bits of parchment."

For the first time since we'd left Trenčín, Benedict turned to look at me, his gaze so intense I thought it might knock me off my horse like a punch to the stomach. His scar rippled when he spoke, gleaming like fresh bone against crimson skin stretched taut by the cold.

"A woman should learn in silence with all subjection," he told me. "She should submit herself to her master with all respect, not only to the good and gentle, but also to the cruel."

In the afternoon we rode into a deep forest, the branches gnarled and withered, reaching up toward an ashen sky filled with storm clouds that were cracked and brittle. Our progress slowed as the trails became more narrow and twisted, and I was forced to keep my head low to avoid the sharp branches that slapped at us in the cutting wind.

I was thirsty and asked Benedict if we could stop for a few moments at a small river we were approaching. He grumbled his approval and I stepped down from my horse, careful not to slip on the patches of melting ice. Lifting the bottom of my dress, I cupped my hands and knelt at the riverbank, sipping the icy water until my throat hurt.

"Fill this." He rode over and handed me a ceramic flask.

I pulled out the stopper and leaned forward, pushing the flask as far down into the depths as my arm would extend. The water gurgled and glugged like a baby cooing, and tiny bubbles broke on the surface. I scooted closer to the edge, pressing my fist into the mud so I wouldn't tumble into the river.

And right then—as I bent forward to jiggle the flask, to fill those last remaining bits of space—my mother's handkerchief fell out of my dress. I lurched forward with a gasp, but it spun through the blustery air and landed in the middle of the river.

There was nothing I could do but crouch there at the mucky edge. I had one hand committed to duty, the other to balance. In my panic I almost dropped the flask.

"The Countess," Benedict said as he stroked his horse's mane. "We mustn't keep her waiting while you prattle about."

I stood up, put the stopper back in its place, and handed him the flask. He sat there, looking down on me with indifference. I wanted to pelt him with dirty snow and push him off his horse. Instead, I turned away in anger, cursing the swift current as I watched my mother's handkerchief float around a bend and disappear from sight.

I didn't speak for the rest of our travels. While Benedict drank from his full flask, I clasped the reins and glanced behind me every so often, as if hoping my handkerchief had tired of its swim and was now following me home like an obedient lapdog.

Except I wasn't going home. I was traveling to a distant kingdom where I would meet the Countess and begin a new life. I would be handed expensive fabrics and asked to weave a masterpiece. In some ways I still felt dizzied by all the attention, like I had stepped inside a soothing dream. But as Benedict and I journeyed farther and farther into the dense woods—increasing the distance between Mama and me, and everything I had ever known—the more tense I became, eyes widening as I shifted around on my horse with fidgeting hands and sidelong glances.

Čachtice Castle sat high on a steep hill, and as we entered the village I could see it rising above me, the banks covered with flowers and plants in various stages of decay. The left side sloped away to a field covered in clods of dirt and straggly weeds, the edges of which bordered a gloomy forest. The entire right side was perched on a precipice with enormous roots and branches that protruded from giant crevices zigzagging through great slabs of rock.

In front of us, a winding dirt path snaked its way up to an iron gatehouse, lodged in place by a thick stone wall that stood thirty feet high and encircled the expansive grounds. Keeping watch at both ends of the castle were two gothic towers, each stretching high into the sky, their pointed tops piercing the storm clouds that swirled above us.

I followed behind Benedict, my face stinging from the frigid air. We passed through the center of the village where a large crowd was gathered. Benedict explained that a peasant boy, not yet fifteen, had stolen livestock from the Countess. For his punishment he was sentenced to be sewn alive inside a dead horse.

I watched, horrified, as the boy was stripped naked in the street and his hands tied behind his back. His legs were burned with red-hot irons, and my stomach lurched at the long wisps of smoke rising into the air. I pressed a fist into my mouth and fought back the urge to vomit, shaking my head as black spots swam before my eyes.

The boy was beaten by the local magistrate, his back lacerated by a bullwhip, his face kicked in until he choked on his own teeth. I wanted to look away, but I had never seen anything so grotesque. I was captivated by noblemen in fine clothes slinging curses and insults, by the mob of dirty children who assaulted him with stones and rotten apples.

As our horses climbed the hill, I turned to glance behind me, watching as three guards dragged the boy into the village square. They pulled out their swords and cut long, forceful strokes into the underbelly of the decomposing animal. They ripped open a large flap of skin, peeling it back to expose a jagged hole, the edges stiff with ice and matted with congealed blood. I saw bones poking out, the ribs curved inward like pincers. The stomach and intestines spilled out onto the street, and then the boy was shoved inside the horse—head first, thrashing from side to side—his screams fading to silence as needle and thread entombed him.

CHAPTER III

A GIRL MY OWN age met us at the gatehouse. Benedict handed her his coat and hat, and asked if my room had been made ready. She nodded, said the Countess was expecting us, then collected my coat and mittens. I swung myself off the horse and steadied both feet on the ground, my legs wobbling as the boy's piercing shrieks continued to beat against my skull.

The courtyard in which we stood was a vast puddle of brown slush. Goosebumps rose on my arms and legs as a freezing wind whistled through large cracks in the crumbling stone walls. A few chickens ran around—clucking and pecking at the soggy ground—and a mangy dog growled at me before creeping closer to sniff my dress. I lifted the green hood off my head and lowered it onto my shoulders, feeling dwarfed by the huge castle now looming over me.

We stepped inside the foyer, which was cold and musty. I had expected it to feel warm and cozy, but the windows were small and high up, providing little sunlight save for dusty streaks that barely had strength enough to gleam. Immediately, I noticed there were mirrors everywhere. Small ones sat atop fireplaces and tables, while full-length ones hung from the walls, their beveled borders edged in shimmering jewels.

I saw few servants, and those who passed me did not look up, but rushed by carrying linen sheets and crystal goblets, or copper chamber pots. The main corridor was long and narrow, lit by large torches mounted on both sides of the ancient walls. Their distorted flames flickered into the murky passage like monstrous fingers beckoning me to follow.

We climbed a lavish staircase to the third floor of the west tower. The corridors were more expansive here, and the windows were wider and taller, filling the hall with pockets of light that reflected off the stone floors. My leather sandals slapped against the ground with each hurried footstep as I strove to keep up with Benedict, who seemed to glide through the darkness.

We reached an oak door at the end of a long passage. It was partway open, but Benedict rapped on it several times.

From inside the room came a voice. "Enter."

I'd thought royalty was supposed to sound prim and proper—smooth like a well-ironed tablecloth—but her Ladyship's command was strong and confident with a sinister tinge lurking just beneath the surface, as if a sheet of ice had crusted over a pond and might break open at the slightest disturbance.

Her voice put me on guard, knotting my stomach and raising the tiny hairs on the back of my neck. I looked at Benedict, waiting to follow him into the room, but he stepped aside and motioned for me to go in alone. I touched my pendant and smoothed out my windblown dress. Then I pushed open the heavy door.

The bedchamber was as large as the cottage I shared with my mother. There were oriental rugs and paintings, and the entire room smelled of jasmine. To my left was a writing desk covered with papers and quills and candles; a bookcase stood beside it, every shelf stacked with leather-bound volumes. To my right, a chest of drawers towered above me, the handles made of pure gold, the black walnut inlaid with mother-of-pearl. I stood with my mouth hanging open, my eyes swimming in every direction, wincing at this explosion of color that dazzled me into silence.

Across the room, in front of three large windows draped with red damask curtains, the Countess lay on a four-poster bed. Her back was to me, and she was propped up on one arm, a black satin sheet wrinkling beneath her.

She was naked.

A servant girl, maybe ten years old, stood on the other side of the bed, holding a large oval mirror in her small hands. The Countess was staring at her own reflection, her nose almost touching the glass. She turned her head left and then right, running a finger across her cheek and down the long curve of her neck.

"Come closer," she said to the mirror, "so that I might see you better."

I took a few steps closer and stood straight, hands clasped at my waist. I detected a faint whiff of ginseng, and when she shifted her position I noticed her porcelain skin glistening, as if oils had been rubbed into the shallow wrinkles just beginning to crease her thighs and lower back. Her dark brown hair, flecked with gray, shone in the bright candlelight; it spilled out of a tight bun onto a plush velvet cushion that rested against an ornate, carved headboard.

She sat up and turned to face me. Right away, her amber eyes bore into me, dominant and demanding. She pursed her lips and looked me over in complete silence before finally saying, "Indeed, Miss Darvolia was right. You are quite lovely."

I curtsied. "Thank you, Countess."

She gazed into her mirror. "Alas, time has no respect for beauty. When you are young, it offers you compliments. When you are old, it attacks you with insults."

My stomach rumbled and I realized I hadn't eaten in hours. I was suddenly thirsty, too. I wanted to run outside and fetch a bucket of water from the well.

The Countess patted the empty space beside her. "Come, Maria. You have a small voice, and I would like to hear you better."

I sat down next to her. My hands were cold and clammy. I folded them in my lap, trying to wrap them in the thin folds of my dress.

"Leave us." She waved the servant girl away. "And close the door behind you."

Once we were alone, the Countess sat up on the edge of the bed. She took my chin in her hands and peered into my face. "My, what pretty eyes you have. And such a milky complexion. No blots or blemishes. It's not often one can pluck a pearl out of the muddy water." She inched closer, grabbed a coil of my hair, and held it against her nose. "Lavender, no?"

"It grows wild behind our cottage," I said. "My mother uses it to make oils."

She crossed her legs and sighed, swinging her bare foot in tiny circles. "I was young once, too. Now, alas, I am forty-nine." She waited for me to respond, her fingertips pressed together in a steeple.

I swallowed hard and cleared my throat. "Time has been exceedingly kind to you, Countess."

"One must bathe every day." She stroked the side of my face, and I shuddered at the coldness of her fingers. "It keeps the skin soft and smooth."

I stared down at my fidgeting hands, afraid to glance up.

"Do you know why you are so exquisite, Maria?"

I shook my head no.

"Because you have not yet tasted the pleasures of love. You are sixteen and unmarried, a vessel that has yet to be filled." She stood up and looked down at me, her arms folded across her chest. "Tell me, have you ever lain with a man?"

My cheeks burned. "No, Countess."

"How fortunate for you," she said, smiling. "Nothing will gray your hair and wrinkle your skin faster than a fluttering heart."

I looked down at the crumpled bed sheet. The Countess acted as if I'd been spared a special kind of pain, but my inexperience with boys stemmed more from an obligation to help Mama than from an aversion to the flirtations I enjoyed while wandering the streets of Trenčín. And while I certainly took pleasure in those piercing whistles and lingering stares, I doubted a few heartaches would catapult me into antiquity any faster than the sun could rise and set in a given day.

The Countess must have sensed my unease because she laughed. "But listen to me harping on about age and beauty. I didn't invite you here to prattle about pleasantries. We have business to discuss." She picked up a red silk robe lying at the foot of the bed and motioned for me to help her. I held up the robe and she slid her arms inside, watching herself in the mirror as she did so.

"In addition to your enticing looks, Maria, you have a reputation for being a skilled seamstress." She walked over to the middle window and pushed aside a damask curtain so she could watch the steady drizzle that had begun to fall. "I wish to capitalize on the latter while admiring the former."

I curtsied. "Thank you."

"You will sew three gowns for me. One red, one yellow, and one orange. All made of silk—with lace cuffs and a V-shaped collar—and the necklines stitched with four diamonds. Do you understand?"

"Yes, Countess."

"I will supply whatever materials you require. I expect you are accustomed to chalk because it is cheap, but here you will learn to hold a pencil instead of a pitchfork. I don't expect you to be educated, but I do expect you to draw lines and circles. Surely, such simple tasks won't confuse you. If you dissatisfy me, however, I will be forced to demonstrate other uses of a pencil, in which case you'll be digging pieces of granite out of your arms and legs."

My knees trembled, but I managed to stand tall. "I understand."

"Cost is no issue," she continued. "I have secured a private room in which you may work without distraction. You may also be asked to help out in the kitchen and to assist the other servants." She frowned. "I must warn you that most of them are not agreeable. They complain, as children are prone to do, about trivial matters. Unfortunately, as the poor become more afflicted, they become more resentful, and I have no tolerance for those who constantly criticize and complain."

"Yes, Countess."

"Good. You will begin making measurements tomorrow morning. My children, Ursula and Katherine, will be visiting at the end of the summer, and I would like your work to be completed by then."

"As you wish," I said.

She turned away from the window and looked me up and down, perhaps still deciding if she wanted my dirty fingers to touch her expensive fabrics.

"You will remain on the castle grounds at all times," she said. "You may not travel into either Čachtice or the forest unless you have my permission. And you will refrain from venturing into the east tower of the castle. If you disobey any of these orders, you will find in me the strength of a man."

"Yes, Countess."

"We have boundaries for a reason, Maria. In Čachtice there is cholera. In the forest there are wolves. We have many girls working here at the castle, and it would be a shame to lose them to foolish disobedience before they've had a chance to become useful."

My hands were clammy and my throat was on fire. I could feel sweat collecting under my arms. I didn't want to see my reflection, so I averted my eyes from the half-dozen mirrors spread about the room. Instead, I studied the paintings and tapestries covering the high walls, admiring the intricate patterns and designs. Above the writing desk in the corner hung a coat of arms engraved on polished oak. Compared to the Countess, it was rather plain and ordinary, nothing regal or formidable, just alternating red and white triangles stacked atop one another.

She noticed my interest. "That is the Báthory family crest. As you can see, it depicts three horizontal teeth surrounded by a dragon biting its own tail. Sometime around the year 900 AD, a warrior named Vitrus journeyed into the village of Ecsed to fight a ferocious dragon that was living in the swamps. He killed the dragon with his lance, delivering three powerful thrusts, and as a reward he was given a majestic castle and all the surrounding lands. The nobles honored him with the name 'Báthory,' which means good hero."

"He must have been very brave and important," I said, trying to curry favor. "Like a modern-day Odysseus slaughtering the Cyclops."

She glared at me. "The Báthory family is one of the most noble and respected families in all of Hungary. Our reputation is built upon dignity and order, not myth and legend."

"Apologies, Countess." I clasped my hands together to keep them from shaking. "I didn't mean to offend."

She gazed up at the coat of arms, then chuckled to herself as if remembering a clever jest. "The Greeks like to concern themselves with painted masks and embroidered tragedy, but we Báthorys prefer hard-fought victories, secured with fierce determination and an uncompromising attitude. Remember that, Maria, and next time you will not be so quick to forget your place."

My stomach groaned like a dying animal. I blushed and bit down on my lower lip.

The Countess walked across the room to one of the full-length mirrors. It had been built with wooden supports on which she could lean her slender arms. She stood like this—slanted forward and staring at her own reflection—for several minutes, not saying a word. Finally, she sent me away with a careless wave of her hand. "Have Benedict take you down to the kitchen. I don't want you cutting a hole in my expensive fabric because of hunger pains."

Benedict was waiting for me in the hallway. I followed him through the narrow corridors—back down the wide staircase, across the foyer, and toward the back of the castle—until we entered an enormous kitchen that opened up onto the rear grounds. He left me without saying a word. I stood off to the side, trying to stay hidden while I clutched my empty stomach. The room was hot and stuffy, and it contained more life than I had seen up to this point in Čachtice Castle. Half a dozen cooks, their faces baked red with sweat, hurried from one end of the room to the other, chopping vegetables and plucking chickens. Servants carried in buckets of water from outside and swept feathers out the door along with rinds and peels; they washed forks and knives in a large stone sink that overflowed with gray, soapy water.

Above me, pots and pans hung from ceiling racks. To my left, silver plates and goblets were stacked on shelves, surrounded by flasks of red wine. There were barrels filled with olives, and jugs containing olive oil. Oranges and lemons were scattered on a side table, a plate full of walnuts teetering on the edge. To my right, two wooden spits were being turned by a boy who couldn't have been older than ten; huge chunks of beef and lamb roasted above the blazing fire. A cast-iron cauldron stood in the corner, bubbling and steaming as one of the cooks stirred the fragrant broth with a gigantic wooden ladle. Next to her, a young girl ground herbs in a mortar.

In an adjoining room, much smaller, there were cabbages and turnips and different types of melons and strawberries and grapes. Thick loaves of bread spilled out of straw baskets, and garlic bulbs were strewn across a bench as if forgotten. In a third room, a live turkey sat in a cage on the floor while chickens and pheasants lay dead across a bloody counter. An old woman held a dead rabbit by the hind legs. Her cheeks were pinched and sunken, and blue spider veins stretched across her wrinkled face. She ripped out the stringy guts and dropped them into a bucket that sat at her feet.

"Are you lost, dear?" she asked me.

"No," I said, smiling. "Just stunned. I've never seen so much food. It's enough to feed an entire village for a year."

"You should have been here when her Ladyship's daughter married Count Drugeth. That feast called for two hundred pounds of peppers, fifty pounds of ginger, twenty-five pounds of garlic bulbs, one thousand lemons, five hundred oranges, and three hundred pounds of honey, all purchased in Vienna and shipped here in wagons. Not to mention one hundred calves, fifty sheep, thirty lambs, one hundred pigs, two hundred rabbits, five hundred chickens, three hundred ducks, and five thousand eggs." She laughed. "Just thinking about all that food makes my stomach hurt."

In response, my own stomach rumbled, almost knocking me off my aching feet. I curtsied to the old woman and headed back to the main kitchen where a tall, burly woman glowered at me. She had straight blonde hair, streaked with white, that reached past her broad shoulders. Her face seemed square and jagged—as if I might cut my finger by swiping it across her cheek—and I could tell by the orange gown she wore that she was not a servant.

"Don't wander away without an escort," she said. "Čachtice Castle is quite large, and it's not uncommon for one to become lost and forgotten among the halls and corridors. Do you understand?"

"Yes," I said.

"Good, because no one has time to search through the castle whenever you get curious." She leaned forward, her face inches from mine. "We have many servants working here, which means it is easier to replace you than it is to find you." Her breath was hot and rancid, as if something had crawled inside her mouth and died.

"Apologies," I mumbled.

She handed me a hunk of bread and a cup of water. I thanked her and devoured the bread in less than a minute, ripping it apart like a wild animal while flakes of buttery crust fell onto my dress. I chugged the lukewarm water, some of which dribbled down my chin, then wiped my mouth with my sleeve.

"Delightful." She looked disgusted as I offered her the empty cup. "I hope your sewing is better than your etiquette."

Her name was Helen Szentes, and she was Countess Báthory's most trusted confidant. She managed the servants, tended to daily purchases and business transactions, and had served as a nursemaid for each of the Countess's three children.

"Do they live here in the castle?" I asked her.

She seemed taken aback, perhaps unaccustomed to servants asking questions. "They are older and no longer require my assistance. Several of them are married, and one is away at boarding school." She stated these facts as though rattling off a list, then pressed her hand against the small of my back and guided me past the busy cooks and servants.

We walked through the postern gate and stood at the rear of the castle, looking out over the expansive fields. Cattle and pigs were penned inside tall wooden fences while chickens wandered around, pecking at clumps of brown grass that poked out from the slushy snow. In the distance was a large pond stocked with fish, and off to my right was a large herb garden dotted with scarecrows.

"When you are not sewing gowns, you may be asked to pick herbs or tend to the animals," Helen told me. "You may be asked to assist with the linens, or to help the cooks in the kitchen." She looked me up and down. "It's good that you have some meat on your bones, girl. Hopefully you can carry a bucket of water without twisting your ankle."

"I'm a hard worker, miss. If I slip and fall it will be from health, not laziness."

When Helen spoke again her words sounded thin and pointed, like sharpened knifes. "Idle hands are the devil's workshop, Maria, and the Countess does not take pleasure in delays or excuses. Work hard, accept without question, and you will be provided for. Disregard your responsibilities, and you will soon find yourself an unwanted guest."

I bowed my head. "Yes, miss."

The sky was darkening, and I realized I was exhausted from all the instructions and conversations. My feet hurt from walking through the castle, and my hands hurt from gripping the horse's reins. Already, I missed the warmth of a roaring fire in the stone hearth. I wanted a bowl of stew and a mug of hot cider. I wanted Mama to brush my hair while she hummed her folk songs. It seemed days ago that I had said goodbye and rode away from our cottage.

Helen and I moved back inside, out of the drizzling rain. She gave me an apple and a sprig of grapes, which I washed down with another cup of water. This time I tried to be more graceful in my manner of eating and drinking, and in return I was rewarded with an apathetic look instead of a scathing insult.

Afterward, we walked through the rest of Čachtice Castle, or at least those parts where I was allowed to stray. Several sections on the ground floor were under guard and servants were forbidden to enter them unless instructed by the Countess. The rooms I did see were filled with silk tapestries and opulent furniture that the Count had claimed as trophies during his many years spent fighting the Turks. There were Persian rugs spread across the drawing room and crystal chandeliers hanging from the beams in the Great Hall. There were gold harpsichords and coral vases decorated with emeralds and rubies, and many of the floors were laid with polished white marble. I felt dizzy from spinning around so much, my eyes trying to take in as many luxuries as possible before another decadent room presented new treasures to admire.

The servants' quarters were located on the second floor, an entire wing at the back of the castle, and by the time we climbed the spiral staircase the sun had set. The long dark shadows that once stretched through the corridors had now pooled into an inky blackness that made it difficult to see as I followed behind Helen. Soon, candles were being lit in pewter holders, and the passageways were awash with splotches of yellow and orange that writhed across the walls in a ghoulish dance.

"Do all the servants sleep in this part of the castle?" I asked her. It was common knowledge, at least in Trenčín, that servants usually slept where they worked. Cooks slept in the kitchen, stable hands slept in the stable, maids slept in the pantry, and so on.

Helen stopped in front of a small oak door near the top of the stairs. "The Countess does not like complications. She prefers to know where her servants are at all times. She becomes angry when they wander off."

I stared down the hallway at a long line of doors, each with a large rusted lock bolted to a wooden frame. At the end of the corridor one could turn left or right, where even more doors were waiting to be opened. "How many servants live here?"

She pushed open the door and motioned for me to enter. "You must be very tired after such a long journey."

Inside the room were a small bed, a nightstand with a candle and a tinderbox, a chamber pot, and a large spinning wheel. There was one window to the left of the bed, tall and narrow and round at the top. It was barred with iron grating. The glass was caked with dirt.

At the foot of the bed was a wooden chest, the front carved with the Báthory coat of arms. Helen pointed to it. "The Countess has provided you with some dresses, as well as a pair of leather shoes." She glanced at my pendant. "You are welcome to store any valuables. I can assure you they'll be quite safe."

I bent down and opened the chest. Inside were two dresses—one gold and the other black—as well as a gray linen kirtle and a wool nightgown. On the bottom were leather shoes with wooden soles for support; unlike my own cracked sandals, these new shoes were soft and smooth and the color of rich soil. I smiled, feeling welcome for the first time since my arrival. "Thank you for your graciousness."

She waved her hand in the air as though I was acting absurd. "It is a matter of necessity. Without proper shoes and clothes, you may fall ill and become bedridden. And you cannot sew with precision while lying prostrate and suffering from fever."

"What time tomorrow shall I begin my needlework?"

"Sunrise. You will go down to the kitchen, where the cook will supply you with some food, and then I will personally escort you to the Countess."

Then she closed the door and was gone.

I sat on the bed and placed my hands on my lap, listening to Helen's footsteps disappear down the passageway. I removed my hood—delighted in how its bright green fabric injected warm color into that drab room—and stowed it away at the bottom of the chest. Then I slipped off my blue dress and stepped out of my cracked sandals.

I put on the wool nightgown, lit the candle, and walked over to the window. My bare feet were cold on the floor, and I shivered. I held up the candle, trying to look outside, but the rain—and the bright light reflecting off the foggy glass—made it difficult. I reached my hand through the iron bars and rubbed a small circle of visibility. Pressing my forehead against the bars, I could barely make out the forest in the distance. Below me was a sheer drop, at least one hundred feet down, to a collection of jagged rocks that sloped away from the castle walls.

I blew out the candle and climbed into bed. I pulled the sheet up to my face and nestled into the straw mattress, my body humming with nervousness and excitement as I remembered all I had seen and heard since my arrival. For the longest time I tossed and turned, worried about beginning my measurements in the morning and hoping the Countess would be satisfied with my skills.

Outside, the wind blew hard, rattling the window and moaning through the tops of the trees. I drifted off to sleep, knees hugging my chin. I dreamed I was trapped inside a rotting horse, screaming in the night as I clawed my way past broken ribs, tearing apart the stitches and seams, and ripping through layers of frozen skin.

Hours later, I awoke to muffled voices outside my door. At first I didn't know where I was, and I rolled over to shake my mother, certain there were intruders lurking outside our cottage. Sitting up, I rubbed my eyes and heard heavy footsteps creeping past my room, moving away from the spiral staircase and toward the servants' quarters at the end of the hall.

I got out of bed and tiptoed across the cold floor, reaching out in the darkness until my fingers grasped the latch.

The door was locked.

CHAPTER IV

I EXPECTED ONE OF the servants to bang on my door as soon as the first rays of sunlight skimmed across my bedroom floor, but the only sounds in the castle were maids speaking in hushed tones as they hurried through the halls with linens and trays and buckets of water. Turning over on my side, I looked out the window and saw nothing but thick white fog. I blew into my hands, which were cold and stiff, and sat up to rub my sore feet. I wondered if Mama was still asleep in our bed, wrapped up in a wool blanket, or if she was sitting by the fire with a cup of hot cider, listening to oat porridge bubble over the rim of a cast-iron pot.

I sat on the bed for a few minutes, letting the sleep drain out of me, then I slipped on the gold dress and the leather shoes. Shivering, I smoothed out the wrinkles in the dress and ran my fingers through my hair to untangle any knots. There was no pitcher or basin to wash my hands and face, and there was no mirror, so I arranged myself as best I could. Since I was feeling restless—and unsure if I should wait for someone to fetch me—I decided to walk down to the kitchen to ask one of the cooks for some food and water.

I feared the door might still be locked, and even pulled extra hard on the latch, but it swung right open to reveal a gloomy hallway with torches mounted on the walls. A few maids and servants passed by, most offering a quick nod in my direction, but for the most part the castle seemed silent and empty. I hurried down the stairs and passed through the Great Hall, admiring the long wooden tables and benches, the oil lamps hanging from the walls. Here, the Countess hosted feasts and visited with nobles, talking politics and weddings while, above in the minstrels' gallery, musicians played their lutes and gemshorns. The entire room smelled of mint and chamomile, no doubt spread across the floor to cover the more unsavory scents of ale and sweat.

As I left the Great Hall—heading down a shorter flight of stairs toward the kitchen—someone walked up behind me and grabbed my hair. It was a boy who looked to be around eighteen years old, stocky and handsome with olive skin. His brown eyes matched the unkempt hair that curled around his ears and tapered down the back of his neck, disappearing into a red cotton shirt that was covered with pieces of straw. He twirled a strand of my hair around his thick callused finger. "As soft as spun sugar. And just as delicious, I'm sure."

"Excuse me?"

He pressed the curl against his nose. "Not rank or musty, either. Quite tempting, in fact."

"Must a lady pass inspection to walk down the stairs?" I asked, trying to push past him.

"Come now, all I want is to introduce myself like a proper gentleman." He was not angry or threatening, but dominating in a mischievous way.

"Then do it from a distance. Surely, the farther away you stand, the more I'll miss you."

He fingered my silver pendant, his knuckle pressing against the hollow of my throat. "You must give me some sign of affection, otherwise I'll be forced to follow you around all day until my confidence is restored."

"I doubt you suffer from lack of confidence," I said. "Quite the contrary, in fact."

"Do you wish for me to leave?"

I nodded. "With every wish I'm granted."

He leaned against the wall, his eyes wandering over my body without the slightest restraint. "I'm no magic lamp, but rub me the right way and I may still reward you."

"Perhaps you require fresher air to cool your spirits," I told him. "A fire in the heart sends smoke into the head."

He laughed. "Come, Maria. Let us be friends."

I held out my arm to halt his advance. "How do you…"

"Peter!" A voice shouted from below, and I turned to see Anna Darvolia limping up the stairs. She was wrapped up in a black coat, her short bony fingers protruding from the dark holes of her sleeves. "Stop badgering the help," she said to him. "Can't you see the girl is unaccustomed to flattery?"

"She plays coy," he said. "But there is an eagerness to her reluctance."

Anna moved past me and placed her hand on Peter's arm. "Go heat some water for her Ladyship's bath. And tell the kitchen to send up a tray of cheese and nuts along with a bottle of wine."

Peter nodded, cast another glance in my direction, and rushed down the stairs two at a time.

Anna turned to me. "Where should you be right now? Surely not standing here like a simpleton."

"I don't know, miss." My heart was pounding, and I felt completely turned around, unsure whether I should go upstairs or downstairs. "I'm supposed to begin my measurements for her Ladyship's dresses, but Helen hasn't come to collect me."

"Then perhaps you should make yourself useful in the kitchen, instead of cavorting through the halls."

"Yes, miss."

"It seems Peter has taken a liking to you, despite the bewildered look on your face and the dirt smudged across your forehead."

I looked down at my shoes. "Apologies, miss, but I haven't had a chance to wash since yesterday morning."

"You were not brought here to wash yourself," she told me. "You were brought here to sew. If you wish to splash water on your cheeks, then do so in the kitchen. And be quick about it."

"Yes, of course."

She peered into my face. "Such dark circles under your eyes, Maria. Did you have a restless night? Perhaps one too many nightmares?"

"No, I slept fine."

"Then maybe you feel uneasy?" Anna grinned, revealing teeth that were cracked and brown. "No doubt you are unaccustomed to such luxurious surroundings. Are you afraid you'll prick your finger and bleed all over the fabric? Or forget how to thread a needle?"

I clenched my fists. "No, miss."

"Some girls become lonely without their mothers to cradle them," she said. "They become anxious and agitated. They lose focus and neglect their duties, which angers the Countess. Be careful you don't suffer distractions." Then, without another word, she pushed me aside and disappeared up the stairs, her heavy footsteps echoing through the mirrored halls.

The kitchen was crowded and hot. There was a roaring fire in the hearth, and the smell of fresh-baked bread hung in the air. Servants swept up straw and scrubbed the floors; cooks dipped long ladles into kettles and pots, stirring stews and sauces while they added salt and pepper and various spices.

The old woman I'd met yesterday shuffled over to me, took my arm, and sat me down at a small table in the corner where a young girl was chopping a large pile of red onions. The old woman patted me on the back, then returned moments later with a glass of milk and a piece of hot bread dipped in honey.

"Drink up," she told me. "It's no health if the glass is not emptied."

"Thank you," I said.

I ate the bread and sipped the milk. The girl continued her chopping, pushing down on the top of the blade with dramatic grunts and glancing up every now and then as if she wanted to say something. I couldn't see her face because it was hidden by long red hair in corkscrew curls, which she brushed out of her eyes with a dirty sleeve, her tiny hands fluttering in every direction like an injured bird. While she deposited the pieces of onion in a clay bowl, I drummed my fingers on the table and watched the doorway, checking myself for fallen crumbs in case Helen showed up in a foul mood.

"What village are you from?" the girl finally said.

"Trenčín. You?"

"Dubnica." She looked up and smiled. "I'm Sandra."

"Maria." I studied her face, which was round and smooth. "How old are you?"

"Thirteen." She put down the knife. "Do you work here in the castle, or outside in the stables?"

"In the castle. I arrived yesterday."

"Are you a scullery maid?"

I shook my head. "A seamstress."

Her green eyes narrowed as she looked me up and down. "There aren't any seamstresses in the castle. Washerwomen do all the stitching."

"I'm not here to mend rips or patch holes," I told her, raising my palm as if to ward off her accusations. "The Countess has asked me to sew her a series of special gowns."

"With silk and lace?"

"Yes." I drank the rest of my milk and pushed the empty glass to the side.

The girl shrugged. "Perhaps she wants to impress all those young men who shower her with jewelry and compliments."

I imagined the Countess lying upstairs in her darkened room—her head propped up on a satin pillow—watching herself in the tall mirror. "How empty she must feel since the Count died."

Sandra glanced around the room to make sure no one else was listening. "She has her circle of vultures. Mostly Helen and Benedict, and that old witch, Anna."

"Who is Peter?" I still felt his hand against my throat.

"A manservant who stays close to the Countess." She picked up an onion and chopped it in half, dropping the skin onto the floor where a scrawny dog began licking it.

"Is he...one of the vultures?"

"He's a man, which means he pecks for attention wherever he can get it."

"How long have you been working here?" I asked her.

"Three months, I think."

"Do you always work in the kitchen?"

She nodded. "Usually. There's always food. And it's not so lonely."

"Or so cold." I looked around at the servants, all of whom wore disintegrating dresses, most of which were dotted with holes and frayed at the edges. "Why doesn't the Countess provide you with better clothing?"

Sandra looked uncomfortable. "If you have grumblings, keep them to yourself."

The old woman returned to the table and tossed me a woolen cap. "Cover those raven locks," she said. "I don't want them seasoning my goulash." She winked at me and picked up the empty glass.

"Thank you." I put on the cap and tucked my hair underneath it.

"Someone needs to watch over you girls." She put her arm around Sandra. "Especially during these dark days."

"The cholera?" I asked.

The old woman bent down and cupped my face in the palm of her hand. "Oh, there are worse things than a plague, dear."

I looked to Sandra, but she had gone back to chopping her onion.

"Remain attentive, and always do as instructed," the old woman told me. "And if you must suffer, it's best to do it in silence."

Before I could question her further, Helen entered the kitchen and scolded one of the servants for not working fast enough. The poor girl—who couldn't have been older than twelve—had been peeling and cutting potatoes at a table by herself, and her small hands were struggling with the large knife.

"Chop, chop, chop, you shirker!" Helen shouted. "Before I skin you myself!"

At the sound of that shrill voice booming across the room, the girl spun around and her elbow knocked a bowl of lentils onto the floor.

"You clumsy fool!" Helen kicked aside the broken pieces of clay and backed the terrified girl into a corner. "If you can't pull your weight, then you can trudge home through the ice and snow. You'll likely freeze to death before you're halfway there, but it won't be a total loss. The wolves need to eat, too."

I noticed that the other servants had ceased talking and were busying themselves with newfound interests in other parts of the kitchen. I picked at a piece of dried orange rind with my fingernail; the old woman disappeared into one of the adjoining rooms with an armful of fresh fruit; and Sandra leaned forward to quicken her chopping, her button nose just inches from the table.

When Helen had finished her tirade—and delivered a hard slap to the sobbing girl—she shoved past the other servants and approached our table.

I stood up and curtsied. "Good morning, miss."

"The Countess is not feeling well. She needs her rest and must not be disturbed."

"Yes, miss."

"You will work in the kitchen this morning. There is meat that needs to be hung, and vegetables that need to be chopped."

I nodded.

"In the afternoon you will sweep the floors, then you will clean out the ashes from the fireplace."

"Will I not sew today?"

"When the Countess has regained her strength and wishes to see you, I will send for you. In the meantime," she wiped away a glob of honey that had dripped onto my sleeve, "I trust these menial chores will help you feel less homesick."

I stared past her at a reed basket hanging on the far wall, my face growing hot. I was brought here to sew and stitch—to fashion elegance out of spools and spindles—and instead I was being banished to a hot and noisy kitchen like a child who couldn't be trusted with valuables. It seemed no matter how dignified I tried to present myself, the Countess and her circle of vultures were sure to treat me like a simple farm girl whose sole function was to serve and submit.

After Helen left, I sat back down and crossed my arms. My eyes watered from Sandra's pile of chopped onions. "Čachtice Castle certainly lives up to its cold reputation," I said, wiping the tears from my face. "The only warmth I feel is from the roaring fire, and now I've been tossed into that, as well."

"You are a servant," Sandra said, "and you're here because you need money. If you leave, they'll just replace you with someone else."

I glanced over at the girl that Helen had just berated, her tiny hands still shaking as she choked back a series of gasping sobs. Shuddering, I pulled at the hem of my dress, twisting the fabric as I prayed to God that a few passing insults were the worst stings I would suffer during my stay at the castle. I did not want those vultures to swoop down on me from all directions, picking the meat off my bones with their power and fury.

Sandra lowered her voice. "A couple of months ago a girl complained about the cold and asked Helen for some clothes that weren't thin and ripped. When the Countess found out, she had the girl dragged into the kitchen and whipped until the skin on her back was hanging in strips."

I became lightheaded and closed my eyes.

"When the girl regained consciousness," she continued, "Helen and Benedict held her down while the Countess stuck pieces of oiled paper between her toes and lit them on fire."

My stomach felt like someone had kicked it in with a leather boot. "And then what?"

Sandra looked at her half-chopped onion and shrugged. "No one's complained about the cold since."

I placed my palms flat on the table, remembering all the stories I'd ever heard about the Countess. Ever since my arrival, something in Čachtice Castle seemed to be pressing down on me and I felt wary and apprehensive, afraid of what I might see if I looked over my shoulder and peered into the darkness.

"It's not unusual for the Countess to fly into fits of rage," Sandra whispered. "She is very particular about what she wants and how she wants it done."

"But...why..." I swallowed the lump in my throat, trying to steady all the questions that piled up in my head. "The kitchen?"

"Most punishments take place in the kitchen," she said. "It's a lot easier to wash away the blood."

CHAPTER V

I THOUGHT THE PEASANT life had hardened me—I thought that watching my father collapse on the side of the road had wrapped an iron bar around my heart—but what I witnessed at Čachtice Castle sickened me. I now understood why servants hurried from room to room with their heads down, why they preferred to be alone, and why they rarely said a word unless questioned by someone of authority.

The Countess and her vultures regularly beat the girls, and I soon noticed that most had bruises and welts on their arms and faces, or burn scars on their hands and feet. Every day I saw dozens of girls, most of them younger than me, covered in bite marks and bleeding wounds. I watched these daily thrashings with bulging eyes and trembling lips—my breath raspy, my skin clammy—cringing in horror every time another agonized scream shattered the silence.

In the past week alone, twelve girls had died, and it seemed that every other day more and more bodies were loaded into wooden coffins and carried outside. Helen blamed the deaths on cholera, and told the servants not to wander the castle alone lest they catch a shiver and fall ill. Sometimes, when I came downstairs in the morning, there was a stack of coffins resting in the muddy courtyard, nailed shut and surrounded by a swarm of flies.

When called upon by the Countess, Father Barosius drove his wagon to the castle, loaded however many coffins were piled up at the gatehouse, and buried them in the church graveyard. Whenever I saw Father Barosius, he looked wretched. There were deep grooves in his leathery face—which was always pinched with sadness and grief—and his fingers trembled as he made the sign of the cross.

Nevertheless, my days settled into a familiar routine. Mornings, I helped Sandra sweep the floors and chop vegetables in the kitchen. Sometimes I stacked logs in the fireplace or emptied the chamber pots. Other times I helped the maids polish the gold and silver. Because the weather had grown warmer with the arrival of spring, Sandra and I carried the tapestries outside and beat the dust out of them with thick boards.

Like me, Sandra was an only child. Her father had died years ago in one of the wars, and she lived with her mother in a small hut that was half the size of the cottage I shared with Mama. Their home, and all of their possessions, had been seized by Baron Helfert in Dubnica, and it was he who had sent Sandra to Čachtice because her mother could no longer pay the local taxes.

We were cleaning ashes out of the fireplace one morning when I turned to her and said, "Have you seen your mother since you've been here?"

"We're not allowed visitors."

"What about writing her a letter?"

"Baron Helfert believes that peasants aren't fit to be educated," she told me, "so I never learned to read or write. Even if I could, what difference would it make? No one here is permitted to send letters, and no one ever receives any."

I thought about my mother, so many hours away and living all by herself, and how she wouldn't be able to contact me if something bad happened. I wondered if anyone in Trenčín had visited her since I'd left, or what would happen if she suffered heart sickness one afternoon, just like my father, and collapsed inside the cottage with no one to help her. I couldn't imagine dying alone, and suddenly I wanted to run home and sit with her by the fire. I felt guilty and ashamed, as if I'd tossed her over my shoulder like a crumpled piece of paper.

"Has anyone ever run away?" I knew that Benedict patrolled the grounds, and that guards were posted at the gatehouse, but given such deplorable conditions it seemed likely that someone, at some point, had attempted to flee from the castle.

"One or two every week," Sandra said, "but they don't make it very far. If hunger and fatigue don't kill them, the wolves certainly will."

"What happens if they're caught?"

She raised her eyebrows. "Pray the wolves reach you before the Countess does."

I shuddered and put my arm around her. "Well, I can't fend off the wolves...or even tame the vultures...but I can teach you how to read and write."

"Really?" She smiled. "But...what if someone finds out?"

I glanced around to make sure no one was watching us. I felt anxious and excited, my palms sweating with anticipation. If discovered, Sandra and I would likely find ourselves in blood-stained pieces on the kitchen floor. Still, I needed to regain some control before I went mad—to exercise some power that might drown out the constant heartbeat thrashing in my ears—and so I spread the ashes on the floor in front of the fireplace. Then, using my index finger, I wrote "Sandra" in large letters, making sure to pronounce and highlight each letter as I wrote it.

"That's your name." I spread another handful of soft, fine ash and scooted back. "Now you try."

She studied the six letters I'd drawn and traced each of her own directly below them, mimicking my own movements and pronouncing every letter in a strong, clear voice. After writing her name a few more times, she clapped her hands twice and gave me a hug.

"I'm sure it seems a bit silly," she said, blushing, "but I'm never happier than when I'm getting my hands dirty."

I held up my own blackened hands. They looked so shrunken and ugly, as if they belonged to someone else. My knuckles were scraped raw from washing the stone floors with a coarse rag, and I'd lost count of how many blisters I'd drained from my palms and the soles of my feet. I was used to calluses and cuts, and the satisfaction of temporary pain when I completed something of value, but there was nothing honorable or redeeming about working at Čachtice Castle.

"I miss planting flowers and herbs," Sandra said as she stared down at the soot we'd smeared across the hearth. "I miss feeling the warm dirt between my fingers and toes, the hot sun shining on my face. I used to spend hours outside every day, running through the millet grass and staring up at the clouds, or wandering into the forest to collect tulips and peonies and blue poppies, sometimes even lilacs and roses. I can name any flower by sight, and most by smell."

"My fingers aren't green," I told her. "I can barely dig a hole, much less seed and water it."

"The trick is to fertilize them with cow manure. It doesn't smell very good, but it keeps the soil moist. Especially for the tomatoes and onions."

I sat in front of the fireplace and pulled her down beside me. "If your mother tends to the garden half as well as you, I have no doubt there will be a spread of beautiful flowers to dazzle your eyes when you return home."

"Perhaps," she said, frowning, "though she won't sweat over them like I do. She's old and tired. Her days mostly consist of living from one meager meal to the next, of washing laundry for snobby ladies and cleaning out the stables for Baron Helfert." She clenched her jaw, and I could tell she was trying not to cry. "Those days spent outside were the only times I ever forgot I was poor and hungry, and that the nobles would sooner spit at me than give me a dirty crust of bread. Here, I'm lucky if I can sneak outside for fifteen minutes, and if I do it's only because I'm emptying a chamber pot or beating a rug against a stone wall."

I put my arm around her. "After Anna came to see me, I thought I would waltz in here with my head held high and astound the Countess with my magic fingers. Instead, I've been wandering around with my nose pressed against the floor, trying to fade into the background."

"I never wanted to come here," Sandra said, "but I couldn't let Baron Helfert put my mother in jail. I heard lots of crazy stories about the Countess…that she had an uncle who believed he saw ghosts and tried to fight them with a sword…or that one of her cousins went insane and spent her days locked up in an empty room, biting herself on her arms and legs until she died from infection…"

I thought back to that cold day in April when I rode up the hill, and how the castle had seemed so tall and imposing, how the entrance had looked like a gaping mouth ready to swallow me up. "There are probably lots of stories locked inside these walls," I told her. "Some buried deeper than others."

Sandra leaned closer, and her voice dropped so low it was barely a murmur. "Do you ever hear the screams at night?"

"Yes." I steadied my voice so as not to seem afraid. "Servants being punished, most likely."

She stared off into the empty fireplace as though the coals were still glowing, and then—after folding and unfolding her hands a few times—she said, "Someone's been locking my door."

"Mine too. Do you think it's the Countess?"

Sandra shrugged. "All I know is that someone locks it just after midnight and unlocks it again right before dawn. The other girls in my room say we're being penned up like animals, and that the Countess will work us till we're empty shells. They say the less useful we are, the harder she'll beat us."

"Girls?" I stood up and wiped my hands on my dress, coughing as clouds of dust rose into the air. "Your room isn't your own?"

"No, of course not."

"How many share your room?" I asked her.

"Six." She tilted her head as if I had just asked the most ridiculous question in the world. "There are six girls in every room."

I closed my eyes and listened to the heavy thud of footsteps overhead. The wind gusted through the chimney to stir the ashes at my feet, and I felt a burning sensation in the pit of my stomach.

Why had the Countess placed me in a room all by myself?

Sandra tugged on my sleeve. "Maria, do you think there are ghosts in the castle?"

"Ghosts don't make loud noises when they thump down the corridor," I said. "And they certainly don't scream like they've been set on fire."

"So you don't think it's a vengeful spirit?"

"Whatever is lurking in the castle late at night is flesh and blood," I told her. "The same as you and me."

"Then perhaps it's best our doors stay locked," she said. "Because I'm terrified to see whatever it is that's waiting for us on the other side."

Once the Countess recovered from her illness, I saw her almost every day, usually in the afternoons. She typically rose at seven o'clock, whereupon servants delivered her a small breakfast of cheese and fruit along with a glass of red wine. They brushed her hair and applied her makeup, which took anywhere from two to three hours. After dressing, she spent at least another hour staring at herself in one of the large mirrors that were spread about her bedchamber. She sat at her desk and wrote letters to various relatives and nobles, sometimes making extravagant purchases and other times reviewing important documents sent from Vienna.

At eleven o'clock the Countess took lunch in the Great Hall, sometimes alone and other times with nobles such as Count Gregory Thurzó—who was a distant cousin—or with any one of the young gentlemen who paraded in and out of the castle bearing expensive gifts and complimenting her Ladyship's beauty.

After lunch she went horseback riding or read books in the library. On Saturday afternoons she traveled into Čachtice for no other reason than to be seen by her subjects, often meeting with the barons who supervised her estates and collected taxes on her behalf. At six o'clock she always sat at the head of the table in the Great Hall—feasting on an elaborate dinner—and then after drinking a small glass of port she retired to her bedchamber for the rest of the evening.

The Countess insisted on order, and she never deviated from her daily schedule unless headaches and eye pain forced her into bed with the curtains drawn. She was prone to such spells and often spent entire days in bed, sipping herbal remedies that Anna created from the many flowers and plants which dotted the countryside. From what I learned during my time in the kitchen, the Countess had been sick as a child, suffering violent seizures, and these episodes had supposedly produced the fits of rage for which she was now infamous.

Though she was vain and sadistic, I admired her determination and self-confidence, how she towered over everyone else, including men. She was tall and slender like a reed, but immovable in her convictions. Now lacking her husband's army and protection, the Countess knew she was vulnerable to attacks and political deceptions, but because she was well-respected as one of the most learned women in all of Hungary, the nobles treaded carefully when moving within her vicinity. She possessed more power and control than I had ever seen in a single person, and it was most evident not in the strength of her voice, but in the horrified stance of those who quivered before her.

Still, the Countess had her concerns, as evidenced by a gossiping kitchen staff and the deepening lines on her forehead. Without the spoils of war to increase her dominance and monetary worth, the Countess was cautious with her assets and kept diligent track of all financial records. It was also rumored that King Matthias owed her over twenty thousand gulden, which Francis had loaned to the crown before his death in 1604. Every few months the Countess traveled to Vienna and asked King Matthias to repay his debt, and when she returned home, always angry and empty-handed, she amused herself by sticking sewing needles underneath girls' fingernails until they passed out from the pain.

I was fortunate enough not to incur her Ladyship's wrath, mostly because I was left to myself and thus had little time to displease her. In addition to sewing her three gowns, I was tasked with mending any clothes that needed repair. This meant fixing the holes and rips in dresses and pants, and sewing buttons onto cotton shirts. Sometimes I returned to my room and found a stack of coats with ragged tears in the sleeves, or linen stockings with holes that needed patching.

Finally, during my second week in the castle—once the Countess had regained her strength—I was summoned to her bedchamber one morning to make the necessary measurements for her gown. When I entered, she was sitting at her writing desk in a white chemise. A tall candle burned beside her, and I detected the faint smell of honey. Several papers were spread out amongst a stack of leather-bound books and a small oval mirror.

"Stand next to the window," she said without glancing up. "I will join you when I'm ready."

I walked across the room, hands clasped, and stood where she had instructed. Next to me, on a table, someone had placed an ivory ruler, a cloth sewing measure, an ink pot with a quill, and several scraps of parchment.

The Countess wrote for several more minutes. Once finished, she blew gently to dry the ink, then folded the letter four times and tied it neatly with string. I watched as she held a piece of red wax to the candle flame, rotating it in slow circles until it began to melt. She then let the hot wax drip onto the letter until a small circle formed—almost as if the letter were bleeding from within—at which point she pressed the wax with a handheld seal and set it on the edge of her desk.

She walked over to the window and let her arms hang loosely by her side. "Don't dawdle, Maria. I have other business to attend to. Fires are raging across the countryside and all the surrounding areas are being threatened by the Turks. I have letters to send and villages to protect. I suggest you measure both quickly and accurately."

"Yes, Countess." I took the strip of cloth and stood directly in front of her, measuring the fullness of her chest until my hands were clasped behind her back and we were locked in a strange embrace, the room quiet save for the wind gusting outside and the rustle of her chemise as I rubbed against it. I felt uncomfortable when my fingers brushed against her breasts, but I lowered my head and kept my eyes on the measuring cloth. The scent of honey was stronger now, lingering on her skin, and to combat the awkward silence I mentioned the sweet fragrance permeating the room.

"What you smell is beeswax," she told me, motioning toward her desk. "The candles are from Paris. You're most likely accustomed to tallow candles, which is all your family can afford. Tallow candles are made from animal fat and have a foul odor that upsets me."

I dipped my quill in the ink pot and wrote the measurement on a scrap of parchment. Then I asked her to stand up straight and bend at her waist so I could record the crease line. I scribbled down the numbers— careful to document them in a legible and orderly fashion so I wouldn't misread them later—and instructed her to stand with her feet together so I could measure her hips.

"Lard might be sufficient for peasants," the Countess said as I knelt to wrap the measuring cloth around her backside, "but beeswax burns longer and isn't as smoky. I don't wish to greet my guests smelling like a dirty hearth in some hovel."

"Yes, Countess."

"I have always desired purity," she said. "Purity leads to beauty, and beauty leads to reverence."

I stood up, jotted down a few more measurements, and took the ruler off the table. "You're very wise."

She put her hand on my shoulder. "Do you know what is better than wisdom, Maria?"

"No, Countess."

"A woman. And do you know what is better than a good woman?"

"No, Countess."

"Nothing. You cannot depend on anyone in this world. You must seize power at every opportunity. Even your own shadow will leave you when you're in darkness."

I busied myself with measuring her waist, then I finished my measurements by calculating the dress length, which involved using the ruler to record the distance from her collarbone to her hemline. When I had finished, I explained to her that each gown—with all of its intricate designs and patterns—would take roughly five weeks to design and sew, given no complications. She looked over my measurements, then informed me that the other two gowns would be worn by her daughters, Ursula and Katherine.

I picked up the scraps of parchment. "But you told me they won't arrive until the end of the summer. How will I complete the other gowns by then? Won't I need to take their individual measurements as soon as possible?"

She was watching herself in the full-length mirror and did not bother to turn around when she answered my question. "Let me worry about that, Maria. Finish sewing the first gown. Then, if I'm satisfied with your work, you may play some more with your ruler."

I dictated a list of materials I needed, including a pair of scissors, a basket of pins and needles, several pieces of chalk, and a small table on which to lay my supplies. The Countess instructed me to work in my room and away from the other servants, an order I was not quick to forget when she looked me in the eyes and said, "When you are in your room, you will spin and sew. You will work diligently and carefully." She walked over to her bed, grabbed a knife off the breakfast tray, and touched the tip of it with her index finger. "I expect to be awed, and if you disappoint me, I will cut you deeper than you can possibly imagine."

My room was set up in a matter of days. Helen provided a large table so I could lay out the parts of each gown as I assembled them, and the Countess sent Peter to Vienna to purchase all the materials. He returned two days later with dozens of bags and boxes, winking and gloating as he entered my room to unload yards of linen, silk, and lace. I sat at my spinning wheel and chewed on my fingernails, watching the room grow smaller and smaller as assorted fabrics rose up before me in colorful mountains.

Peter had continued to smother me with kind words and furtive glances, sometimes snatching the woolen cap off my head so I was forced to chase him down and retrieve it. I never knew where he might be hiding. He appeared in the kitchen when I helped Sandra wash the plates and goblets; he tapped me on the shoulder while I was outside emptying the chamber pots; and when I returned to my room at the end of the night, exhausted and ready to fall into bed, he was waiting by my door smelling of musk and sweet hay, tucking stray hairs behind my ear and demanding that I give him a kiss for his troubles. Though I often pushed him away, approaching his interest with annoyance and skepticism, there was a knot in my belly whenever we touched.

"Why do you insist on teasing me?" he asked one night as I opened my door and slid past him.

"Because you insist on chasing after me at all hours," I said, yawning. "It's a wonder you're not constantly winded."

He smiled. "Then let me come in and catch my breath."

"No, I need to sleep. I can't afford mistakes while I'm sewing. If my measurements are wrong, or if I tear the fabric, the Countess will shatter my bones."

"Always an excuse," he said. "No matter where we are, no matter what time of day, you're always hiding behind a wall."

"My walls don't topple so easily," I said. "Especially when you keep trying to crash through them with reckless abandon."

Peter let his hand rest on my arm. "And what would you have me do?"

I shrugged him off, tired and confused. I was unsettled by his closeness, yet I adored the flood of attention. His adulation might have appeared more grating had I endured it in Trenčín, but here at the castle—surrounded by so much death—it became a soft light that glowed in the penetrating darkness.

"Remove one stone at a time," I told him. "Perhaps a bit of patience will lead you down a more direct path."

"Like the one that's led you here to Čachtice?"

I shifted from one foot to the other. "Necessity and obligation have brought me to the castle, not my own free will."

"Don't be modest, Maria. You have heart and grit." He laughed. "And maybe some grit in your heart, too."

"Yes, but it toughens me." I looked past him, down that long corridor which led to the back of the castle where girls wanted to sleep through the night without being awakened by unearthly screams. "One needs to be tough if she hopes to survive in this horrid place. Every day girls are beaten and whipped, or dying of cholera. They're afraid to peek around corners or talk above a whisper."

"I know, Maria. I've lived in this castle since I was a young boy. I've listened to more screams…and I've seen more blood splattered on these floors…than you could possibly imagine."

"The Countess has never beaten you?"

"She's kept me alive," he said. "She treats me like a son."

"But…what about your parents?"

"They were gypsies. Killed on the Austrian border when I was a child. The Count found me wandering in a field."

"I'm sorry." I reached out and squeezed his shoulder. "The Turks are vicious and ruthless. I know many families that have suffered at their hands."

Peter said nothing for a moment, and then he touched the pendant hanging around my neck, his fingers skimming the smooth silver. "A gift from an admirer?"

"No, from my father."

"And where is he?" There was a hard edge in his voice. "Out fighting the Turks? Or perhaps the nobles?"

"In a grave by our cottage."

His hand dropped to his side and he leaned against the door frame, silent.

"I was ten years old. The two of us were returning home from the market. As we rounded the bend, he clutched his chest and staggered forward, gasping and coughing, his face turning blue, and then, before I knew what was happening, he collapsed on the side of the road...and then..."

I tried to control my breathing, my emotions tipsy and ready to spill over at the slightest provocation. "I knelt down and grabbed his shirt, shaking him as hard as I could, and when he wouldn't wake up, I ran all the way home. I know I should have run back into the village to find the doctor, but..."

"Maria, don't..."

"Maybe he would have had a chance," I said. "But I was so scared, and all I could think about was Mama waiting for us, and how she hated when we were late because it made her worry."

He wiped a tear from my cheek. "There's no shame in behaving like that. People get turned around all the time."

I looked away, embarrassed. "Yes, but at some point they stop spinning so their lives can come back into focus."

"Is that what brought you here?" he asked me. "The chance to stand on firmer ground?"

"I'm old enough to march in a straight line, but lately the world seems so slanted, and all my steps seem so crooked." I crossed my arms and stared down at a rusty brown stain on the floor. "I just want the chance to shed my old skin and see what grows back in its place."

Peter leaned into me, so close I could feel his breath on my face. "And what will you do with this new skin?"

CHAPTER VI

THE CHILLING SCREAMS BECAME so frequent they often woke me from a deep sleep. They always began sometime after midnight, when my door was locked and the castle had settled itself into an eerie silence. Sometimes they were so loud I had to cover my ears or put the pillow over my head; other times they were so low they sounded like wind whistling through the stone wall behind our cottage. Each night, I would pull the sheet up to my chin and stare into that impenetrable darkness as terror entered my bones. Then, jaw clenched and stomach churning, I trembled myself into a fitful slumber.

During the day, the screams were less intrusive, and thus less unsettling. They blended with all the other clatter that flooded through the castle, an unending stream of Helen shouting orders, dogs barking at the gatehouse, minstrels entertaining lords and ladies, knives slicing through piles of fresh vegetables, and servants hurrying from room to room with linens and chamber pots and pewter trays piled high with plates and goblets.

I continued with my sewing and embroidering, cutting yards of gold fabric and sitting at the spinning wheel until my fingertips were cracked and callused. My eyes were bloodshot from lack of sleep and strained from threading needles in the dirty light. I'd lost weight from stressing about exactness and precision, and I was constantly sweating for fear of tearing the expensive fabric, but by the end of May I'd completed the first gown, which the Countess demanded to see as soon as I stitched the last diamond onto the neckline.

Because she refused to enter the servants' quarters, I laid the gown across my open arms and carried it to her bedchamber, careful not to brush any part of it against the grimy walls. Upon entering, I saw the Countess sitting in a chair by the window with her hands folded in her lap. She wore a scarlet dress with a white ruffled hem. A servant was brushing the Countess's hair in long, even strokes. The girl looked to be about fourteen. Her eyes were red, and she was marked with fresh bruises.

"Place the gown on the bed," the Countess told me, "so that I may examine it."

I did as she instructed and stepped back so she could inspect my work. She walked over to the edge of the bed and bent forward. Her hands skimmed over the sleeves, across the midsection, and down the waistline. She leaned closer, her nose inches from the fabric, and circled the top of a diamond with her index finger. She muttered something to herself and then carried the gown over to a tall window where she held it up to the light.

"Lovely," she said. "You've exceeded my expectations."

I looked away to allow myself a smile while she returned the gown to the bed.

"I was right to bring you here, Maria. You will be put to good use."

"Thank you, Countess."

"I know your time in the castle has not been easy," she told me, "especially being so far from home, but if you continue to please me with work of this caliber, then you shall be rewarded within my circle." She stood in front of me and cupped my face in her hands. "Remember, we must first descend if we wish to be raised."

"Yes, Countess."

She trailed a cold finger down the side of my face. "I can't believe you have never had a lover, Maria. A young woman as pretty as yourself has certainly gathered a collection of admirers, no?"

"Perhaps," I said, smiling, "but if so, I never offered much in the way of encouragement."

While I certainly enjoyed such starry-eyed attention, the Countess would never understand that I had no time for romance when chores needed to be done and mouths needed to be fed. While the boys in Trenčín were following me through narrow streets and spinning their silken words, I was gathering vegetables in the garden and spinning fine clothes for wealthy landowners.

She walked over to a silver basin and splashed water on her face. "My own marriage was based on politics rather than love. There was no courting, no promises or lingering stares. I was engaged at eleven and sent to live with my husband's mother, who oversaw my education, which consisted of memorizing religious texts and learning how to hold a fork properly. She was a dominating woman who adored her son and eschewed change, and so it was difficult for her to embrace my presence in her household, especially when I married Francis at fourteen." She dried her face on a small piece of cloth. "Can you imagine being married at such a young age, Maria?"

"No, Countess."

"My husband, may he rest in peace, could barely read and write in Hungarian." She turned to me, her arms crossed. "In terms of honor and prestige, the Báthory name far exceeds that of Nádasdy, yet my duties as Countess were to have children and to be seen in public. Not an easy task when one's husband is constantly off at war fighting the Turks."

"Did you love him?" I asked, and immediately clamped a hand over my mouth, certain I had crossed a line. I took a step back, expecting her to strike my face with the back of her hand. I was certain she'd grab my hair and drag me into the kitchen where Helen would crack her whip until pieces of me flew across the room.

But the Countess did not lunge at me, nor did she glare at me with those cold eyes. Instead, she walked over to one of the mirrors and gazed at herself for several seconds before saying, "My husband was a fine soldier, but a terrible lover. To be fair, he had his strengths. He commanded countless armies on the battlefield, increased our lands throughout Hungary, and amassed a wealth of gold and silver…and his victories certainly granted us protection by the crown…but he left me alone to age in this castle."

"A lesser lady would have crumbled," I told her, still mortified by my interruption.

She motioned for me to come closer. I walked forward and kept my hands in front of me, still afraid she might lash out. But when I stood beside her, she pointed down at the silver basin. "Look beneath the water. What do you see?"

I peered through the water. "It looks like a woman…in a seashell?"

"That is Venus, the Roman goddess of beauty. She is the embodiment of love and sexuality." The Countess dipped her fingers into the basin and stroked the carved image on the bottom. "Venus is stepping out of her shell, wringing the water from her hair. And as the water in the basin lowers, she slowly appears, revealing herself as the most perfect symbol of eternal youth."

I stared down at Venus, thinking of Peter and how his breath tingled my skin whenever he whispered into my ear.

The Countess sat in her chair and looked up at me, smiling. "That is how you continue to be a formidable presence, Maria. You rise up from the depths, no matter how far you fall. You strive to endure. And you don't depend on others to carry you. Because they'll inevitably stumble when you need them most."

"Yes, Countess."

She snapped her fingers and the servant girl walked back over to resume brushing her hair. I wasn't sure if I should stay or leave, so I stood still, pretending not to notice that the Countess was watching me the entire time.

The girl raised a thin trembling hand, her fingers clenched tight around the brush, her knuckles stretched white. She began each stroke at the end of a long curl, moving up from the bottom, her hand at the roots to prevent from pulling too hard. She was nervous—as evidenced by her flushed face and the slight rasping sound whenever she sucked in a breath—and every time the Countess sighed or shuffled her feet, I saw the girl's arm shake.

The air in the room was hot and stuffy. I felt perspiration dot my forehead, and I wiped my hands on my dress. Somewhere in the castle I heard shouting, and outside a dog barked. After a few minutes I raised my eyes to look out the window, praying for the courage to find my voice so I could ask the Countess to excuse me.

Just as I was about to speak, my mouth already open, the words bunched together on the tip of my tongue, the servant girl glanced up, her lips quivering, and we gazed at each other from across the room.

I smiled.

She smiled.

And that's when her hand slipped.

The hard bristles snagged on a tangled knot of hair, and her Ladyship's head was yanked back.

"You little whore!" The Countess leapt up like she'd been set on fire and struck the girl across the mouth, knocking her to the ground.

Had I been less afraid, I might have bolted from the room. Instead, I took a step back and said not a word.

The girl threw her hands over her face, yelling that she was sorry and promising it would never happen again.

The Countess turned to me. "This worthless wretch can't seem to use her fingers properly." She grabbed a pair of scissors from her desk and sat atop the terrified girl, pinning her to the ground. "Maybe this will help to loosen your fingers, dear." Holding the girl's bony wrists, the Countess began stabbing her fingers one at a time, raising the scissors high into the air and driving them down into the flesh and bone, oblivious to the piercing screams, ignorant to the drops of blood now splattered across the ivory rug.

I felt dizzy and sick to my stomach. I turned toward the bed, my entire body reeling.

"Perhaps it's not your fingers at all," the Countess said. "Perhaps it's your arms that are giving you trouble." She plunged the scissors into the girl's arm and dragged the blade from wrist to elbow. The soft skin tore open like paper shredding, leaving a jagged gash that spurted blood onto her Ladyship's dress.

I gasped and struggled to breathe. I wished I was a shadow on the wall. My legs shook, and I gripped the bedpost to steady myself.

Little by little, the gut-wrenching sobs tapered off until the girl was curled up on the rug, whimpering apologies while she pressed her mangled fingers against her chest. The Countess sighed with exasperation and threw the bloodstained scissors onto the desk. They landed with a heavy thud, spraying tiny red droplets onto her letters and books.

"Maria," the Countess said, "go inspect my gown." She turned to the crying girl. "If there is but one speck of blood on the fabric, I will pour out my indignation upon you."

I whispered a prayer, walked over to the bed, and picked up the gown. I held it in front of the large window so as to see it better in the morning light. It was clean, and I exhaled a long breath as tears welled up in my eyes. There was not a single red stain anywhere, and I relayed this to the Countess.

"Excellent," she said. "Now go and find Helen. Tell her to send another servant up to my room. I wish to change out of this ruined dress, and I require someone with less clumsy hands."

I laid the gown on the bed and took a small step toward the door, waiting to see if further instructions followed.

After a few seconds, the Countess looked up. "Don't just stand there, Maria. Do as you're told. My scissors are in a happy mood, and while your fingers are extremely valuable to me, other parts of you are quite expendable."

I found Helen in the kitchen, though I didn't remember arriving there. I didn't even remember leaving the bedchamber. I'm sure I passed dozens of servants in the hallway—and I must have walked down the grand staircase and into the Great Hall—but I had no recollection of the path I had traveled. Everything seemed slow and hazy, as if I were wandering through a thick fog, cold and alone.

When Helen left with one of the servants, I sat down at a table and cried until my eyes were sore and my stomach ached. The girl's screams still echoed inside my head, and every time I closed my eyes I saw her red fingers clutching the ivory rug. I stared down at the deep grooves in the table, wishing I could crawl inside one and disappear. Some of the older women pressed me to eat, but all I could manage were a few sips of water.

At some point I left the kitchen and walked outside, straight to the gatehouse, which, of course, was locked. I gripped the iron bars and looked down the road toward Čachtice. I pushed with all my strength, grunting until my muscles were sore, though I knew the gate wouldn't yield.

After rattling the bars a few more times, I heard footsteps behind me. I turned to find Benedict watching me. He was frowning, and his arms were crossed.

"Return to the castle," he said.

I moved away from the gate. "I need fresh air. A walk will do me good."

He motioned toward the courtyard. "You may explore the gardens…or even the fields…but I can't permit you to travel into the village."

"I wish to see my mother."

"You may bring that up with the Countess the next time you speak with her."

"If I write a letter, may I give it to the messenger?"

"You may give it to the Countess," he said, "and she will see that it arrives in Trenčín."

"Why are servants not allowed to leave the grounds?" I asked him.

Benedict stepped closer, towering over me, and when he spoke his voice was low but harsh. "Do not question those above you, Maria. Ever."

"Or what?" I screamed. My entire body was trembling. My breaths—so sharp and quick in the frigid air—were becoming more erratic.

He took another step toward me, and I backed away. "Or you may find yourself lying in a place where there is never fresh air."

I moved farther away and realized he was circling me, that my back was now to the castle while he stood in front of the gate, his fingers clasped around the hilt of his sword.

"I'm not a child." I held my hand at arm's length. "But if you prefer to be cautious, then perhaps one of the other girls can accompany me."

"There is an outbreak of cholera in the surrounding villages, and the Countess does not want to risk exposure." He grabbed my arm and led me back to the castle. "You will remain in the castle where your safety can be guaranteed."

I tried twisting out of his grip, but he dragged me up the hill. I yelled and cried and kicked his leg. He cursed and wrenched my arm. Pain exploded down the left side of my body, and I thought my shoulder would be torn from its socket. I wanted to rake my fingernails across his face. I wanted to give him a third nasty scar.

Once inside, Benedict tightened his grip, silencing any servants who approached us with concern. I thought he would pick me up and carry me upstairs. I thought he would throw me in my room, lock the door, and be done with my foolishness. But as soon as he veered off from the grand staircase, I knew he was bringing me into the kitchen, and my body went limp.

I knew for certain he was going to beat me. I had questioned him, I had disobeyed his orders, and I had attacked him. Would he whip me until I lost consciousness? Would he beat me with a heavy club? Only the previous week, one of the new servants had interrupted the Countess during a dinner party, and for that small mistake Helen had driven two needles through the girl's upper and lower lip, rendering the child unable to speak until the needles were removed several hours later.

Benedict sat me down in one of the chairs and held my arm so I couldn't escape. "The girl is hysterical," he told the women. "Most likely overworked. She has been sewing like a fiend and has barely had time to rest."

He whispered something to one of the women, and she rushed off into an adjoining room, only to return moments later with a large goblet. "Drink," he commanded, and I was so tired that I gulped down the sweet red wine in one mouthful, afraid of what might happen if I refused.

The woman took the empty goblet, and the rest of the servants went about their work. After a few minutes, Benedict let go of my arm and I slumped down in the chair. My insides felt warm and calm, as if I'd slipped underwater. My breaths became slower and less frequent. I waited for him to strike me, or to burn me with red-hot tongs, but he stood there silent, tapping the toe of his boot against an empty cage that someone had set down beside the table.

My arms and legs seemed disconnected from my body. I struggled to speak, my tongue thick in my mouth, my thoughts jumbled and murky.

My eyes began to close and I felt myself tumble from the chair onto the floor, my cheek scraped raw against the rough stone.

And then there was darkness.

CHAPTER VII

I WOKE UP GROGGY and sore, still shrouded in the cold blackness that had swept over me like a wave. My mouth was dry, my right cheek stung, and my upper lip was cracked and swollen. When I rolled onto my left side, a searing pain blazed through my shoulder and radiated down the left side of my back. I moaned, my voice barely a ragged gasp, and wiped several beads of sweat from my forehead. The air, hot and stuffy, pressed down on me, and for a brief moment I thought I'd been buried alive.

I stretched out my hands and felt coarse cloth. Only then did I realize I was lying in my bed, wrapped in a bundle of dusty blankets. Several pieces of straw poked out of the mattress to scuff my aching legs. I threw off the covers and sat up, squinting into the bright light as I swept the hair from my eyes. I planted my bare feet on the cold floor and stood up with a slight wobble, then glanced down at my bruised and naked body. Someone had undressed me and left my dirty clothes atop the sewing table. Worried, I reached up and touched my throat, relieved to find my father's pendant still hanging around my neck.

Despite a few bruises and the throbbing pain in my shoulder, I was not otherwise injured. I walked over to the window and inspected myself as best I could, but there were no cuts or scratches anywhere on my skin. I'd expected several burn marks, perhaps even a fresh scab or some missing fingernails, but it appeared, at least for the time being, that I had escaped punishment. In all honesty, I was surprised to have woken up at all given my reckless behavior.

I heard servants moving about in the hallway and someone shouting downstairs. Judging from the lengthy shadows crawling along the base of my bedroom wall, I guessed it to be sometime past eight o'clock in the morning. I rifled through the wooden chest for clean clothes and dressed without delay.

I wanted to walk down to the kitchen, where I was sure to find a cup of hot cider and a piece of bread, but yesterday's actions had yet to be addressed, and at some point I would have to explain myself to Benedict and Helen. Or even, God forbid, to the Countess.

Though my stomach was grumbling, I decided to avoid the kitchen and wander around the castle until my thoughts became clearer. But when I stepped out of my room, Peter was waiting for me in the hallway, leaning against the far wall with a mischievous grin.

"You look worse than a drowned cat," he said.

I managed a weak smile. "I have no energy, and my head feels as though it were stuffed with sawdust."

He handed me an apple and a small piece of cheese. "I have no doubt, given yesterday's spirited performance. You're lucky Benedict didn't break your legs."

I held up the apple, which was red and shiny. "I hope I don't find a nasty green worm inside."

He laughed. "It's better than finding half a worm."

I wolfed down the cheese and bit into the apple, not bothering to wipe away the warm juice that ran down my chin.

"Come along, little troublemaker." He grabbed my hand and steered me toward the stairs. "Someone wishes to speak with you."

My knees buckled, and my stomach pitched forward, but I followed him through the passageway, certain I was marching toward my own destruction.

The Countess was sitting at her desk, writing letters. I glanced around the room and saw no sign of yesterday's incident. The soiled parchment had been cleared away, and the blood-splattered rug had been replaced with a beige one containing handmade diamonds in an Oriental pattern. The scissors—now gleaming in the bright sunlight—rested on the edge of the desk.

Peter did not leave the room, but stood beside me, waiting for the Countess to finish composing her letter. I stared down at the spot on the rug where the girl had lain screaming in a crumpled heap, her thin fingers torn apart. I felt the corners of my eyes fill with tears. I wiped them away with the sleeve of my dress as the Countess stood up and approached me.

"You may finish eating," she said, and I realized I was still clutching the half-eaten apple in the palm of my hand.

I curtsied and took a small bite, wondering if the apple had been dipped in poison. I wanted to throw it away, but knew I would anger the Countess even further by appearing to be wasteful. I bit into the tough red skin and chewed on the sweet white flesh, fighting to keep my eyes open while she studied me with a look I found both distasteful and unsettling.

When I had stripped the apple down to its core, Peter took it from my hand and dropped it into his pocket.

"How do you feel?" the Countess asked me.

"Tired," I said.

She reached out and gripped my injured shoulder. I cried out as a sharp pain exploded down the length of my arm.

"Benedict tells me you wrenched this arm during your theatrics," she said.

I blushed. "Yes, Countess."

"A pity it wasn't your tongue." She stepped closer, her long pale fingers locked together as she looked me up and down. "I trust you'll find it difficult to thread a needle with your arm in such disrepair?"

"My injury is not severe. It's just a strain."

"Don't appeal to my charity by showering me with assurances."

I shivered and looked straight into her eyes. "I promise it will be healed in a day or two."

"Promises," she said, "are pitiable excuses. They are nothing more than placeholders for future disappointments."

I glanced over at Peter, who was gazing out the window. He seemed bored by our conversation, a vacant expression drifting across his tanned face. I opened my hand as if drawing him toward me, wanting him for support lest I crumble under her unpleasant stare.

"I am upset," she said, "because I have spent significant time and money to bring you here as my guest. I have clothed you, I have fed you, and I have provided you with rewarding work that less fortunate souls would kill to acquire. And what have you done to repay me? You have damaged my property during a foolish attempt to run away."

"Property?"

"Your sewing arm. It belongs to me, everything from your bony shoulder to the tip of your middle finger. And now it is damaged." She frowned as though my arm were nothing more than a withered vine. "If I thought the horrid thing was completely useless, I would cut it off myself and feed it to the dogs."

"I had no intention of snubbing your Ladyship's hospitality," I told her. "I felt dizzy and needed fresh air. I thought a walk in the woods might raise my spirits."

"You know the rules, Maria. They are short, they are simple, and they are to be obeyed at all times." She clucked her tongue in a disapproving manner. "I would have thought your time spent here in the castle might have washed the rustic off you, but, apparently, what's bred in the bone will come out in the flesh."

"I'm sorry, Countess. I got scared."

She put her arm around my waist and led me to the bed. We sat down next to each other, and I crossed my arms over my chest. My muscles were tense, but my legs were quivering. I felt a strong desire to flee.

"I need you strong and healthy, Maria. You are no use to me battered and beaten. Nor can I afford extensive delays in the construction of these gowns." She looked at herself in the mirror. "I am losing my beauty as quickly as you are gaining yours, and it displeases me. Don't add to that displeasure by insulting my generosity."

"No, Countess. Of course not."

"I take it we can expect no more tantrums?"

"None."

"No more impulsive urges to run home and suckle from your mother?"

I pictured Mama standing in front of the fire, the bronze wind chime hanging on a post outside, the haycock leaning against the old wooden fence, and suddenly my insides felt stretched tight, as if someone were ripping them out of my chest.

The Countess leaned into me and sighed. "I don't like to repeat myself. If you continue to be difficult, then the next point I make will be with the sharp edge of my scissors." Her breath was hot, and sweet like wine. "Do you understand?"

I exhaled and found my voice. "Yes, Countess."

"You have no further desire to leave the warm confines of my castle?"

"No, none at all."

"Because you are quite happy here?"

I nodded.

The Countess put her palm under my chin and lifted my eyes to hers. "Say it, Maria. Say those five little words and we can be friends again."

I opened my mouth, lips trembling. "I am quite happy here."

She turned to Peter. "Peasants are so predictable. They pretend not to like grapes when the vines are too high for them to reach."

He smiled, but said nothing. I hated him for looking so calm and detached, for remaining quiet while she berated me as if I were a small child. But, really, what choice did he have? It was unwise to question the Countess, or to disagree with her. It was understood by every servant in the castle that to resist her was to invite more pain than even the most loathsome human being deserved. No matter what she said, no matter how cruel or insulting her words might be, the best response was an agreeable one that underscored her intelligence and authority.

The Countess rose from her bed and walked to the door. I followed behind her, head down, aware that Peter had left his place by the window to join us. "Since I am not a disagreeable person," she said, "I will allow you that fresh air which you so desperately crave."

I looked back and forth between her and Peter, not quite understanding her intent. "You mean I can…I have your permission to venture beyond the castle walls?"

"Yes, but Peter will stay by your side to ensure you don't wander off. The forest can be quite treacherous, and it would be a shame if you were to injure yourself further."

"Thank you, miss."

She waved her hand as though my gratitude were offensive. "I will make use of you however and whenever I can. I will not have you sitting in your room and staring at the wall because your arm hurts. You are here to be productive, not lazy."

"Yes, Countess."

"Miss Darvolia wishes to make an herbal treatment for my headaches, and she requires sage. There is a patch of it deep in the woods to the east of the castle. You will each take a basket and a pair of scissors, which you will collect from the kitchen. And don't pull up the sage by the roots. Cut it off low on the stem."

I nodded.

The Countess put her arm around Peter and kissed his forehead. "Make sure no harm comes to her."

"Of course."

"And be back well before sundown. The wolves are feisty when the moon rises." She looked at me with hard eyes. "Dawdle too long, Maria, and you will find yourself torn into so many pieces that Peter will have to carry you home in his own little basket."

It was beginning to rain by the time we entered the forest, not a steady drizzle, but scattered drops that dotted my arms and face. A stack of black clouds hovered overhead, barely visible above the leafy treetops, and a strong wind gusted through the thick shrubs and gnarled branches, almost ripping the basket out of my hand.

The air was cool and smelled of pine needles. I held out my arms as we traipsed through wide open spaces, savoring a lightness in my body that I hadn't felt in weeks. It felt good to be away from the castle—away from the Countess and her brutality—and for a brief moment I considered running away. I could live off berries and roots. I could drink from streams and rivers, traveling northwest until I reached Trenčín. I imagined Mama opening the creaky door and rushing outside to meet me, both of us crying as I fell into the safety of her arms.

But for how long?

Even if I survived the wolves, I would not survive the Countess. She was relentless in all her wants, and she would never stop searching for me, no matter how long it took. Even if I did manage to find my way back home across all those hills and mountains, Mama and I would still have to pack up our belongings and flee across the country.

And how could I run away with Peter standing beside me? He was faster and stronger, and he would surely catch me. Nor did I expect him to simply look away and let me dart off into the forest. The Countess had ordered him to watch over me, and if he returned home alone, she would surely torture him.

I stared down a long, windy trail and felt myself push off with my toes, ready to dash into the undergrowth. I heard twigs snap beneath me and the distant crack of thunder. But then I glanced over at Peter—his eyes set hard on the path ahead—and I crumbled at the thought of his broken body growing cold on the kitchen floor.

I hesitated—feeling angry and confused and defenseless—and tripped over a knobby root. As if sensing my helplessness, Peter picked me up and brushed the dirt from my scraped knees. He took my hand and pulled me closer, his fingers curled tight around mine as he led us deeper into the forest.

I walked as if in a trance, stopping to look at the red dahlias and gazing up into the darkening sky to watch a flock of black terns shoot over the treetops. Several times we heard wolves in the distance, and we crouched low until their howls faded away. It took us almost an hour to reach our destination, but I relished the delay. I was in no hurry to return to the castle.

The sage bushes were scattered beneath a cluster of towering oak trees. They were scraggly and unkempt, their grayish leaves a pale imitation of the vibrant green ones that shaded us from above in a soft canopy. Peter and I bent down, wiped the rain from our eyes, and cut pieces of fresh sage, snipping low at the stems like the Countess had instructed. We dropped the pieces into our damp baskets.

"Why can't we pull it up by the root?" I asked him an hour later as I massaged my sore shoulder. "It would be so much easier."

"Because we want the plant to grow back. This patch has been here for hundreds of years."

"Is Anna…" I straightened up to brush the hair out of my eyes. "Is she a mystic? Or is she…a healer?" It occurred to me that I still didn't understand her position at the castle, or why she was so valued as one of her Ladyship's confidantes.

"She is skilled in herbology," he said. "As you know, the Countess is prone to severe headaches and fits of malaise."

"Fits of rage, you mean." I set my basket on the ground and stretched my aching back. My fingers were stained green and smelled earthy. "She's more concerned with vanity than vigor."

Peter rose and looked at me, his eyes moving up and down as he took in my entire body. A slight smile teased the corners of his mouth. "Don't fault the Countess for lamenting her youth, Maria. Once, she was as beautiful as you are now. Men idolized her, and killed each other for a scrap of her attention."

He stepped forward and ran his fingers through my hair. He placed his hand on the small of my back and pulled me toward him. "You and I have no idea what it feels like to grow old…the sweetness draining out of our voices, our bodies wasting away like wood splintering."

I choked down my nervousness and stared up at the swollen sky. My entire body tingled.

"The Countess would give anything to shine inside those darkened halls like sparks through stubble, to merit much more than a fleeting glance or a consoling touch from an eager admirer." He kissed my cheek, his whiskers chafing my soft skin.

"She has her share of suitors," I whispered, my eyes half-closed. "I watch them coming and going, their arms weighed down with jewelry and trinkets and false bravado."

Peter laughed. "They believe her love will propel them toward positions of power, whether in the high courts of Vienna or in their own villages."

"They're banging their heads against a stone wall," I told him. "Nothing can get into a closed fist."

"Are you jealous?" He kissed me a second time, more firmly now on the corner of my mouth. "Or are you still stinging from that tongue lashing you received earlier?"

I pulled away and crossed my arms. "Apologies for being irritated, but I'm not accustomed to seeing a girl's fingers sliced open on account of a tiny mistake."

"That girl," he said, "despite your noble intentions to make her a martyr, has committed several mistakes since arriving in Čachtice. And she did not die."

"How can you be so callous?" I sat on the grass and leaned against an oak tree, stretching out my legs until I heard my knees pop. "If the girl is careless, then send her home, but don't…" I pushed the ghastly image from my mind. "Don't act dignified and righteous by pretending that what happened up in that room was necessary."

"Not necessary, but certainly expected. Everyone knows the Countess has a temper. The girl should have been more guarded in her presence."

I ripped up a handful of wet grass, shredded the blades into pieces, and tossed them into the air. "That girl has probably lost the use of both hands. At the very least, her fingers will be scarred and misshapen for the rest of her life."

Peter sat back down and put his arm around me. "I don't mean to be indifferent, Maria, but I've lived in the castle since I was a young boy. I've learned that silence equals survival. I have my fears, the same as everyone else…"

"But you won't live in the castle forever. At some point you must leave. Where will you go then?"

"I have no family outside of Čachtice," he said. "I'm just a poor orphan that the Countess found crying in a field, half-dead in the middle of winter. But at least here I'm clothed and fed and protected. And I'm educated, which means I'm acknowledged and listened to by everyone around me, even those with royal blood. Here, I serve a higher purpose. I'm as valuable as a gold coin."

I palmed an acorn and felt its roughness, then slid it inside the pocket of my dress. Papa once told me that carrying an acorn would ward off sorrow and pain, and right now I was carrying too much of both on my small shoulders.

Peter tapped the scissors against his leg. "Come, Maria. We should finish before the storm rolls over the mountains. The Countess has been kind in allowing us this pleasant diversion, but her graciousness extends only so far."

CHAPTER VIII

WE RETURNED TO THE castle in the late afternoon. The rain fell harder and thick clouds choked out the last remnants of sunlight. Bolts of lightning streaked across the dark sky and thunder boomed in the distance, shaking the muddy ground as we approached the gate with our baskets full of sage.

Father Barosius stood in the gatehouse, arguing with Helen. She pointed to five coffins stacked atop one another in the courtyard. He stepped away from her and made the sign of the cross. She leaned forward, poked him in the chest, and again pointed to the coffins. When he made to climb up into his wagon, Helen grabbed his beefy arm and pulled him toward the castle, slinging insults at his shuddering frame, her blonde hair whipping itself into a frenzy as every other word was slapped away by the biting wind.

Peter nudged me. "We should take these baskets to the kitchen so the sage can dry out."

"Shouldn't we bring them to Anna?" I yelled into his ear, my head bent low to avoid the downpour.

"If she's here, she'll collect them," he said, "but until then the baskets have to remain in the kitchen."

I was about to question him further, but we had just entered the castle and found the corridor blocked by Helen and Father Barosius, who were now arguing in the foyer. Peter pulled the heavy door closed and stood beside Helen.

"Don't question the Countess," she told the priest, "or it will go badly for you."

"I have tolerated her strange funeral requests for far too long," he said, "and I will not remain quiet over this matter."

"These allegations are nonsense."

"It is not customary for the coffins to be nailed shut before I collect them," Father Barosius said. "If you wish for these poor souls to rest in consecrated soil, then you must allow me to prepare the bodies before they are taken to the cemetery."

"These bodies don't require preparations," she said. "The girls died of cholera, which is why the Countess instructed me to nail down the lids. There is an epidemic at hand, and we must keep it at bay before we lose any more of your precious souls."

"I have always followed your instructions…despite my misgivings…but there are too many girls dying under mysterious circumstances."

"Peasants are full of sickness and disease. They track it wherever they go, like a mangy dog with fleas." Helen glared at him. "Would you defy her Ladyship's orders because your heart bleeds for a few miserable girls who cough up whatever food they're lucky enough to eat?"

"I don't pretend to know exactly what it is that lurks inside this castle," he said, "but I do know that beating all across this countryside gallops something like a beast. And it lives behind these ancient walls."

"Is it more money you want?"

Father Barosius held up his hand, and a look of intense sadness spread across his weathered face. "I cannot, in good faith, continue down this path."

Helen stepped in front of him, her eyes thin as razors. She motioned outside. "There are five coffins waiting to be loaded into your wagon."

"I will bury no more bodies for you."

She spat at his feet, then turned to Peter. "Bring the Countess."

Peter handed me his basket. "Take these to the kitchen, Maria." Then he hurried down the corridor and sprinted up the stairs as though his feet were on fire.

Helen—noticing me for the first time—gave me a shove. "Be quick about it. And stay there until you're needed elsewhere. I don't want you gallivanting through the castle. You're likely to tumble down the stairs and break your scrawny neck."

I brought the baskets to the kitchen and placed them on one of the tables, away from all the cooks and servants who were hurrying around with sharpened knives and cast-iron pots and slabs of fresh meat slung over their shoulders. I slunk off to the corner and shook out my wet clothes, wringing the water from my hair and warming my chilled feet by the fire. I looked for Sandra, but she wasn't there, so I sat by myself and ate an apple that one of the cooks gave to me.

When there was nothing left but a brownish core, I tossed it outside to the dogs and stood up. I knew I should return to my room, but I hesitated. Whether I was afraid for Father Barosius, or perhaps because I'd been cursed with my father's stubbornness, I found myself creeping along the passageway toward the foyer, tiptoeing around splashes of firelight and trying to remain in the shadows as much as possible.

Before I was halfway there, I heard the Countess's voice, cold and steady. Her words rumbled through the passageway and cut through whatever heat had warmed me in the kitchen.

"What is the nature of this intrusion?" she asked.

Father Barosius cleared his throat. "I can no longer take any coffins that have been nailed shut, your Ladyship."

There was silence. I took a few steps forward, crouched low to the floor, and glanced around the corner. The rough stone pressed against my face, and in between flashes of lightning I glimpsed Helen standing off to the side, her hands clasped together.

The Countess towered over the priest, her bone-white complexion almost translucent in the flickering candlelight. "You have picked an unfortunate moment to become pious, Father."

"The pious are never lacking in fight," he said.

She laughed. "You speak as if we were engaged in deadly combat. I have merely asked you to remove some coffins and to bury them in your churchyard."

"It offends God," he told her. "I am sworn to give the deceased a proper Christian burial, and I cannot attend to that if the bodies aren't properly prepared. They should be washed and anointed with oils, then dressed in a shroud."

"If they have stopped breathing, then they are adequately prepared for whatever judgment they receive."

"These circumstances are highly suspicious, and there are rumors in the village concerning the manner in which these young girls have lost their lives." His voice was growing stronger now, and his fingers clung to a rosary around his neck. "Last week, four girls died in one night. When I returned to the church I felt as though the devil were sitting on my shoulders. I broke open two of the coffins. The bodies inside were unclothed. They were bruised and mutilated."

"You are a priest, not a doctor. All I ask is that you drop these coffins into the ground, spit out a few prayers, and shovel some dirt. My directions are not complicated, nor are they confusing." The Countess glowered at him. "What is confusing, however, is your sudden insolence. It distresses me, and I don't like to be troubled by petty affairs."

Father Barosius took a step back, his hands trembling. "My unease has been festering for quite some time, your Ladyship. Too many girls have died, and I can no longer turn a blind eye."

She waved her hand as though swatting away a minor annoyance. "Your concerns are tenuous at best. One of the girls stole a knife from the kitchen and murdered the others for a fistful of jewelry. When confronted with these facts, the deranged girl barricaded herself in one of the bedrooms and killed herself."

"And what of the other girls?" he asked. "Am I to believe that cholera has killed hundreds this past year alone?"

The Countess stepped forward, her face wrapped in the encroaching darkness. "You will believe what I tell you."

"I cannot. As a humble servant of God, it's my duty to ensure that these poor girls don't leave this world with their eyes open and their mouths agape."

"Would you risk infecting the entire village with cholera?" she asked him. "Do you want the graveyard to be a red sea of stinking remains? No, I won't be held responsible for a plague."

"We need only exhume the other bodies," he said, "to find that the marks will almost certainly identify the manner of death."

"There was a time when your tongue was still and your pockets were heavy with gold," she said. "But now, having uncovered some torn-up bodies, you've suffered an attack of morality. I ask for cooperation. Instead, you have the rectitude to accuse me of impiety."

"I have been silent for far too long, and I fear the Lord will punish me along with you."

"Punish me?" She slapped him across the face. "Don't ever question the worth of a noblewoman, especially one from such a renowned family. I am a Báthory, one of God's elect, you pestilent swine."

Father Barosius staggered backward and rubbed his stinging cheek. "The devil has exercised in you his mighty works of unbelief, and only God knows an account of all your crimes."

She gripped his whiskered chin, her nails digging into his blotchy skin until droplets of blood appeared. She stared down at him, her voice a low throaty growl. "I will make you pay for this intolerance."

He turned, then—almost tripping over his green robe—and pushed past Helen, his fingers still clutched around the rosary. Muttering a rapid succession of prayers, he wrenched open the door and disappeared outside, swallowed up by the battering rain. In his place, a strong wind gusted into the room, scattering the rushes and dried herbs that carpeted the floor.

The Countess ran to the entryway and beat her fist against the thick wooden door. "May the devil make a ladder of your backbone," she screamed into the howling wind, "that I may climb up it on my way to Heaven."

I stayed hidden in the passageway, my face pressed against the stone wall. I peered around the sharp corner at the towering figures standing before me. Slanted rain beat against the large stained-glass windows, and the flames above me wavered in the damp air, rising and falling in quick tortured bursts as if twisted by an invisible hand. I scooted closer and squinted, rubbing my tired eyes as the foyer grew dark with the approaching dusk.

The Countess looked at the back of her hand and massaged the skin in slow circles. She walked over to a large mirror and gazed at her reflection. She touched the side of her face with the tips of her fingers.

Helen closed the door and shook raindrops from the hem of her dress.

"The priest will talk," the Countess said, "but no one of importance will listen."

"And what if the wrong ears should latch on to his mumblings?"

"No one connected with the king will ever fret over the death of a peasant, regardless of how many are buried in the churchyard."

"And the bodies?"

The Countess was quiet for a moment. She touched a deep wrinkle above her left eyebrow. Then: "We must demonstrate more caution now that the priest has developed a conscience. Tomorrow morning, once the storm passes, bring the bodies into the deepest part of the forest and leave them for the wolves."

Helen nodded. "And what of our precious butterfly? She has been flitting around the castle since she first arrived, hardly the timid creature that you..."

"She is nothing more than a fuzzy caterpillar," the Countess interrupted, "and we are keeping her warm in this stone cocoon."

"The girl is too brash," Helen said. "Too friendly with the other servants. We can't afford to let her wander the castle."

"What are you suggesting?" the Countess asked. "That we lock her away in the highest tower?"

"Only that we should guard her more closely. She's simmering in ferocity, and must be contained."

The Countess leaned into the candlelight and stroked her long neck. "My skin doesn't look as fresh as it did a week ago. I wish it to be brighter and suppler."

Helen took her hand and led her out of the foyer. They marched down the hallway and up the grand staircase—their chins jutting out and heads held high—like proper ladies taking a turn about the room.

"I shall have some food and wine sent up to your chamber immediately," Helen told the Countess, "and then I will make the necessary preparations for your evening bath."

I waited until the sounds of their footsteps died away, and then I rushed up to my room, glancing behind me at every moment to ensure I was alone. I'd been ordered to remain in the kitchen, but I didn't want to see anyone or talk to anyone. I was worn out and on the verge of tears. All I wanted was to throw myself down on my bed, shut my eyes, and disappear inside the folds of those filthy blankets.

I shut the door and lit a small candle, which I carried over to the barred window. Outside, the rocks below were shiny and smooth, polished like black onyx, while off in the distance—beneath a horizon smudged gray by passing storm clouds—large branches thrashed around in the pelting rain.

Staring into the forest, I wondered if I should have run off when I had the chance, if I should have braved the hungry wolves and nature's unleashed fury. But I soon realized the futility in such a hurried escape. For despite the lure of home, I knew that finding solace in my mother's arms would not take away my fears or troubles, and it made little sense to flee one storm only to charge headfirst into another.

In that small and terrifying moment, I knew only one thing for certain: If I escaped from Čachtice Castle, the Countess would find me; and when she did, I would surely know pain unlike any I had ever experienced.

I paced back and forth in my room for the next twenty minutes, and then I lay down and tried to fall asleep. I rolled onto my side, wrapping myself up as best I could, but my shoulder ached. Frustrated, I lay on my back and stared up at the numerous cracks that spider-webbed across the ceiling, thinking about poor Father Barosius.

Suddenly, the door was flung open and Helen stormed up to me with arched eyebrows. Her pointed finger threatened to impale me.

"You were given simple instructions, which you disobeyed. Tell me, Maria, is it terribly difficult to sit in one place and do absolutely nothing?"

I stood up and curtsied. "No, miss."

"Your orders were to stay in the kitchen and wait until I summoned you. Was I unclear in any way?"

"No, miss."

"Perhaps you believe you're better than everyone else? That you can disregard the rules on a whim?"

"The kitchen was hot and stuffy," I told her. "I felt lightheaded and didn't want to cause another disturbance."

Helen smiled. "Disturbance? You, my dear, are an annoyance at best."

"I'm sorry, miss."

She poked me in the chest. "You're always sorry. Ever since you arrived here at the castle you've been throwing that word around like bread to the birds."

I stared down at the floor, my hair falling over my eyes.

"You have seen what happens to little girls who misbehave, haven't you?"

"Seen, heard, and even smelled." A hint of anger crept into my voice. "Enough for a dozen lifetimes."

She scowled. "You are either a stupid girl who requires far too many examples, or an obstinate one who prefers to set her own."

I chewed on my bottom lip and swallowed the knot in my throat. I wondered if she could hear my heart thumping against my chest.

"Did you come straight here?" She moved closer and looked straight into my eyes. "After you left the kitchen?"

I tried to appear as innocent as possible, though my hands were fidgety. "Of course, miss."

Helen reached out and grabbed a hank of my hair, jerking it down so I was forced to glance up. "Or did you linger in one of the corridors? Perhaps eavesdropping on conversations that don't concern you?"

"No, I came straight upstairs and shut my door. I passed no one. I heard nothing."

She watched my face for several seconds, as if my brazen lies might rise to the surface in a rush of guilty blood. "You are not to leave this room tonight. Do you understand?"

"Yes, miss."

"If you feel ill..." She motioned toward the chamber pot in the corner.

I nodded.

"And if you disobey me again, I will disfigure your beautiful face with something more imaginative than a pair of scissors." She ran a finger across my face and down my bare neckline, tracing a slow circle in the hollow of my throat. "Perhaps I will smear your body in honey and make you stand outside all day in the hot sun, to be stung by bees and other insects."

Helen watched me, relishing the look of horror as her words found their mark. Then, after an unrelenting minute—satisfied that she'd once again regained her precious authority—she left the room and shut the door behind her.

I heard a key turn, and the rusted lock clicked into place. I sat at my table in the corner, surrounded by heaps of fabric and a silver tray strewn with shimmering diamonds. Shadows crept along the walls, thrown into the corners by a sputtering candle whose feeble light was no match for the bursts of lightning that continued to pound the landscape. For several hours, rain pelted my window in great sheets of water while peals of thunder exploded from atop the castle towers, reverberating through my very bones as I trembled in the darkness.

I wandered in slow, shuffling circles, crisscrossing the room as I fought hard to push away all the horrid thoughts that kept spiraling through my mind. I tried patching holes in a dress, but my stiff fingers could not steady themselves to thread a needle, and my tired eyes—red and swollen from such a tumultuous day—could barely see the table in front of me, no matter how hard I squinted.

Exhausted, I finally climbed into my rickety bed. I laid my head on the dusty pillow and curled up with the stiff blanket between my legs. Outside, the wind roared and shook the glass window. A yellow moon hung low in the rumbling sky. I turned away from the iron bars and closed my eyes, praying for sleep to wash over me.

Instead, I tossed and turned for hours, sleeping in fits and starts, my body slick with sweat.

A series of nightmares prowled my chaotic thoughts: A swarm of bees covering my naked body in a buzzing black gown, their sharp stingers puncturing my tender skin—

Then I was standing in the kitchen while dozens of girls were held down and beaten, blue welts rising up with every tormented scream, the crack of Benedict's whip slicing open their exposed backs like scissors cutting paper—

Then I was gasping for breath in the courtyard, running toward a mountain of coffins that towered above me like an impenetrable wall, blocking out the sun as warm drops of blood rained down from threadlike clouds that rushed across a purple sky—

The ground shook with a tremendous boom, and I found myself in the Countess's bedchamber, my mouth sewn shut while she gazed at her reflection in a large ornate mirror studded with rubies and—

I snapped to attention and sat up in bed, short of breath and shivering in the humid air. My eyes opened wide. They wandered across the tiny room. The candle had burned down hours before, and there was nothing left but total darkness and the foul odor of tallow wax. I peered closer into the murkiness. My fingers clutched the blanket—one bare foot dangling off the side of the bed—and in between the brilliant flashes of lightning I caught sight of a faint movement that froze my body with absolute terror.

Someone was standing in the corner.

CHAPTER IX

I SHUDDERED AND FELT the straw mattress crackle beneath me. A few strands of hair had fallen in front of my eyes, and I brushed them away with a trembling hand, peering into the deep blackness. I tried to make out any distinguishable features that might identify the intruder. Whoever was standing next to the spinning wheel did not move or make a sound, but hovered there like a ghost, watching me.

I pulled the blanket up to my chin. Even if I had wanted to scream, I doubt I would have been able to squeeze the air out of my lungs.

Several hours seemed to pass, though it was only a matter of minutes. The bed shook with thunder, the window rattled in its iron frame, and the lone figure stood stone still. Finally, I wet my lips and called out, "Hello? Who is that?"

The only sound was a sharp clap of thunder followed by a bolt of lightning that filled the room with a bluish tint.

I sat up straighter—prepared to reach out and grab the candlestick for protection—but the person expelled a long raspy breath and took a step forward. The wooden floor creaked in protest as the shape loomed closer, one hand reaching out in the thick gloom. I scooted back, my head hitting the wall, and threw up my arms, anticipating a violent attack. Instead, the mysterious stranger opened my bedroom door, cast one last glance in my direction, and glided into the hallway, an inky silhouette that flowed away into the long darkness as its footsteps receded with muffled pulses.

I flung off the blanket and let out a long piteous moan, then swung my feet onto the floor. I hurried over to the door—prepared to drag the sewing table in front of it for protection—but when I gripped the splintered wood in my hands, I felt small and powerless, certain that a flimsy table would not prevent someone from barging into my room if she was determined to do so.

Outside, bolts of lightning continued to slash the landscape in thin, jagged strips. I sat on the floor and hugged myself, wallowing in my vulnerability. I rocked back and forth like a small child, my forehead pressing into my knobby knees.

From somewhere below I heard what sounded like several voices. I felt my heart quicken. I was frightened that the mysterious stranger was now returning, and this time she would not be content to just hang back and stare. Panicked, I leapt up and clasped the Celtic love knot, treasuring its comfort and warmth as I caressed the thin silver chain that hung around my neck.

Since my arrival, this cramped space had been my only refuge from the castle's daily horrors, and now it had been infected, as if someone had bagged up months of misery and pain and dumped it onto the floor beside my bed. My panic turned to anger and I punched the door, scraping my skin across the rough wood. Leaning against the table, I swept a tangle of damp hair from my forehead and rubbed my eyes—white knuckles digging into closed lids until tiny red spots exploded across my line of vision.

My stomach felt queasy, as if I might become ill at any moment. I wanted to crawl back into bed and hide under the covers, but knew I shouldn't dismiss what had just happened. Someone had snuck into my room for a reason, and I needed to understand why. Otherwise, I might end up slashed and crippled, thrown inside a pine box, or dragged into the deepest part of the forest where my body would be torn apart by wolves.

My father always said that fear is only as deep as the mind allows, and standing there in the center of my room I realized that if I wanted some answers, I would have to reach out in the night and grasp for them.

Which meant I would have to follow the mysterious stranger.

I put on my leather shoes and grabbed the scissors off the sewing table. I jammed the blade into the thin metal plate bolted to the door and wiggled it back and forth until it separated from the wood. I pulled out the scissors and thrust them as hard as I could into the tight space, wrenching the plate toward me until it snapped free and fell to the floor with a resounding clang.

I pushed open the door and poked my head into the hallway. It was deserted. I closed my eyes and listened. All was quiet save for the thunderstorm now beginning to move south and out of the valley. I contemplated lighting a candle, but didn't want to draw attention to myself, so I tiptoed down the corridor, away from the servants' quarters and toward the grand staircase.

Taking small cautious steps, I felt along the wall with my right hand and crept down the stairs, careful not to slip or fall, letting bright splotches of the fading firelight lead me into the Great Hall, which seemed endless and imposing as it stretched into the night. Strange noises—a succession of creaks and clicks and taps—seemed to amplify around me as if something was waiting in the darkness and ready to pounce. I stood still and searched for a flicker of movement, listening for the tiniest sound, anything that might guide me in the right direction.

I had begun to lose hope when I heard a soft padding that echoed from one of the side passageways. It was a long, narrow hallway I had never explored, the Countess having declared it off limits to every servant in the castle. I ran as fast as I could through the cold air, sinking into the shadows while the soft leather shoes deadened my frantic footsteps. The front of my thin nightgown was soaked through with sweat, and the bottom dragged along the ground with a ghostly swishing sound.

As I drew closer, the padding became a calculated thumping. Only now there was another sound that resonated throughout the hallway, one that sprung up like a sudden rush of wind, a sound I'd heard many times since arriving at Čachtice Castle.

It was a terrifying and blood-curdling scream.

The sound came from deep within the castle; it filled the passageway, barreling toward me like a wave. It seemed to come from nowhere and yet from everywhere, pressing down on me from above while rising up from the floor beneath me.

I pushed forward, turning right and then left, slamming into a wall whenever I hit a dead end. Several minutes later—my shoulder aching, my knees scraped raw from stumbling and falling—I stopped and squinted. There, up ahead, hanging in the air like a dying ember, I spotted a pinprick of light. My fingertips, chafed from rubbing against the stone walls, brushed against cobwebs, and I sensed a slight shift in balance, as if the ground had become steeper and I was moving downhill. The light grew larger as I approached, becoming a bright yellow circle before finally assuming the shape of a long, wavering flame that cast the cramped space in a dull yellow glow.

I drew nearer to a wooden torch, secured high on the wall in an iron sconce. I glanced around for the mysterious stranger, expecting at any moment to feel someone's hot breath raise the hairs on the back of my neck, or for cold clammy hands to wrap around my slender throat.

I shuffled forward a few more feet and it was there that I finally stopped, for the corridor ended abruptly. Hanging on the wall before me was a giant red and white tapestry portraying the Báthory coat of arms.

The weak light spread across the corridor in shallow pools. I moved through them with careful steps, running my hands down the length of one wall and then the next, searching for the opening to another corridor. There was nothing but cold black rock and a damp, musty smell. I was exhausted and beginning to feel disoriented. I moved faster while the screams around me pierced the silence like needles puncturing skin. I knelt down on my hands and knees and felt across the cracks in the floor for a hidden trapdoor. There was nothing except dead bugs and pieces of old straw. I looked up and stared at the ceiling, wondering if there was a void through which the mysterious stranger might have climbed.

When I had exhausted all possibilities, I stood in front of the giant tapestry, shivering as I pressed my face into its dirty cotton. The stitching felt rough and bumpy. I wanted to cry at how miserable and alone I felt. My body was sore and achy. I wanted to collapse on the stone floor and fall asleep, but I knew better than to be caught wandering the halls when morning came.

I took a step back and studied the tapestry. The top half was covered with enormous cobwebs while the lower half billowed out ever so slightly, the faded colors brushing against my legs.

And then my mouth fell open as I stared down at the rippling fabric, as I realized that a tapestry shouldn't billow when it's underground.

Not unless...

I moved to the far corner and looked behind the tapestry, noticing a spacious gap about three feet wide. I stepped inside the chasm and braved my way forward, struggling to breathe as the heavy air crushed me from all sides. I thrust out both hands and my fingers skimmed the rough rock wall, traveling over bumps and cracks until they slipped into emptiness.

Turning right, I found myself standing in front of a dark passageway. There was no light emanating from within, though the air was cooler and a faint breeze tickled my nose. I leaned forward and peered into the abyss, trying to see what lay beyond. I took a step forward, hesitant, for the screams were growing louder now, horrifying and heart-wrenching, leading me deeper and deeper into the bowels of Čachtice Castle.

Light from the torch behind me trickled into the darkness. I could see only a few inches in front of my face. I put another foot forward, hand stretched out before me, and realized I was standing on the edge of a stone step. The stairs seemed to disappear into the earth, and there was a low howling sound, as if even the wind felt trapped and was trying to break free.

I walked down crumbling stairs that were slanted and uneven, forced to press my fingers against the wall for support. The air became colder as I descended. Soon, I stepped onto solid ground once again, creeping forward as I twisted and turned through a labyrinth of narrow tunnels. I stumbled over rocks and banged into jagged walls. I breathed in dust and wiped beads of sweat from my stinging eyes. And then the corridor straightened out, a thin ray of light focused my vision, and up ahead I saw figures moving about inside a vast underground chamber.

The room was circular. Dozens of flaming torches were mounted on the walls. Several cages hung from the low ceiling, and lying on a large table was an assortment of whips, pincers, and rusted branding irons. In the center of the room, looking ominous in the flickering firelight, sat a copper tub, smooth and round like an egg.

Hanging above the copper tub—upside down, with thick chains wrapped around her ankles—was a servant girl. She was naked. Her hands were tied behind her back, and the front of her body was bruised and covered with whip marks. I recognized her as someone who worked in the kitchen, though she'd been absent for several days. Sandra told me the girl had been confined to one of the cholera rooms at the back of the castle. Instead, she was right in front of me, screaming and crying, both lips purpled and split open. Her legs were crisscrossed with blistering burns from a branding iron, and a row of jagged teeth marks ran down the side of her stomach from where someone had bitten into her.

Suddenly, Benedict stepped out from behind the table, his strong strides slicing through the heavy shadows that ran across the chamber floor. He reached up and wrapped his muscular arms around the girl's waist, holding her still despite her constant struggles. She thrashed from side to side while he stood there silent, the veins on his arms bulging out.

From another passageway—a yawning gap cut out of ancient stone—Helen stepped forward into the firelight and approached the tub. She carried a small dagger, the handle encrusted with rubies. Grabbing a fistful of the girl's hair, she yanked back her head, exposing the pale neck. Then, in one quick movement, she ran the knife across the girl's throat until it opened up like a smile, the blood draining out of her and spilling into the tub below.

I bit my knuckles to stifle a scream. My knees shook and I slid to the floor, vomiting what little food was in my stomach. Fearing I might faint, I pressed my forehead against the cold wall, watching the girl's body writhe for a few more seconds, her mouth open wide in a hideous gurgle. Her eyes glazed over as the gushing torrent of blood slowed to a steady stream and then to a trickle. She stopped convulsing, and the heavy chains clinked together as her lifeless body swayed back and forth like a pendulum.

Benedict unchained the body and carried it out of the room. Minutes later he returned with another girl, just as battered and bruised as the first. He tied her hands and strung her up, ignoring the heavy sobs that choked her. Like a cook handling meat in the kitchen, he held her with a disinterested look while Helen reached up and slit her throat.

This gruesome process continued for the next thirty minutes—I counted seven girls—until the tub was almost full, the smooth golden rim now stained with drops of blood. When the last corpse had been slung over Benedict's shoulder and carried out of the room, the Countess appeared, gliding out of the shadows. She wore a red silk robe, and her hair was pinned up in a tight bun. She removed her robe and handed it to Helen. Then, taking Benedict's outstretched hand, she stepped into the tub and lowered herself into the pool of blood.

The Countess closed her eyes and exhaled in a languorous ecstasy. She leaned back her head until it rested against the curved rim. Though her face was obscured by the shadows, I saw that she was smiling, her eyelids fluttering as she rubbed the warm blood into her arms and breasts.

After several minutes she sat up and cupped her hands together, then dipped them into the blood. She splashed it onto her face, letting the thick liquid run down her neck in sluggish rivers. She rubbed it into her cheeks and smeared it across her forehead with the tips of her fingers. Several drops splashed onto the floor, but the Countess—usually so orderly and precise—didn't seem concerned. Instead, she leaned forward to let Helen wash her back, her face tilted up toward the set of chains dangling above her.

She sank lower into the tub and raised her feet high into the air, one at a time so Helen could wash them with a small cloth. Sitting there in the small circular tub, her skin looking as white as milk in the firelight—her body speckled with fresh blood—the Countess looked like she had just been born.

I wanted to run for help, but there was no one within arm's length to pull me out of this nightmare. Sandra and the other servants were locked in their rooms, and Father Barosius was tucked away safely at his church. As for Peter, I had no idea where in the castle he slept, and it suddenly occurred to me that I'd never bothered to ask him.

Besides, even if I did find solace in the arms of a friend, who would believe me?

Yesterday, the entire kitchen had witnessed me suffering a breakdown. If I ran through the castle shouting tales of torture and murder, the Countess was sure to attack my mental stability and brand me as a grumbling peasant who had strayed too far from home. Worse, I might find myself hanging from those heavy chains, my good intentions bleeding into the tub along with the rest of me.

I hid in the shadows, afraid to move. When the Countess had been scrubbed and washed, every pore and wrinkle tended to, she sank even deeper into the crimson pool, her head barely visible above the glinting rim. She closed her eyes and was still for several minutes, the entire room silent save for occasional ripples of blood that splashed against the sides of the tub whenever she shifted her weight.

"Music." She motioned toward the dark recess from which Helen had entered the room. "Bring me something to stir my soul."

Benedict left the chamber and returned moments later, dragging a young girl by the hair. I recognized her as the same one whose fingers the Countess had stabbed with the scissors. He threw the poor girl to the ground and shoved her inside a small cage. Dozens of sharp metal spikes jutted into it from all sides, and they sliced open her tender skin as she thrashed about in agony. The cage was too short for her to stand inside, but too narrow for her to sit down. She was forced to bend her body in a grotesque shape, as if all her bones had been broken.

Benedict locked the cage, and I saw that it was attached to a pulley. He took hold of a rope lying on the ground and pulled with all his strength until the cage rose into the air. The girl screamed as the cage swung from side to side, the spikes shredding her arms and legs and ripping apart her small hands as she held them out for protection.

Benedict pulled on the rope. The cage rocked back and forth, jostled in every direction, until the girl's desperate cries tapered off. Streaks of blood ran down the iron bars. They dripped onto the floor as her face, now slashed and unrecognizable, spun back into view. Her fingers—which stuck out of the cage at odd angles—spasmed for several seconds. Her body—bent forward as if offering a silent prayer—gave one final shudder.

I felt consciousness slipping from my tenuous grasp. My hands were numb, and my lips were cracked from constantly licking them. I pinched my cheeks, sucked in a lungful of air, and twisted the skin on my arm until tears ran down my face.

Benedict lowered the cage to the floor. He unlocked the door, reached in with careful precision, and pulled out what was left of the girl. Her skin hung in tatters off exposed bones. Grabbing one of her arms, he dragged the body across the floor, his footprints leaving a bloody trail as he disappeared inside the darkened tunnel on the far side of the room.

The Countess dipped her fingers into the warm blood. She rubbed it into her lips and down the bridge of her nose, massaging the lines and creases that threaded across her face. She smiled and stared up at the spiral patterns etched into the ceiling.

I knew I should return to my room. I would have to answer for the broken lock on my door, and I needed time to create an excuse that wouldn't sentence me to death or endanger the other servants. Reaching up, I grasped an outcropping of rock and willed myself to stand. I grit my teeth until the waves of nausea broke, then I shuffled backward into the receding darkness.

My eyes were still focused on the Countess—ready to retrace my path through that intricate maze of tunnels—when I heard the footsteps behind me. A hand clamped down onto my shoulder and I froze, certain my heart would burst. Turning, I stared into the hard eyes of Anna Darvolia. Her face seemed wizened and blackened, as if carved from the very same rock now surrounding me.

Seizing my hand, she pulled me into the room, toward the tub and the Countess and the overpowering smell of death. The hem of my nightgown ripped as I pitched forward. My bare knees scraped against the floor. I cried out in pain and covered my face with my hands, refusing to glance up as everyone encircled me. Any moment now, I expected to be strung up on those chains, or to be pushed inside that awful cage and swung around the room for musical entertainment.

Amid the deafening silence, the Countess spoke: "It seems Maria is afraid to be alone in her room. She wishes to surround herself with friends."

Benedict reached down and lifted me to my feet. Struggling to stand, I gripped the edge of the tub and forced myself to meet her gaze. She extended her hand and laid it on my arm, which was spotted with goosebumps. Drops of blood dripped off her fingertips and splashed onto my nightgown.

"You were told to remain in your room, and to stay there until the morning," she said.

"I…yes, miss."

"Were my instructions mystifying?" she asked. "Or were you merely sleepwalking through the castle?"

I glanced over at Helen. She looked like she wanted to wrap her hands around my throat and squeeze until her knuckles turned white. Even in that frigid chamber I could feel her rage. Her eyes—normally wide open—were now tiny slits, and bright red splotches dotted her cheeks.

"I woke up...the storm outside..." I whispered the words as though I didn't trust their integrity. "There was...someone...standing in the corner."

The Countess laughed. "How wonderful that someone cares enough to watch over you, to make sure that no harm befalls you in the midst of such dreadful weather." She patted my arm as though placating a small child. "Your mother would be delighted to know we're taking such good care of you."

I stood there panting, my heart wedged in my throat, until the Countess glanced over at Benedict and Anna, whereupon they hurried across the chamber floor and disappeared inside the dark entryway.

Standing in the center of the room, I saw that the ceiling was lower than I'd imagined and decorated with various pictures. Some resembled the moon while others were clearly crosses. There were several large triangles, surrounded by what looked like leaves on a branch, followed by another series of smaller upside down triangles that wrapped around the edge of the ceiling in an ornate border.

Peering closer, I saw that etched into the center of the ceiling—directly above the Countess, and spreading outward like the rays of the sun—was a sequence of large luminous stars that revolved around what appeared to be a goat head and a chalice.

Several large mirrors had been hung on the walls to reflect the firelight, and across from me was the table laden with branding irons and knives. In front of it sat the cage studded with iron spikes. As far as I could tell, there were only two entrances to this horrid tomb, both carved out of solid rock: the one to my left leading back to the castle, and the mysterious one to my right that had swallowed up Anna and Benedict.

The Countess sank back into the tub. "Despite my best efforts, it's apparent that Maria no longer enjoys the confines of her cozy room. She dislikes it so much, in fact, that she's developed an uncanny ability to pass through locked doors as if she were a ghost."

"But the person...in the corner..."

She raised a hand and I backed away, thinking she meant to strike me. "Helen, please find more suitable accommodations for our restless spirit. Someplace where she feels less of an urge to skulk around the castle." She spoke the word "suitable" as though it were an ugly blemish, and again my heart raced and my knees shook until I was certain I was going to collapse on the ground in a heap of hysterics.

Helen handed me the blood-stained cloth, cast me another fierce scowl, and stomped out of the chamber.

The Countess sat up and instructed me to wash her back. I became nauseous and felt the room spin, as if my entire world was sliding off a steep ledge. Somehow, I dipped the cloth into the warm blood, squeezed it out, and ran it up and down her back in broad strokes. She reached up to move her hair aside so I could wash the nape of her neck, which I did in vigorous circles like Mama used to do when scrubbing dirt off my face.

"You must think me a monster," she said matter-of-factly.

"No, miss…" I dunked the cloth into the tub and began to wash her arms. She spread them out on either side as though she might fly away at any moment.

"You have never felt vulnerable, Maria. You possess nothing of value, thus you have nothing important to lose. But I, on the other hand, have money and property and political positions, all of which I intend to pass on to my children." She turned to look at me. "Do you know how difficult it is to maintain power and control when men are trying to get close to me so they can seize my money? They play games with their words and gestures, believing a smile will unlock my heart. They think wearing a codpiece will ingratiate themselves into my bedchamber, that they can simply lie their way to divine power instead of claiming it as a birthright."

She lowered her arms and leaned back again. I noticed that several stray hairs had slipped free from her bun; they spilled over the back of the tub like a waterfall. Some of the edges had clotted together and were tinged red with flecks of blood.

"Since my husband's death, many men have tried to take advantage of me, including King Matthias. But the Báthory name is not easily won, and I refuse to be conquered by a few measly thrusts that are doled out halfheartedly by some panting ruffian."

The Countess cupped her hands, lowered them into the dark red pool, and splashed blood onto her face until she looked ferocious in the smoldering light. "The only true love I've ever known is with the beauty bestowed upon me, and even that is being scraped away by time." She touched the side of her face. "Do you not see how youthful I look after bathing in the blood of these peasants, how my skin seems fresher and smoother, my wrinkles less noticeable?"

"But...they're innocent children..."

"They are pure. Which means their blood has not yet boiled over from the constant stings of unrequited love. It has not been corrupted by hate and jealousy." She smiled. "Their blood is fresh and chaste, like water gurgling out of an underground stream, and I indulge in it because that is my right."

The Countess reached for my arm and stood up to let the blood run down her body. Patches of it clung to her skin. She remained standing there for several minutes—her body shimmering pink in the firelight—and then she stepped out of the tub with a drowsy sigh, whereupon Anna emerged from the darkness with a silk shawl that she wrapped around her shoulders.

Anna plunged her gnarled hand into the crimson pool, fumbling around in its depths until she withdrew a small brass plug. Immediately, the blood began to drain out. Confused, I peeked underneath the tub and noticed a wide chasm cut into the floor like a jagged vein. The blood was now filling it and flowing away toward that dark entryway, which I now realized was at the far end of a sloping floor.

The Countess must have noticed me watching, for she pointed toward the black recess and said, "The boundaries that divide life and death are often as delicate as a shadow, but they become more pronounced as we age. Every blemish and pockmark, every turn of gray, is yet another painful reminder that Death approaches with hands of stone."

I glanced at the copper tub ringed with red, at the rusted chains hanging from the ceiling, and at the cage in front of the table with its spikes still wet and glistening.

"But I will not sit idly while the years continue to slip past." She pulled the shawl tight around her shoulders. "If I am to secure my holdings, then I must maintain my youth."

I took a step forward and tried to see through the cobwebbed gloom, past the jagged hole carved before me in the ancient earth, but my tired eyes would not adjust to the dimming firelight. I wanted to look away, but I couldn't. I had seen young girls pulled from its gaping mouth, and I had watched their lifeless bodies dragged back into it. I wanted so badly to be standing on the other side—to know exactly what I was facing—but the thought of what lay beyond seemed more ghastly to me than anything I had yet encountered.

Amidst the deep echo of crackling flames, the drain shuddered and the tub emptied its vile contents with one last gasp. As if in response, the Countess took my hand and led me out of her secret chamber, back toward the castle from whence we'd come.

As we began our ascent, she turned to me and said, "You are an intelligent girl, Maria. And intelligent girls understand that words must be used with restraint. You will remain silent about everything you have seen. You will not even whisper it to your own reflection. And if you cannot hold your tongue, then I will rip it out to ensure your compliance."

"Yes, Countess." Sickened, I followed her into the darkness, up winding stone steps and through narrow passageways, contemplating everything I had seen that terrible night, and dreading wherever it was I might now be going.

CHAPTER X

EVER SINCE ANNA HAD come to our cottage on that cold day in March, I had dreamed of impressing the Countess and rising above my position. I wanted fancier clothes and important responsibilities. I wanted to be addressed by name and looked directly in the eye when spoken to, as if I was worthy enough to command attention.

And when I finally received what I thought I'd always wanted, I was more miserable than ever.

The morning after I stumbled into the secret chamber, I was removed from the servants' quarters and brought to an even smaller room, which was located right next to her Ladyship's. While I no longer had a window or a nightstand, I did gain a four-poster bed that belonged to one of the Báthory children. It was built out of cedar, and instead of a lumpy straw mattress—infested with lice and fleas and swarming with spiders—I now had a comfortable one stuffed with wool, atop which lay a soft coverlet filled with down feathers plucked from geese that roamed the castle grounds. There was also a white linen blanket—embroidered with the family's coat of arms—and a long slender pillow that cooled my cheek whenever I lay down to sleep.

From the highest floor of the castle the screams that had kept me awake were now almost nonexistent, nothing more than bits of anguish stirred up by a steady breeze that swept through the long winding corridors. Which would have been a blessing had I not been forced to stand inside that chamber and listen to young girls beg for mercy while they hung above me like meat on a hook. I worked with these girls in the kitchen; I picked vegetables with them in the garden. Every morning, I passed them in the corridors and offered a smile, trying to raise their defeated spirits. Out of pity—or perhaps a selfish longing that raged inside of me—I reassured them that one day soon they would return home to their families.

And now pieces of them were spilling into a copper tub, running through the Countess' fingers whenever she cupped her hands to splash their fresh blood all over her face.

My daily routine had shifted to the point where I often felt shaky and bewildered, as if I were stumbling through a haze in no discernible direction. I was now permitted to sleep until ten o'clock, whereupon I hurried down to the kitchen, ate some bread and cheese, and assisted the other servants in their chores until midday. I spent the afternoons alone in my room, stitching expensive fabric and mending torn clothes.

If the Countess was not happy with her appearance, I went to bed early. On those occasions, Helen woke me just before three o'clock in the morning and together we proceeded downstairs and disappeared behind the tapestry. The Countess preferred to indulge in her atrocities when the castle was steeped in silence. She wanted privacy, not because of what people might think—peasant deaths would not prompt an uproar—but because she believed atmosphere was as crucial as blood in drawing beauty out of her aged skin.

I watched Benedict lead more and more girls out of that dark entryway. He strung them up by their thin ankles, and with one quick swipe Helen slit their throats. I closed my eyes as their gasps and screams gurgled into silence. Then, clutching the washcloth, I plunged my hands into their warm blood. I bathed the Countess until she was satisfied that her pores had absorbed every drop, and I assured her that my detailed cleansing had restored elegance to every line, wrinkle, and crevice.

For the next hour she lay submerged in that still and awful red, reminiscing about the golden luster her skin once possessed. She shared quaint stories of her childhood at Ecsed Castle, and she swore to preserve her magnificence, no matter how many bodies she was forced to dispose of.

After the tub had been drained—and the Countess was dried off and wrapped in her shawl—we returned to her bedchamber where Anna prepared yet another bath, this one containing hot water mixed with rosemary, lavender, calendula, and yarrow, all of which were meant to soothe and rejuvenate the newly tempered skin.

Finally, around five o'clock in the morning—tired and sore and freckled with blood—I crawled back into my bed for a few hours of sleep, my restlessness punctuated by thoughts of Mama and our rustic life in the cottage. Oftentimes, despite sleeping on a cloud of feathers, I awoke clutching my chest, struggling to breathe while I massaged the ache in my heart that grew so strong I feared it might one day split me in half.

The Countess became more agitated and volatile, for the wrinkles were not disappearing as fast as she wished. One morning she woke up with a sharp pain in her side and ordered Anna to fetch more girls from the surrounding villages. Soon I was summoned every night to the underground chamber, and my arms became so sore that I had difficulty performing my daily chores.

Sometimes, I snuck away to an empty room and stared out the window, wishing I could wash away the shadows that had soaked into my skin. I prayed for an opportunity to go outside and feel alive. I wanted to sweat in the sweltering sun while I tended to the animals and hauled buckets of water out of the well. I wanted to walk through the dandelion meadow at dusk, lazing under a hot and copper sky.

But the Countess said it was not safe for me to leave the castle, and so I confined myself to my room as much as I could. When I wasn't stitching, I sat on my bed and gazed at the gray walls, counting cracks in the stone and remembering stories my father told me, like the one about the pilgrims traveling to the shrine of Saint Thomas Beckett at Canterbury Cathedral, or the poem about the green knight in Camelot whose head is chopped off on New Year's Day.

I was locked away in the highest tower, surrounded by giants who wanted to grind my bones. The wolves crept closer to the castle, feasting on more and more bodies as the Countess became ever so ravenous in her desire to remain young. And as their howls grew louder—drifting through the walls late at night—I felt terrified and alone, more separated than ever from those who might sympathize with my plight.

All I had in the world—apart from my Celtic love knot—was the old cedar trunk, a table loaded with fabric, and a spinning wheel with a cracked spindle.

And the antique mirror, which—unbeknownst to me—would soon become my salvation.

Benedict and Peter had hauled it into my room one afternoon while I was busy cutting fabric, a full-length mirror set into a thick panel of solid red oak. They pushed it against the wall, grunting and cursing while I tried to recognize the dour-looking girl trapped behind the polished glass. Peter cast me a secret glance and I smiled, wishing he would stand next to me so I could lean into him for support. Since our trip into the forest, we had not been able to meet for more than five minutes at a time, and I was tired of one-sided conversations in which I was scolded or lectured.

Later that night, the Countess walked into my room and stood in front of the mirror. "This belonged to me when I was a child," she said. "And when I traded up for something more grand, I gave it to my daughter, Katherine."

"Thank you," I told her. "You're most gracious."

She laughed. "I am not doling out niceties, Maria. Nor am I in the habit of bestowing my most prized possessions to peasants." She ran her finger along the edge of the oak frame. "This is a work of art. It belongs in a castle, not in some shabby hovel infested with rats."

I sat on the bed and said nothing.

"You are moody," she said. "Perhaps you are tired. Or perhaps you miss your tiny window overlooking the forest." She waited for me to respond, and when I didn't she pointed to the mirror. "No matter. Here is something far more useful than a hole cut into a wall."

"I have too many tasks to complete," I told her. "I can't afford to sit in front of a mirror." Too late, I realized I had spoken with a hint of disdain, and so I said, "Your ladyship would be most displeased if I neglected my work."

"A woman should take pride in her work, yes, but she must first take pride in herself." The Countess turned left and then right, tilting back her head to admire the smoothness of her neck. "You must learn to appreciate your own beauty, Maria. You are careless with it. You must protect it; otherwise your reflection will soon look unpolished."

I glanced down at the dried blood under my fingernails, which were broken and bitten.

"I had your loveliness once," she continued, "and it grew stale as the years unfolded. I sat in this castle, staring out a window, waiting for my husband to return from his battles." She moved closer to the mirror, her lips almost kissing the reflection. "He left me alone to wither away like some forgotten flower deprived of sunlight."

I wasn't sure if she wanted sympathy or praise, so I clasped my hands together and held them against my chest.

The Countess walked over to the bed and took a lock of my hair in her hand. "You don't understand how exquisite you are. You are a spectacle, more precious than jewels." She brought the black curl to her nose and inhaled as if she were delighting in the fragrance of an entire garden. "I would claim your beauty as my own if I could."

"You flatter me," I told her, "but you are far lovelier."

"It's not enough to be pretty, Maria. You must flaunt it with a confidence that others find intimidating and extravagant. Otherwise, you'll become foolish and let love sneak up on you, as I once did. I was young and brash, and I didn't understand that love has the remarkable ability to make you smile while it slowly kills you."

The Countess left soon after, and I resolved to not even glance at the mirror. Instead, I covered it with a piece of blue linen cloth. I did not want to face myself—the pale complexion and sunken cheeks, the hair tangled in knots—and be reminded that all of my grand ambitions were nothing more than pockets of misplaced naivety. I had been lured by the splendor and majesty of Čachtice Castle, forgetting that while honey may be sweet, no one licks it off a briar.

Because it was summer, there was no need to clean ash out of the fireplace, and so it became harder to find ways to teach Sandra her letters and numbers. Sometimes we wrote words in the dust that collected on tables; other times we would reach into a burlap sack to grab handfuls of lentils that we'd then arrange on the floor to spell out whatever words fitted our mood; occasionally, we ventured outside, using sticks to carve our names in hard dirt that had been baked clean by a blazing sun.

Sandra was a quick learner, and it was wonderful to watch her scribble down letters, and then words, and finally short sentences. It afforded her a power at the castle that no one could take away from her. No matter where we were, whether in the kitchen or in the Great Hall, I found words for her to sound out and pronounce. In the library, I made her read aloud all the titles on the lower shelves, and though she asked to flip through the pages of a book, I wouldn't allow it. I knew too well the nobility's attitude on peasants being educated, and I didn't want anyone to discover us reading.

As Sandra became more confident in her reading and writing, she also became more vocal in expressing her own opinions. She was especially critical of Baron Helfert and the taxes he demanded, as well as the deplorable conditions in the debtors' prisons. When engaged in conversation, she now leaned forward with an eagerness that threatened to topple her over at any moment. She was not so quick anymore to glance down the corridor before asking a question, nor was she eager to lower her eyes and whisper away her feelings while we sat in the crowded kitchen and peeled potatoes.

Teaching Sandra redirected my attention in a way that kept my mind sharp, allowing me to focus my strength on daily routines and habits rather than on the cruel images that paraded through my mind. After enduring several weeks in that underground chamber, I began to have raging headaches. At least twice a day I needed to lie down, shut my eyes, and press my fingers into my throbbing temples.

"Maria, you look unwell," Sandra said one morning as we stored fruits and vegetables in the pantry. We wheezed in the hot dusty air, our backs aching as we dragged large crates across the stone floor and stretched our arms high to reach the deep shelves that towered above us. "Do you need to rest?"

I sat on one of the crates still left unopened. "I'm just feeling a bit shattered, is all. I'm working hard to finish the second gown, and my fingers are stiff."

My exhaustion had slowed my work, though the second gown was proving much easier to assemble than the first. It was a gift for the Countess's youngest daughter, Katherine. But she was recently married and unable to return to the castle. Thus, I was instructed to use my own measurements as a substitute since we were both of similar height and build.

Sandra shook her head. "It's a shame you're devoting this much time to gowns that will be worn once and then tossed aside."

"Why do you say that?"

"If you're sewing the same type of gown for three different people, then there must be a special occasion," she said. "And since the Countess rarely sees her children, it only makes sense that your gowns will eventually attract moths instead of attention."

"Her children never visit?"

"If they have, I've never seen them." Sandra scooped up a handful of strawberries and added them to a jar of honey, repeating this action until the jar was full and the entire room smelled sticky and sweet. She sealed up the jar and put it on the shelf next to a larger jar of pickled cabbage. "Besides, Katherine and Ursula and Anastasia are all married. They have their own lands to manage."

"Three? But I thought…"

Sandra clapped her hands. "You've heard the rumors, too?"

"What rumors?"

"Supposedly, the Countess had an illegitimate child with some peasant boy when she was fourteen, the same time she was betrothed to the Count. The baby was given to distant relatives, but the boy was castrated and thrown to a pack of wild dogs."

I stood up and rearranged a row of jars, pushing them aside to make room for several bags of apples. "Does the Countess have any more children? Or just the three daughters?"

"Paul, who's eleven, is her only son. He's usually away at school."

I knew the Countess was a private person, and it was no secret she mistrusted the servants—considering them as scavengers who were fortunate enough to receive whatever snippets she elected to offer—but if she had three daughters, then why hadn't I been asked to sew four gowns?

Sandra pushed an empty crate into a corner of the pantry, chattering away as if she still had my undivided attention. "Did you know that Paul's great uncle is the King of Poland? The Countess is next in line, of course, but apparently she wants Paul to assume the throne, probably because she can't bear to leave this gloomy slab of rock. She's been sending him to Ecsed Castle for years…that's where she spent her own childhood…probably so he can form political alliances and learn how to manage…"

"How do you know all of this?" I asked her.

She laughed. "I'm small, Maria. I can hide in a lot of places."

I pictured Sandra crouched under a table on her hands and knees, peering through a silk brocade that hung over the beveled edge, her knuckles digging into the floor; or standing rigid behind one of the velvet curtains, breath held tight as her blushing ears caught scraps of some private conversation.

But then I pictured her face crumbling in fright when a hand reached into the darkness to seize her wrist. I imagined her small body being dragged down those ancient steps into that bloody chamber. My chest tightened when I remembered how the Countess enjoyed whipping and torturing the girls herself, so she could watch their faces contort in agony as they pleaded for her to stop.

"You can't take chances," I told her. "No matter…"

I froze and peered over Sandra's shoulder, certain I had seen a movement in the corridor, certain I'd heard a slow and steady scraping as though someone were tiptoeing over rough stone.

"…no matter how safe you think you are." I cupped her face in my hands and looked directly into her eyes. "I know you're angry, and that you want to run home and never look back, but don't make the mistake of believing that God is with you inside these walls."

She crossed her arms, though her expression was still soft. "I know you're being protective, Maria, but you're also hiding something. I see it in the way you shuffle through the corridors. And I hear it in your voice…how your words break off mid-sentence…as if something awful has crept up behind you."

I forced a smile. "You think you're being clever, but it's too dangerous. Trust me, please, it's not safe for you to prowl around the castle."

Sandra's voice shrunk to a whisper. "But there's a monster living among us. And I'm terrified that it'll sneak up behind me, that it'll catch me in its jaws and swallow me whole."

"All of us are running from that same monster," I told her, "but understanding exactly what it is won't help you to fight it."

She looked past me, out the door and into the long dark passageway that led from the kitchen into the main part of the castle, her eyes darting back and forth as if she could see strange things moving about in the shadows. "I know that. But I'm more afraid not to face it."

One morning, several weeks later, I stood in the Great Hall—admiring the paintings below the Minstrel's Gallery—when Peter snuck up behind me and threw his arms around my neck.

"Shouldn't you be with the other servants?" he asked. "Helping to store ale in the buttery?"

The Countess was having one of her fits, distressed by wrinkles on her face that had deepened since her last cleansing. She was in bed, raging at whoever dared to approach her, eating strawberries and drinking herbal potions out of a large chalice. Since Helen and Anna were busy attending to her list of demands, I had long stretches of freedom where I could wander the castle.

Peter stepped closer to a portrait of the Carpathian Mountains. It hung at eye-level between two tall windows on a gold baroque frame. "The Countess has a taste for opulence," he said. "A desire to collect delicate things."

Yes, I thought, *and then she slaughters them and leaves their bodies to rot in the forest.*

"She has them shipped here from Vienna and Rome, even as far away as Paris," he continued. "Paintings and sculptures and pieces of furniture, all arriving in large crates packed with straw."

The Countess indeed valued her property. She was constantly buying treasures and trinkets, adamant about what symbolized meaningful beauty, meticulous in ensuring it was not damaged, and specific in explaining where it should reside in the castle so as to enhance her own appearance, as well as to impress visitors with her luxurious and refined tastes. Čachtice Castle was Elizabeth Báthory's private museum, and she alone wished to be the centerpiece.

I pointed up toward the Minstrel's Gallery. "Do you enjoy watching the performers?"

"I like when they juggle," he said. "And when they recite poetry about heroes who slay dragons and rescue princesses."

"I like when they play their harps," I said. "From way up in my room it sounds so gentle and calming, like my mother is singing me a lullaby."

He turned away to look out the window, and I remembered that his parents had been killed when he was only a child. I thought about the songs his mother never had a chance to sing to him, about the myths and stories his father might have shared amid the glow of a winter fire.

And then I thought about Mama humming to herself every morning while she busied herself with sweeping the floor of the cottage. I thought about Papa tucking me into bed at night, smelling of pine and cedar as he leaned in close to relate the legend of the Wondrous Stag.

In the center of my chest, a knot swelled. I clenched my fists, trying to focus on those comforting images, but they were pushed out of my mind by scenes of young girls swinging in cages—all of them beaten and gashed, chunks of pale flesh crusting the metal spikes.

The knot tightened and grew bigger. I clung to the sound of Mama's soft voice, but it was drowned out by the girls' tortured screams, so shrill and piercing in the cavernous chamber, their desperate cries an eerie accompaniment to the constant stream of blood that poured into the tub as each slender throat was sliced open from ear to ear—

"Maria?"

I turned to see Peter watching me, one eyebrow raised, his hand extended as if wanting to console me but not quite sure how I'd react.

And then, without thinking, I did grasp his hand, and that large knot unraveled out of my mouth in a succession of stutters and fragments. It felt like I had been choking on so many words those past few weeks and now, despite my apprehensions, I needed to cough them up before they suffocated me.

"The Countess," I told him. "The tapestry and the passageway. The blood and the iron cages."

He led me over to a chair in the corner, instructing me to take deep breaths. When I regained my composure, he knelt down in front of me. I could tell he was concerned. "Now what's all this about the Countess? Are you having nightmares? You look tired. Perhaps you aren't getting enough sleep?"

"She's killing girls…servants who work here in the castle…bathing in their blood."

He pressed his hand against my forehead and gave me a stern look. "Calm down, or you'll whip yourself into a frenzy."

"In the middle of the night." My voice cracked as I tried to remain quiet. "In a secret chamber, below the castle."

"Your eyes are bloodshot," he said, "and your skin feels hot and feverish. Perhaps we should get you a cup of water."

I leaned forward and gripped his shoulder. "I've watched Benedict drag them into the chamber. I've listened to their screams when he wraps that chain around their ankles. I've seen their throats slit open."

Peter stood up, and when he spoke his voice was low and somber. "I know the Countess can be severe in her punishments, but…"

"These aren't acts of penance," I told him. "She's murdering those girls so she can bathe in their blood."

He scratched the stubble on his chin, his mouth slack as he sucked in a breath. "I've never visited any underground chamber, or seen…"

"But you know the Countess is obsessed with her appearance?"

"That's hardly a secret, Maria." He took a step backward, his gaze unfocused. "It seems so unbelievable, and yet…" He frowned and became still.

"What else do you know?" I asked him.

"A few years ago, not long after the Count died, a servant was bringing a glass of wine to the Countess. She tripped and the glass shattered. The Countess was so angry she slapped the girl and split open her lip. Some of the blood fell onto her hand and later, after she'd wiped it away, she told Helen that it made her skin look fresher…"

At that moment, footsteps echoed outside in the corridor and reverberated through the Great Hall. Peter and I remained silent, wedged into our own private corner, entrenched in the shade. We heard voices whispering, then two servants walked past the entryway carrying chamber pots and wash basins.

I stared down at my fingers. No matter how hard I scrubbed, the nails were rimmed with red, the skin white and pruned from constant soaking. Even my palms seemed pinker, as if blood had settled into the creases to become a permanent stain on my conscience. "So many girls have died," I told him, "and no one has done anything to help them."

"But what would you have us do?" he asked. "Appeal to her motherly instincts? Confess to the priest? The Countess considers them as nothing more than bottles she can uncork at a moment's whim. She'll do as she pleases, and anyone who defies her will be carved into pieces." He ran a callused finger up and down my cheek. "You have beautiful skin, Maria, and if you want to save it, then I suggest you not be so impulsive. You'll stay alive if you keep your head down and tiptoe through each day. Do as you're instructed, and no more. The Countess has set you a task, and as long as she's pleased you won't find yourself in her line of sight."

"Yes, but what if…"

"Throw all this passion into your sewing," he said, "and I promise no harm will befall you."

So that's what I did.

I left the Great Hall and returned to my room. I clasped the Celtic love knot in my hands, running my fingers up and down the chain as if reciting the rosary. I sent positive thoughts to my mother, and I prayed that my father's spirit would fill me with courage.

In the weeks that followed, I kept to myself and spoke little. During the days I continued teaching Sandra her alphabet, and at night I composed imaginary letters to my mother. I steered clear of Helen and Anna when I saw them in the corridor, and I made sure to step outside at least once a day, believing the fresh air would sharpen my senses and dispel the hopelessness which had settled into my bones. I ate as much food as I was allowed—whether or not I was hungry, even waste from the kitchen like scraps of cured beef and crusts of bread—just to make sure I didn't faint from exhaustion or dehydration like some of the other girls.

Left alone for most of the day, I wielded my needle like a sword, the only weapon I had to quell the fear that rose up inside me whenever I allowed my thoughts to drift toward that repulsive chamber. I cut and measured with a fierceness that hardened my tenacity, and instead of lamenting those who died in front of me, I contemplated how I might escape the castle. The sewing needle was a blur in my swollen hand, pushing relentlessly through lace cuffs and silk sleeves. I stitched with such fortitude that by the end of June I had finished the second gown, and the Countess was so pleased she allowed me a glass of wine, a sprig of grapes, and two pieces of chicken for an evening meal.

The day I finished the second gown I began working on the third. The Countess told me Ursula would not be able to visit, and that I should use Helen's measurements as a suitable substitute. I spent the better part of an afternoon scribbling numbers onto parchment and kneeling on the ground, calculating her height and waist and hips. She stood atop a crate when I measured her hemline, glowering down at me like an ill-tempered child and urging me to work faster.

The early summer heat became drier as it seeped into July, and the air thickened with dust. Young girls arrived from nearby villages—only to disappear or suddenly become ill—and sordid tales of vengeful ghosts and malevolent demons intensified among the servants. The wolves crept closer to the castle as more and more bodies were hauled off into the forest, their howls encircling the grounds like a tightening noose.

Even with the scent of death still lingering in the air, my life settled into a familiar routine, following the same well-worn path from sunup to sundown. And while I was not happy in my cryptic surroundings, I did learn how to keep the demons at bay.

Until the beginning of August when Count Thurzó arrived at the castle.

CHAPTER XI

HE WAS NOT EXPECTED. No couriers arrived ahead of him to announce his visit, and no formal letter with an official seal was delivered to the Countess. His appearance was both surprising and unnerving, like a cold snap in the middle of summer. It was not until he reached the gate on that late morning—and was immediately recognized by Benedict—that word was sent to the castle that the Palatine of Hungary had traveled from Bytča to Čachtice and now desired to speak with his cousin.

The Countess had settled down in the library, a grand room at the back of the castle that smelled of dust and leather. Small marble statues stood on pedestals in each corner; large oak shelves stretched from floor to ceiling, revealing colorful books of all shapes and sizes; and the wainscot paneling was gilded. She sat in a chair by the window, reading *The Prince* by Machiavelli, stopping every so often to raise a finger into the air so she could lecture me on ethics and politics and the abstract ideal. Her reading attire consisted of a red satin dress with long tight sleeves, a low rounded neckline, and a winged collar. Her dark brown hair hung loose around her shoulders.

Count Thurzó entered the room with an ivory cape slung over his left shoulder, as if he had just traipsed in from a casual stroll through the garden. I stepped aside as he approached the Countess, though he made not the slightest inclination toward me. Indeed, he didn't even acknowledge my presence.

"Elizabeth, how fare thee?" He folded his cape and laid it on the back of a chair.

She stood up, the book still clasped in her hands. "Well, Gregory. And you?"

He kissed her on the cheek. "A bit lacking in strength and vigor, but I attribute those deficits to an overindulgence of meat and ale rather than to the stacking of years."

"Royalty should never apologize for pursuing decadence." She picked up a small oval mirror and gazed into it, spinning the silver handle as if she were already bored.

"A wise observation," he said. "In the meantime, I will keep telling myself that a gray head is a crown of glory."

I had been staring out the window, watching a blackbird wing across the tops of the trees, but now I took notice of Count Thurzó, for despite his self-deprecating stab at ageing, I had not detected a hint of rust in either his tone or his mannerisms. On the contrary, he seemed as strong and imposing as a Greek column. He stood well over six feet tall, broad-shouldered with a bushy beard and a wide mustache, and when he spoke his voice rose up from deep within his chest to shake the ground like cannon fire.

Though the recent wind had twisted his graying hair into a tangle of vicious knots—and his face had been toughened by the dust and heat—no one could have mistaken the Count for anything other than royalty. He wore a blue doublet made of embroidered and glazed linen, brown breeches fastened about each leg with emerald buttons, and black riding boots that rose to mid-calf. As he spoke, his index fingers cut through the air with each emphatic point, highlighted by gold signet rings that hugged each hairy knuckle.

Standing there before me—in a lavish room filled with books and sunshine—he seemed like an Italian painting come to life.

"To what do I owe the honor of this visit?" the Countess asked him.

He glanced in my direction, then said, "Perhaps you would be so kind as to indulge me in a private conversation?"

She closed her book and placed it on the table next to her chair. "Maria, leave us. And close the door on your way out."

"Yes, miss." I bowed and hurried from the library, marching down the long corridor. But then I stopped and shuffled my feet. I glanced right and left several times, unsure where I should go or what I should do. Part of me wanted to run outside, fleeing to the edge of the castle grounds where I could hide in the shade of an oak tree. Another part of me considered returning upstairs so I could work on the third gown, but it was an especially hot day, and I didn't want to be confined to such a stuffy room. For a brief moment I contemplated heading down to the kitchen for some food and water, or perhaps helping Sandra to complete her chores, but then I heard Count Thurzó say, "Father Barosius," in his deep rumbling voice, and a shiver spread through my body.

I crept back toward the library, tiptoeing with calculated steps, appalled and exhilarated by my defiance. Since it would be foolish to eavesdrop in the corridor—where I was sure to be noticed by Helen or Anna or any servants hurrying past—I snuck into the drawing room next to the library. The curtains were drawn, and it was dark as I made my way toward the small door at the back. I maneuvered across a thick Parisian rug to muffle my footsteps, trying not to cough as I breathed in the mildewed air.

Ever so slightly, I opened the door leading into the library, pulling on the handle until a thin ray of light trickled into the room. I moved closer—pressing my face against the warped wood frame—and watched as the Countess rose from her seat to meet Count Thurzó by the window.

He held up a piece of paper, which he waved in her face. "...and now the priest has set down his suspicions."

"Pure nonsense," she said. "The man howls whenever a peasant is punished for dropping a goblet. He should know they're far too fragile a breed. Slap one across the face and you're likely to break a few bones."

"He speaks of torture and mutilation...right here in the castle...dozens upon dozens of murdered bodies, some even by your own hand."

"The ravings of an old man."

"Perhaps," he said, "but listen to what the priest writes in his letter. 'Your majesty, I wish to make known the serious actions of the noble Countess Báthory; namely that through some sort of evil spirit she has set aside her reverence for God and man, and has killed in cruel and various ways many girls and other women who have lived in her castle. Oh, such terrible deeds, such unheard of cruelties. In my opinion there has never existed a worse killer. But I must not go on, for my heart is bleeding and I cannot speak any more. I must not despair. I must strive to save as many souls as the good Lord will allow me. I have reached out to that dark creature living atop the hill, but when I asked her to accept the call to repent, and to join me in taking Holy Communion, she refused. She has...'"

"He is a hypocrite," the Countess said. "Is Christianity not built upon the ritual of human sacrifice? Did God not purposefully send his own son to be killed in public for all to see?"

"I'm not troubled by your treatment of peasants," the Count told her. "But your husband is a national hero, and you must be careful not to tarnish his legacy. Or the Báthory name. You are kin to bishops and cardinals and kings, and I promised Francis I would look after you and your children. We can't have malicious rumors sweeping the countryside like a plague."

They studied each other in silence for several moments. Finally, the Countess spoke. "And what would you have me do?"

"Be more cautious in your disposals."

She scowled. "I shouldn't have to fret over a pile of rotting corpses just because a priest is upset about his salvation."

"Agreed," he said, "but when the door has been closed…as this one clearly has…then one is often forced to slide across the crack of the sill."

"And what of the priest? Will he…disappear?"

"I have met with Father Barosius," the Count said, "and I have assuaged his fears."

"Meaning?"

"If he has reservations, he must keep them to himself. Or share them only with God."

The Countess took the letter and ripped it up. She placed the shredded pieces on the table next to her chair. "I would be delighted to handle this matter myself."

"I've already given him a stern warning. There is nothing else you need to do, except be thankful that his letter was directed at me. I doubt the king would have echoed my sentiments."

She sat down and crossed her arms. "Matthias is more concerned with becoming Holy Roman Emperor than with investigating a few suspicious deaths among the peasantry."

"True, but he savors his status, and he won't tolerate any report…justified or not…that threatens his future holdings."

"And here I thought you had come to bring me good news," she said. "Perhaps to tell me that the king has agreed to repay the money he borrowed from my husband."

"Don't push him, Elizabeth, or he'll become even more persistent in his excuses."

She slapped the arm of her chair. "I have shown infinite patience, Gregory. I have been considerate and courteous…even allowing him the use of my lands to house soldiers…yet whenever I broach the subject of his debt he becomes slow of speech and tongue."

"Matthias will repay you when he is ready."

"I find it fascinating that he has the funds to buy paintings and sculptures," she said, "and that he's made several offers to purchase my estate at Ecsed, yet, somehow, he's unable to scrape together the hefty sum Francis loaned him to finance his war against the Turks."

"Francis was smart enough not to refuse the king's requests," the Count said, "and you would do well enough not to demand your own."

"I fear he has no intention of honoring our agreement."

"It would appear so," he said, "but at least you can take solace in knowing you are wealthier than the king."

The Countess leaned back and closed her eyes. "There is little comfort in that."

"Because your husband is dead?"

"No," she said, "because I am a woman."

Count Thurzó walked over to the chair and put his hand on her arm. "It's pointless to stress about things over which you have no control. The priest has been mollified, and Matthias is busy granting concessions to the Protestants. If you are careful…in whatever private activities you pursue…you can spend your remaining years enjoying a tranquil solitude here in Čachtice."

She shook off his hand and leapt up like a wild animal suddenly released from a cage. "Am I aging so terribly that you believe I'm soon to be forgotten?" she yelled. "Is my outer self simply wasting away while the sky above me darkens?"

"I meant no offence," he said. "Merely that you look tired."

The Countess smoothed out the front of her dress. "I assure you, cousin, that despite the rapid advancement of years, I still retain some semblance of my youth."

He bowed. "Quite right, Elizabeth. You are as luminous as ever."

"Good. Because I'm not yet ready to feel the soil falling over my head."

"Let us hope not," he said.

She walked over to a mirror hanging on the wall and gazed into it, caressing her flushed cheeks as if afraid they might shatter at the slightest touch. "They say there is a fountain…somewhere across the ocean…that will restore the youth of anyone who bathes or drinks in its waters."

"Yes, Herodotus wrote of it."

"Many men have died searching for it," she said. "Can you imagine anything more tragic? Spending years of your life in a foreign land…chasing points on a map and pursuing imaginary relics…only to die while desperately wishing you could live forever."

"People shouldn't battle so fiercely over the apple of discord," he said. "It's not natural. Besides, we may discover someday…when we're old and crumbling…that death is no different than life."

She turned away from the mirror, her mouth set in a thin hard line. "Will you stay the night? I'll have the servants prepare a banquet and make up a private room."

"No, I must go. I'm on my way to Vienna to speak with the king. Ottoman troops have been assembling at the border, and he wishes to discuss military action."

"His highness seems eager to please the House of Hapsburg. I daresay he'll soon be crowned by the pope, at which point he'll declare himself to be first among equals."

He picked up the ivory cape and slung it over his shoulder. "Matthias succeeds where others have failed because he prefers to rule with a strong hand and an outstretched arm."

"How honorable," she said, making no effort to mask her derision. "Perhaps with a bit more effort he can stretch that arm in my direction."

Count Thurzó kissed the Countess on the cheek and offered her a farewell bow. "Don't jest, Elizabeth. The king believes…as do all of us who reign…that the thunder of our power lies not in diplomacy, but in our ability to crush the serpents and scorpions that rise up from beneath our feet."

I returned to my room before Count Thurzó left the library, and while I didn't see the Countess for the rest of the afternoon, I did hear her wandering the castle in a frightful mood. She screamed at servants and slammed doors. She kicked tables and hurled expensive objects in every direction. The hallways were strewn with slivers of glass and chunks of marble, and there were occasional streaks of blood from where an unfortunate girl had chosen the wrong time to walk down the corridor.

Finally—exhausted and lightheaded—the Countess retreated to her bedchamber sometime after four o'clock. She called for me soon after, and I entered with hesitation. She stood naked in the waning light, studying her reflection in the large mirror. She moved aside hair and folds of skin, exploring every square inch of her being like a madman trying to dissect a rainbow.

"Tell me, Maria, am I still a rose? Or have I become a prickly thorn?"

"You are a rose in full bloom," I said, hoping to encourage her attitude. "No one would dare accuse your beauty of being ragged."

"Then why must I be subject to insults and insinuations as if I were drawing my last breath?"

"Everything possesses beauty," I told her, "but not everyone can see it."

She picked at some dry skin on her elbow. "Do you know what happens to your body when you die?"

"No, Countess."

"It begins to liquefy," she said. "Your skin becomes discolored…gray blue and mottled…until it tightens around your skeleton, afraid to let go. Eventually it splits open…oozing what's left of your insides…and then large pieces separate from your muscles to slide off your fat and bloated corpse like some foul-smelling river."

I looked out the window, trying to focus my attention on something beautiful like a white-tailed eagle or a cluster of dandelions, but all I saw was a pile of young girls. They were stacked atop one another like firewood, their hair matted with blood while shards of bone glinted in the darkness.

"You look ill," she said, watching me in the corner of her mirror. "Do the mysteries of the human body unsettle you?"

"No, Countess. I just prefer to ignore death until it's screaming in my ear."

"I'd expect someone like you to be accustomed to the sight of a stiffened carcass," she said, laughing. "I daresay they're as common as acorns falling from a tree in most villages."

Tears sprang to my eyes, but I held them in. I clutched the Celtic love knot and rubbed it between my fingers. "My father once told me that as soon as we start thinking about death, we're no longer sure of life."

"A quaint bedtime story, no doubt." She raised her arms high in the air, examining the sides of her chest. "Did you know that the ancient Egyptians would use incense to fumigate their bodies? Or sand mixed with oils to scour away the dirt?"

"No, Countess."

She put on her silk robe and turned to me. "Though my methods may be unorthodox, I'm clearly not the first woman who has labored hard to preserve her natural features."

"Your efforts have been valiant, and the results have been impressive." I sharpened each word and dropped it into her lap with careful accuracy. I needed to guide her mood away from anger and self-doubt, otherwise the cages underground would soon be filled with girls waiting to have their throats cut.

In recent weeks her temper had boiled over until it burned everyone around her. More and more servants were being dragged into that dungeon on a daily basis, and still the Countess complained about her complexion, about the onset of wrinkles that only deepened the more she worried. In the past week alone she had bitten one girl on the cheek and whipped another with such force that the poor thing had died from her wounds the next afternoon.

Now, she returned her gaze to the mirror. She pulled down her lower eyelid—exposing the red underside—and studied the white part of her eye for several minutes. "Perhaps Gregory was right," she said. "I do appear a bit tired."

"Your Ladyship must not forget the humidity." I fanned myself with an open palm to emphasize the oppressive heat. "It wraps us up like a heavy blanket and stifles our spirit."

"Then I will shake it off," she said. "As I have done so my entire life. I am not one to back down from adversity, Maria."

"Yes, Countess."

"As a child, I suffered from bouts of convulsion. My mother…who was not one to show affection…never believed in the curative power of singing folk songs, or of kneeling beside me at night to pray. She was a woman of action."

I remembered all those times when I was sick with fever—the coolness of Mama's hand resting against my forehead while she fed me porridge; or how she carried me atop her shoulders when I twisted my ankle in the gully beside the cottage. She and Papa had taught me to cook and clean and sew, but they also surrounded me with whatever books they could buy or borrow. At night they tucked me into bed with tales from faraway lands, urging me to imagine "what could be" instead of "what had been." I cultivated those dreams over many years, and I had chased them over the Carpathian Mountains.

I knew in that moment, listening to her pitiful rant, that I had survived for this long inside Čachtice Castle—had stomached countless murders and bloodcurdling screams, and braved the unknown darkness that stretched before me at the rise of each new day—because my roots were strong.

She dropped her hand with a surrendering sigh and turned away from the mirror. "My mother would boil the leg bone of a deer and grind it into a fine powder. Then she'd mix the powder with wormwood and stir it into the water. Several times a year I was forced to drink that vile concoction. And do you know what my mother would whisper to me every time she pressed that cup to my lips?"

"No, Countess."

"That the mills of God grind slowly, but surely. Which means time is inescapable, and we must do all we can to rail against its constant intrusion. To remain idle is to admit defeat. That is why I'm a woman of action, Maria. And that is why I'm not afraid to dirty my hands or spill a little blood on the floor."

"Yes, Countess."

"If you have beauty, you have hope," she said. "And if you have hope, then you have everything." She walked over to the bed and struck one of the satin pillows with a closed fist. "And right now I'm losing hope because my appearance displeases me."

I stood taller and raised my voice, hoping to quell one of her angry outbursts. "Nevertheless, you remain a sparkling diamond amidst weathered stones."

She gave me a scathing look. "Perhaps I need to bathe more regularly...or make use of younger girls."

"Forgive me for saying so..." Again, I selected each word with the utmost precision. "...but given the importance of these decisions...and their significance on your Ladyship's good health...might it be more sensible to consider them early in the morning, when you're fresher and have more energy?"

The Countess considered this for a moment before pulling back the sheets and slipping under the covers. "I will rage against the night to ensure that my beauty is never separated from my body." She seized her handheld mirror from the bedside table and pressed it firmly against her chest. "Just as heat cannot be separated from a fire."

CHAPTER XII

COUNT THURZÓ'S SURPRISE VISIT set the entire castle aflame with rumors. By the time I arrived in the kitchen—sometime after six o'clock and looking for something to eat—the gossip had only intensified. Sandra sat at a table in the corner, chopping a head of cabbage. She was ensconced in shadows and whispering with Viktoriya, a pallid servant her own age who tended to weeds in the courtyard and fed the various animals that grazed in the fields behind the castle.

I broke off a hunk of bread, ladled out a bowl of goulash, and joined them at the table.

"...because so many of us have disappeared," Sandra was saying.

Viktoriya glanced around the room, then leaned in closer. "Maybe that's why the Countess was so angry this afternoon."

"No one has disappeared." I dipped my bread into the bowl and took a soggy bite. "Servants are removed from the castle when they die, sometimes in the middle of the night. There's a cholera epidemic, and the Countess doesn't want to bury the entire household."

"What about the screams?" Sandra asked me. "And where has the priest gone?"

"If you were vomiting for hours at a time, and writhing in constant pain, you'd be screaming, too," I told her. "Be thankful you're both healthy, and not stretched out on a bed with flies hovering around you."

"Who's been removing the bodies from the castle?" Sandra asked. "And where? Surely, not the graveyard? The priest hasn't been here in weeks."

"There's more going on than just an outbreak of cholera," Viktoriya said. "We've all seen the Countess throw hot wax in someone's face.

We've all seen Helen kick someone to the ground and then beat her with a piece of wood until the cracks in the floor are filled with blood and…"

"Yes, they're wicked. They're the most pitiless and vindictive people I've ever known." I tried to sound agreeable, but my voice was tired and my hands were clenched in frustration. "Which is why you mustn't provoke them. They don't need excuses to hurt you. They'll do it because they can."

"Some people say the castle is cursed," Viktoriya said. "That those who died fell asleep with their mouths open…that their souls escaped from their mouths in the form of a mouse that runs around the castle all night long…that if the mouse doesn't return by morning then that person will never wake up and she just dies in her sleep."

Sandra gathered several cabbage wedges and dropped them into a clay bowl. "I've heard talk that a strigoi is roaming the castle."

"A strigoi?" I said.

She nodded. "A demon that preys upon you, usually when you're alone or asleep. Sometimes they're invisible, other times they transform into a black cat. They devour your blood until you're shriveled up like an old prune, and…"

"Nonsense." I dipped my crust into the bowl and took a large bite, wiping hot juice off the bottom of my chin. "You're scaring yourselves even more by grabbing hold of ancient superstitions."

Viktoriya laid her hand on my arm. "Strigoi are real, Maria. There was one in my uncle's village a few years ago. It killed a lot of children. Eventually, everyone went to the cemetery and broke open its coffin. They found fresh blood on its lips. They had to burn the body and scatter the ashes in a river."

"You both put too much faith in deeds of the devil." I ate a spoonful of goulash and brushed a wisp of hair from my eyes. "You should toss aside these wild illusions, otherwise they'll dull your senses, especially when you need them most."

"Why won't you tell us what you know?" There was a spiteful edge to Sandra's voice I had never heard before.

"Because I'm in the dark as much as you are."

"Liar." She chopped the cabbage with quick ferocious hacks, her cheeks bright red and puffed out in annoyance.

I scraped the last bit of goulash from the bottom of my bowl and finished the crust of bread, which sat heavy in my stomach. "Why can't you understand that I'm trying to protect you?"

"You're hiding something," Viktoriya said.

The headache I'd felt earlier was now returning, and I was in no mood to coax it away with kind words. "What would you do if I told you the Countess concocted some diabolical scheme to lure us all here?" I asked them. "What if you suddenly discovered that there are dozens of strigoi creeping around the castle in the middle of the night? Or that every servant who's died during the past few months has fallen asleep with her mouth open, and that's why there are so many mice running around the kitchen?"

Sandra put her arm around Viktoriya's shoulder. "What would happen if all the servants decided to march out the front gate and return home without ever looking back?"

I waved my spoon in their faces to show I was serious. "You'd be cut down before you ever made it to Čachtice. And then, while you were buried in some shallow ditch, or rotting in the forest for the wolves to feed on, Anna would collect dozens more girls…young and innocent and naïve…who would welcome the opportunity to work here because they don't want their families to go hungry."

Sandra had just opened her mouth to continue arguing when a tremendous crash erupted behind me. Everyone in the kitchen froze, their eyes wide open as jagged pieces of clay flew past us and hit the wall. The entire room settled into an uncomfortable silence, save for water boiling in cast-iron pots and slabs of beef hissing on the rotating spits.

The Countess stood in the entryway. She looked at no one in particular, yet her eyes seemed to fall on every single person in the room. "My dinner…" She pointed down at her feet where a piece of chicken lay on the dusty floor, surrounded by dates and raisins that had fallen from her plate when she'd thrown it across the room "…is cold."

No one spoke. No one took a breath. The servants nearest to the Countess—those who had been skinning the chickens and seasoning the beef—cowered in the dim light while the servants farthest away—those who were uncorking wine and pouring glasses of ale—slunk off into the shadows or hid behind tables and crates.

The Countess took a long deep breath and balled her hands into fists. "How long must my dinner sit on a table, growing stale and collecting dust, before someone has the sense to bring it up to me?"

No one answered. No one had the courage to meet her gaze.

She kicked a grape and sent it skidding across the uneven stones. "Which one of you ingrates is responsible for ruining my meal?"

A dog wandered in from outside. It sniffed its way along the floor and devoured her food.

"I will not ask a second time," the Countess said.

The servants remained silent. Their ashen faces looked ghostlike in the murky firelight.

She stepped farther into the kitchen, her dress swishing along the floor. "If one amongst you lacks the decency to admit incompetence, then I shall be forced to punish all of you."

A minute passed.

I sat up straight like a proper lady and stared down at a shriveled onion skin lying on the floor. I sucked in a great mouthful of air, held it deep inside until my lungs began to burn, and then I exhaled through pursed lips. Sweat rolled down my back and my leg itched, but I dared not move. I wanted the guilty servant to step forward; I wanted the Countess to abandon her retribution and return to her bedchamber; I wanted my mother to take my hand and lead me back to our small cottage in Trenčín.

And then—just when I thought the Countess might fly into another tirade—there was a sharp clanging sound that startled everyone in the kitchen. The floor beside me reverberated with a metallic ping, and I realized that the chopping knife had slipped out of Sandra's hand and skidded under the table.

I bent down to retrieve the knife, but no sooner had I reached for it than the Countess appeared beside me, her arm extended and her palm open.

"This is precisely how accidents happen," she said as a smile played across her full lips.

I placed the knife in her waiting hand. "It was an accident, your Ladyship. I bumped the table when I shifted my chair."

She ignored me and turned to Sandra, whose face had grown pale. "Perhaps it was you who let my meal grow cold?"

"No, miss," Sandra said, her voice barely a squeak. "I've been chopping vegetables."

The Countess touched the point of the knife with the tip of her finger. "You enjoy playing with sharp objects?"

Sandra looked at me, her eyes pleading for help, but I was too afraid to move. Part of me was terrified that the Countess might light my friend on fire or rip out her fingernails. But another part of me—a part I despised—felt a surge of happiness and relief, grateful that it wasn't me everyone in the kitchen was now pitying.

"You must be careful when handling knives," the Countess said, "otherwise you're likely to slice off a finger or a toe. And then what use would you be?"

"I'm a hard worker, miss," Sandra said. "I always do exactly…"

"If you damage yourself, then you're nothing more than a crippled burden. You become a heavy load that takes up space, like that sack of flour sitting over there in the corner. You become worthless to me, just another rancid piece of garbage that stinks up my castle. And do you know what happens to garbage?"

Sandra shook her head. "No, miss."

"It gets tossed outside for the wolves to find."

I clutched the edges of my seat, fearful that the meal I'd just eaten might erupt all over the table. I squeezed the splintered wood as hard as I could until the nausea passed, until I didn't feel so hot and feverish.

"In ancient Egypt," the Countess said, "a pharaoh...much like royalty today...was considered a god in human form. And when he died, his servants were buried in the tomb along with him. They were sealed up in the darkness with his most valued treasures. Sometimes, they were buried while they were still alive...drugged and wrapped in bandages...stacked neatly atop one another like bottles of wine in a pantry." She placed her hand on Sandra's shoulder as if comforting her. "Those servants died so they could attend to their master in the afterlife. They understood the concept of loyalty and dedication, and it was a source of pride...even a mark of respect...to be buried with someone so illustrious."

The Countess glared at everyone in the room, and there was no disguising the look of utter disgust that was splashed across her face. "And what do I receive instead of respect? Insolence and a cold dinner."

No one spoke.

"You're nothing more than a pack of lazy children," she yelled. "God help me if I had to be buried with you miserable lot for all of eternity."

No one breathed.

She returned her attention to Sandra. "Do you know what servants would do in ancient times when they disappointed their masters? When they lost the respect of their friends and family...when they wanted to redeem themselves from the shame of having failed?"

"No, miss."

"They committed self-murder," the Countess said. "They found creative ways to end their own lives, whether by swallowing a poisonous spider or ramming a hot poker down their throat." She loomed closer, boring into Sandra with those piercing eyes, each speck of yellowish-brown a raging storm. "Did you know that in the Mayan culture they often hanged themselves?"

The Countess didn't wait for a response, nor did she demand one. "I agree it sounds a bit primitive...and not always guaranteed to be a success…but it does possess a certain simplicity that I find absolutely charming." She held up the knife and stared at it for several seconds, smiling as the slender blade flashed in the firelight. "The Mayans believed that wrapping a noose around their neck would allow them to live in eternal paradise with their gods. Other times, they threw themselves into limestone sinkholes, which they thought were gateways to the underworld. It was considered respectable. It was seen as honorable." She grasped Sandra's chin and squeezed hard. "Do you even know what respect and honor mean?"

Sandra opened her mouth to speak, but all she could muster was a slight gurgle, an awkward jumble of air and saliva that sounded like she was choking to death.

The Countess leaned against the table. "But in Rome, they were fond of cutting open the veins in their wrists. They used razors and daggers, or sometimes just ordinary knives like this one. They soaked themselves in hot water because it pumps up the veins…makes them fat and round like earthworms…and then they took the edge of the knife and slowly cut into their wrist, slashing down the entire length of their arm…almost to their elbow…until the veins split open and all that regret and shame came gushing out."

Thick tears streamed down Sandra's face. I watched her chest heave in and out, snot running down her upper lip where it dribbled past her chin and onto the cutting board. I wanted to reach out and save her, but I didn't know how.

"Perhaps your friends would like a demonstration." The Countess grabbed Sandra's hand, yanked up the sleeve, and laid her bare arm on the dirty table, palm side up.

Sandra was too scared to struggle or protest, not even when the Countess pressed the tip of the blade against her bony wrist, not even when a single drop of blood bloomed on her fair skin. It was only a puncture, but the Countess pressed a bit harder, and then harder still, and soon a steady line of blood trickled down the side of Sandra's arm and dripped onto the table.

"Pardon me," the Countess said. "I seem to be making a terrible mess." She pretended to bear down with more effort—twisting the handle back and forth as though the skin wouldn't yield to the metal—and then she jerked the knife upward in a jagged movement. The blade skimmed along Sandra's palm and left a long crimson gash.

I wanted to look away, but I found myself hypnotized by the sheer brutality, so abrupt and unabashed that I felt as if I were floating above the room and watching a nightmare unfold.

Sandra's eyes glazed over. A small moan dribbled out of her mouth. I felt certain she would slide off her chair, and that she'd crack open her head on the hard stone floor.

"I daresay I'm becoming as careless as one of my own servants," the Countess said. "Make sure you clean up this stain before it damages the wood." She reached out with her free hand and dipped three fingers into the small pool of blood, moving them back and forth as though she were massaging the weathered oak.

For a brief moment I wondered if the Countess would rub the blood into her face. But then she tightened her grip on the knife and bent forward, repositioning the iron point until it came to rest against a bright blue vein that snaked down Sandra's arm like a tiny river.

The Countess glanced up at me and smiled, and I knew in that instant—as sure as there was breath in my lungs—that she would thrust the knife as hard as she could into that soft flesh, driving it deeper and deeper until blade collided with bone.

CHAPTER XIII

THE COUNTESS RAISED THE knife into the air—the blade glinting in the firelight, her body pulsing with a deliberate fury—and brought it straight down toward Sandra's bloodied wrist, eager to inflict that fatal blow.

I leapt up and screamed, which sounded hollow and tinny, as if I were shouting up from the bottom of a well. And then, oblivious to my own safety, I lunged across the table and grabbed her arm before the blade could sever the skin.

The entire kitchen expelled a shuddering gasp as the Countess turned to me with a face so incensed I felt my strength rush out of me like water spiraling down a drain. She wrenched her hand out of my grip and stepped back, shocked and bewildered. Then she charged forward as if she meant to slice me open. "You care for this measly creature?"

My reckless behavior—spurred by a desire to save Sandra's life—had put me in peril, and if I didn't provide the Countess with a sensible answer, I would soon be tasting my own blood. I scratched my cheek and opened my mouth, but my tongue was rooted firm. The servants stood stone-still, aghast at my silence.

She brandished the knife toward my throat. "You would risk your life for this crude girl who has the strength of a flea and the intelligence to match?"

I don't know what compelled me to wrap my arms around the Countess—whether it was confusion or panic or a heightened sense of self-preservation—but I embraced her like a confidante and placed my mouth close to her ear. "The girl's blood is tainted," I whispered. "You mustn't let any more of it touch your skin."

The Countess neither spoke nor moved for several moments. I lingered there, afraid to let her go, my eyes fixated on a curl of gray hair tucked behind her ear. Finally, she pushed me away and laid the knife on the cutting board. She yanked Sandra to her feet, shoved her against the wall, and said, "Tend to your wounds before you bleed all over the vegetables, otherwise I'll hold your arm over the fire to seal you up tight."

I stepped back from the table, both knees locked and my chin lifted toward the ceiling. I clasped my hands in front of me and tried not to look at Sandra, who hid behind a chair and cradled her injured arm. She choked back a rush of tears that streamed down her sallow face in thin dirty streaks.

"See that my dinner is brought to my bedchamber immediately," the Countess said, pointing to a petrified servant standing beside the oven. "And don't upset me again; otherwise I'll return with a much larger knife and with much less patience."

Deep shadows were creeping across the floor when I walked inside her bedchamber, my heart beating so fast I thought it might lift me into the air. The sun hung low outside the window, a bloody smear ringed with orange and yellow, and I stared at it until my eyes hurt, reciting over and over the explanation I would offer when she demanded that I justify my impulsive behavior.

The Countess grabbed my shoulders. "Were you any other girl, your insides would be spilling out onto the floor. Start talking before my gentleness evaporates. Or I may again find myself in a storytelling mood."

I thought back to our conversation earlier that afternoon, hoping to exploit her paranoia. "When we spoke a few hours ago you were distressed by your appearance...you were concerned that perhaps your evening baths aren't having their desired effect...and that..."

"I'm not forgetful, Maria." She pointed at her face. "I'm frowning, and you know how much I despise puckering my brow. Frowning creates wrinkles, and I already have far too many. Now dispense with your boring introduction before I slice off your tongue and feed it to my dogs."

I steadied myself against the edge of her bed, the hard oak pressing into my hip as if prodding me to continue. "It suddenly occurred to me that it's not how often you bathe that helps to preserve your beauty, but the individual girls that you select."

The Countess sat on the bed and pulled me down beside her. "Explain yourself."

"It's just that...well...certainly the peasant blood has softened your skin...but lately it seems to have lost its potency."

"You believe I've built up a tolerance?" she asked. "That their blood no longer retains any healing powers?"

I slid closer to her, as if sharing a dark secret, grasping for any incentive that might draw her away from murdering so many servants. "You've been indulging in common blood for far too long...blood plucked from hovels and shacks."

"I suppose...that's true." She stared off into a corner like one caught in a daydream, and her mouth hung open, as if astonished that she hadn't realized this crucial fact before now.

"Such blood doesn't befit royalty."

"Yes, you're right." The Countess looked down at the small mirror resting on her bedside table. "I'm a Báthory. I deserve blood that is faultless and pure. Without a doubt, peasant blood is more suited to a slug than to a sovereign."

I looked into her eyes and spoke each word as if it was the only word that had ever existed. "The blood you've been using will not restore your youth. On the contrary, it might even erode your skin if you continue soaking in it. A woman of your stature should drink out of a golden chalice," I said, preying on her conceit, "and not a cracked wooden cup."

"Yes, of course." She seized my hand. "I need blood steeped in beauty and refinement. How can I expect to regain my luster and vitality when I'm splashing around in filth?"

"Their blood might even be responsible for triggering your headaches," I told her. "You've been suffering more fatigue and dizzy spells since increasing your number of weekly baths."

"That must be the reason why my wrinkles have become more visible and pronounced," she said, "and why my skin appears more stretched and loose."

I felt a sudden lightness in the pit of my stomach, and for the first time in weeks I allowed myself a sense of relief.

The Countess rose and went to the window, staring up at the outline of the moon as it shimmered above the trees in the dying heat of the day. "To restore my beauty I need blood that is chaste and untainted, and conferred to me by God himself."

"Unfortunately, you won't find such blood in this castle," I said. "Perhaps there are doctors in Vienna, or exotic herbs that Anna can collect."

The Countess smiled. "I was right to bring you here, Maria. You've been far more useful than I could have ever imagined. And I daresay you'll prove to be even more valuable once autumn arrives."

"Thank you." I bowed my head to sweeten the moment. "And I'm almost finished with the third gown. I should have it completed by the beginning of August."

"Excellent," she said. "I'm sure everything will be ready for the festival."

"Festival?"

"Of course. The autumn equinox on the twenty-first of September. To celebrate the harvest."

"Will your daughters visit before the festival?" I asked. "It might be wise to schedule a fitting in case the gowns require alterations."

"All of my children are either married or away at school," she said. "To see me would require time, which they rarely possess."

I thought of her four children living somewhere on the other side of the Carpathians—nestled like baby birds inside majestic castles that were bestowed upon them by birthright—and I wondered if any of them considered their mother with affection. I wondered if they recalled with fondness their younger days here in Čachtice when they ran through the fields and lazed in the courtyard, unburdened by diplomacy or responsibility.

There was a time when I envied such a life, but that sweetness had soured like an apple cut open to reveal a rotting core. The longer I lived in the castle, the more I pictured Mama leaning against the cottage door, her eyes searching the distant fields and mountains for some indication that her only child would return home. Did she wonder why I had yet to send her a letter? Did she worry that I had succumbed to cholera? Had she tried to contact me?

And what about the money? Was Mama receiving the gold pieces— as well as the monthly forint—that Anna had promised to her, or was that a lie, too? I didn't want to consider the possibility that she was starving to death. There was pickled herring and salted cabbage in the root cellar, and crisp apples sealed up in jars of honey, but how long would that food last? If there was indeed a harvest festival in September, the Countess would expect me to help the other servants prepare for it—and she would certainly demand that I stay through autumn to assist with the reaping and storage of crops—which meant I wouldn't see Mama until at least Christmas. The more I considered all those lonely days stretching into winter, the more I worried that she would run out of food and be forced to forage for nuts and berries.

The Countess reached out to caress my cheek. "I have grown accustomed to my children being absent. Separation is long and painful, but it's also inevitable. You must sever the umbilical cord when your children are young; otherwise they'll clutch it tighter as they grow older, relying on it more and more until it becomes wrapped so tightly around their necks that they choke to death." She closed her eyes and waved me away. "Such is life, Maria. Though it becomes much more tolerable when you realize that a child's love is like water in a basket."

For the next several days I kept to myself, still unnerved by that episode in the kitchen. When I wasn't completing my daily chores, I was hunkered down at the table in my room, cutting and sewing while sweat dripped off the tip of my nose and thick flies buzzed around my head. I was eager to complete the project ahead of schedule—a sure testament to my skillfulness—but stitching the last diamond onto the last gown would create even more questions. Would the Countess allow me to return home? Would she order me to begin work on other desired garments? Or would she kill me?

I saw little of Sandra. Once, she stopped me in the corridor and thanked me for what I had done in the kitchen. She held her injured arm against her chest as if afraid someone might wrench it out of the socket. Her eyes stared past me, and her voice, usually so playful and inquisitive, was now stripped of emotion. Helen had been forcing her to work outside for hours at a time—watering the crops and feeding the animals—and so her skin was red and blistered. Her hair was matted and greasy, frizzled by the scorching sun.

The Countess remained in her bedchamber for most of that week. She continued to gaze at herself in the mirror, and to request her herbal remedies from Anna, but not once did she demand one of her infamous baths. The chains did not rattle, the tub remained empty, and I slept through the night. In the mornings I woke with renewed energy, happy not to have slipped into bed with someone else's blood drying beneath my fingernails.

Finally, after two weeks of relative peacefulness, the Countess gathered all the servants in the Great Hall one afternoon. Standing at the head of the table, a goblet of wine raised high in the air, she made an official announcement:

"It has come to my attention that many parents wish to have their daughters educated in the appropriate social graces and customs. Many of these women will someday marry into royalty, where they'll be expected to host lavish banquets with counts and bishops. They'll govern their own castles and lands while their husbands are off fighting wars, and they may even entertain the king himself. Appearance is just as important as presentation, and while nursemaids are crucial in instilling those initial ideas about right and wrong, there needs to be a deeper understanding about which traditions matter the most, about which behaviors are accepted and which ones are denounced."

The Countess took a sip of wine and placed the goblet on the table. "Therefore, I will open an etiquette academy here at Čachtice Castle. I will accept twenty-five ladies at a time…all from noble and prestigious families…and through my instruction and tutelage they will learn the manners and decorum expected of them. God has appointed me to rule. Therefore, it's my responsibility to ensure that these young ladies understand how best to honor and uphold their sacred lineage."

She removed an orange from a crystal bowl, rubbed it against her gown, and began to peel it. "Tomorrow afternoon, I leave for Sárvár to inspect my holdings and estates. I will also travel to Trenčín, Verbo, and Újhely to meet with potential students so I may select those whom I deem worthy of receiving proper tutelage. When I return, I expect the castle to be warm and inviting for my new guests. I expect fresh hay to be strewn on the floors, and I expect the grounds to be trimmed and the trees and bushes to be pruned. I have also instructed private quarters to be set up for our guests." She finished peeling her orange and placed the bits of rind on the edge of the table in a small, neat pile. "Now leave me."

Helen ushered the servants out of the Great Hall, slapping those who were not moving fast enough. None of the girls commented on her Ladyship's announcement, and if any of them harbored a specific unease I couldn't detect it from the blank looks on their faces. As for me, I shuddered in the shadows, for I knew why the Countess had developed a sudden interest in those jeweled and majestic daughters.

I fell back in line until everyone walked past me, then I moved beside Sandra as she shuffled by. I was hoping to speak with her before we had to separate in the main hall, but Helen was standing by the entryway, watching me with accusatory eyes as if I might steal something and hide it in my pocket. I had just stepped into the corridor—about to turn left so I could hurry upstairs and continue my sewing—when the Countess shouted out from the banquet table and asked me to join her.

I sat down next to her, and she handed me a large piece of the orange. I put it in my mouth and chewed it bit by bit, savoring the pulp and warm juice. Immediately, she held out another piece and I grabbed it, trying not to appear greedy despite the flecks of pith that clung to my chin.

"Anna will be accompanying me on my trip," she told me, "and Helen will stay behind to look after the castle. You will continue working on the last gown, and I've instructed Helen to release you from your other obligations."

"Yes, Countess."

"I've allowed you unprecedented freedom in my personal life, Maria, and you've ventured into parts of this castle that no servant has willingly set foot in. However, while I'm away, I must impress upon you the importance of not straying too far...of not going off on your own. If your eyes wish to rove, let them search for uneven seams in your stitching. If your feet wish to wander, let them treadle the spinning wheel."

"Yes, Countess."

She handed me the rest of her orange and stood up. "I'm not one to scatter compliments, but I'm grateful for your interest in my private affairs. Were it not for you, I would have wasted many valuable years collecting worthless peasants and slathering myself with their gruel." She leaned forward to kiss me on the cheek. "You've provided me with exceptional observations...demonstrating an intellect and cleverness most unbefitting a mere peasant...and for that I thank you. I intend to embrace this golden opportunity until I've squeezed every drop of beauty from those bright blue veins."

I watched her leave the Great Hall, then I pushed away the orange slices and sat in silence with my head in my hands, torn between elation and guilt. She had commended me for my loyalty and cleverness, which certainly boded well for my own safety. But because of my desperate attempt to protect those I loved, more innocent girls would soon be entering the castle, and it was only a matter of time before they met their grisly demise in the lower depths of her Ladyship's chamber.

CHAPTER XIV

THE NEXT MORNING—BEFORE the sun was high in the sky and the castle had woken from its slumber—the Countess called for me and Peter and instructed us to head into the forest.

"Belladonna…a vibrant purple flower with shiny black berries…is blossoming," she said, "and I would like you to collect some."

"The flowers or the berries?" I asked her.

"Both. The flowers will make a nice arrangement for our guests when they arrive, and Anna has a particular use for the berries." She turned to Peter. "It grows most abundant next to the valley at the base of the mountains. You're familiar with that area?"

He nodded.

She ruffled his hair as though he were a small child bouncing on her knee. "Each of you will fill a basket until it overflows, and I suggest you do so before the heat becomes unbearable."

After stopping by the kitchen for boiled dumplings and filling a leather bottle with cold water from the well, we set out to find the belladonna. A slight breeze rustled the trees, and drops of dew still clung to tall blades of grass. My sandals became wet—I could feel pieces of straw and bits of dirt burrowing between my toes—but I didn't care. I was happy to be out of the castle where I could breathe fresh air and stretch my legs. And I was glad to have Peter beside me. I had glimpsed less and less of him during the past month. I liked feeling his hand brush against mine as we trekked through the meadow, the daffodils sweeping our ankles as they bent low in the wind.

"You've been quite the adventurer," he said, knocking into me with a smile.

"Really? I should think that being shut up in a tiny room…with just a mirror and a spinning wheel…hardly qualifies me as an admiral of the high seas."

"I heard about your sudden lunge," he said. "How you grabbed the Countess by the arm…in full view of the servants, no less. You're lucky she didn't crack open your head like an egg."

"I forgot myself for a moment. I became dizzy in the heat and acted on impulse."

We approached the copse of trees that marked the entrance into the old forest. Peter took my hand, and together we stepped over a fallen branch. "You need to be more careful, Maria. Members of the royal family expect to be worshipped and admired. They believe each monarch is a family heirloom passed down from generation to generation, and that any commoner who so much as grazes imperial skin should have her lungs torn out."

"Well, I'm breathing just fine, thank you."

"I cautioned you to tiptoe through each day," he said, "and here you are, barreling through the castle with your head down and crashing into anyone you please."

"I'm not as reckless as you suggest," I told him. "The Countess is pleased with my work, and she values my opinions. And even if she did harbor ill feelings toward me, she'd have little time to act on them. She's far too preoccupied with preparing the castle for her special guests."

"She'll certainly have her pick of girls," he said. "Any family of significance would be proud to boast that their daughter has received special instructions from the Countess."

"But there must be thousands of girls to choose from," I said. "She can't possibly visit every estate. How will she select twenty-five students in just a matter of weeks?"

"She'll start by inviting girls from the lowest nobility," he said. "Those are the families most eager to support the Countess, the ones who wish to ingratiate themselves because they believe it will help them to curry favor with King Matthias."

"But where will they sleep? Certainly not in the servants' quarters?"

Peter swatted at a mosquito that landed on his neck. "The Countess will probably open several rooms in the west wing of the castle. It's been empty since her children moved away, and there's more than enough space to make them comfortable."

For the next several minutes we walked uphill in silence, our feet sliding on the wet ground. Finally, we crested a small ridge laden with pine needles. A bit winded, we stood in the shade to rest our legs, wiping away the sweat that was streaking down our faces and soaking into our clothes. Peter kicked at a stick and sent it spinning down the hill, then leaned against an oak tree, his arms crossed and his eyes closed.

I spun around in the sunlight, comforted by the solitude—a silence punctuated only by wind and birdsongs and small animals darting through the underbrush. I looked up into white clouds that sailed past me, and I basked in the openness that surrounded me, my mouth wide open as I gulped it down like water.

Behind us, the castle's two towers rose up over the trees like giant hands reaching into the sky. To the east, the Carpathians cut a jagged line across the horizon, while ahead of us and over to the west the lush green forest became darker as it dipped into a vale and extended out of sight.

When we started out again, Peter took my hand and guided me along the winding path that led us down into the valley. The fresh air I'd tasted minutes earlier became stifling and now smelled of moss and damp leaves. We pushed aside branches and spider webs as our determined footsteps crushed twigs and decayed bark into the sullen earth. The trees were thicker and more gnarled, taller and closer together, their twisted roots obtruding from the ground like bones piercing skin. Their leaves formed a canopy that obstructed most of the light, pressing down on us until the entire forest assumed an ethereal silence.

Peter threaded his way through the forest, stepping over rocks and fallen limbs, and jumping over hidden roots that threatened to trip us. I followed close behind, clutching a stitch in my side and knowing that if I ever became lost on my own, I would never find my way back to the castle.

"We're almost there," he said. "The belladonna is just beyond that ridge of trees. There's a stream where you can wash your face, and a patch of grass if you want to lie down before we fill our baskets."

"How do you know this area so well?" I asked him.

He turned to face me, his expression one of surprise. "I've explored this forest since I was a boy. I could navigate it blindfolded."

"Is that why you're absent from the castle so often?" I said, smiling. "Because you're wandering the woods like some recluse, collecting herbs and spices?"

He stepped forward and placed his hands on my shoulders. "I didn't want to tell you this, Maria, but..." His large frame blocked out the sun, and he seemed a shadowy outline of someone who had risen up from the ground, like a tormented ghost seeking vengeance. "...after Father Barosius stopped coming to the castle, the Countess ordered me to start bringing the bodies into the forest."

I pushed him away. "But...I thought...doesn't Helen dispose of the bodies?"

Peter snorted. "Helen? She can barely carry a sack of potatoes without whining. I'm the one the Countess trusts." He stared past me in the direction of the castle. "If Helen were told to dispose of those bodies, she'd become lazy and bury them in the courtyard, and then the dogs would be digging up arms and legs every other day."

"But...why do you do it?"

"You say that as if I had a choice," he said, laughing, "but you should know by now that no one ever refuses a request by the Countess. Were I to ignore such a command, someone would leave *my* ripped-up body in the forest for the wolves to devour. Is that what you want to have happen?"

"No, of course not, but...how do you remove them...especially without the coffins? Surely, someone would have noticed a cart loaded with dead bodies."

"There are many ways in and out of the castle," he told me. "Both above and below ground."

I had to remind myself that death and decay were all Peter had ever known while living with the Countess. He had witnessed year upon year of torture and abuse, and his attitude was a symptom of having accepted as normal behavior what any normal person would have certainly regarded as cruel and deviant.

I wanted to cry for him. I wanted to grab his hand and beg him to run off with me. Instead, I marched forward and threw my arms around him. I couldn't imagine loading up those mutilated bodies several times a week—bloated and unrecognizable, the smell of death more pungent in the sweltering sun—and then hauling them into the deepest part of the forest to dump on the ground like rotten vegetables.

"But...how can you continue to serve the Countess," I asked, "knowing she's killed hundreds of girls? Don't you ever feel a pang of regret, or think about running away?"

"Here at the castle I have food, I have water, and I have a place to sleep every night. And for that I'm grateful. Yes, the world is cruel and tragic and unfair...whether it's because you pulled too hard on the Countess's hair, or because you dropped a knife at the worst possible moment...but oftentimes we have to live according to someone else's demands. Otherwise, you might as well just dig a shallow grave and crawl into it."

"You sound like someone who's lost faith," I told him. "As if all the hope had been wrung out of you."

Peter pulled away from me, and a look of sadness streaked across his eyes, as bright and fleeting as a shooting star. "When I was five years old, I watched my parents get knocked off their horses and beaten with clubs…and then thrown into a ditch, their skulls caved in…and what little money they had snatched out of their pockets. I wandered the countryside for days…eating whatever bugs and berries I could find…until I collapsed in a field from exhaustion and dehydration…only hours away from death. And then the Count found me and brought me here to this magnificent castle with its exotic paintings and ornate sculptures and nightly feasts…"

"…And its never-ending chain of murder and torture and savagery," I said.

He sighed like one who's grown tired of explaining. "My life here in Čachtice…which I never asked for…is a second coming, and one that will provide me with the opportunity to seek retribution for what was stolen from me."

"But I'm not here to pursue vengeance," I said. "I'm here to sew a few gowns and, God willing, survive long enough to make it back home to my mother."

He leaned forward and kissed me. His lips were warm like fresh bread, and his tongue circled the inside of my mouth as if it were a key trying to unlock some secret part of me. I rose up on my toes, my hands gripping the scruff of his neck, and pressed myself into him. Our bodies were veiled by the shadows, but I could see his eyes watching me as our faces dripped with sweat in the humid air, his cheeks red as wine.

"I promised to keep you alive," Peter whispered into my ear after we had separated and fought to reclaim our breath, "but you need to stop being so wild. Do what the Countess commands, obediently and without hesitation. And if you can do that, then you just might live long enough to see the leaves change color."

Without another word, he grabbed my hand and we continued down the path toward a bright patch of light that shimmered way off in the distance. Eventually, almost an hour after we had left the castle, the dense forest began to thin out and we stepped into a wide clearing dotted with shrubs, most of which were clustered in the shade of a few large trees. A small stream wound through the gorse and tall grass—the water fresh and clear, and reflecting a hot yellow sun that blazed down on us—while up ahead towered the Carpathians, so majestic and imposing, their craggy peaks scraping the bottom of the sky.

I walked over to the belladonna and examined the long leaves. They were dark green and oval, protruding from a thick purple stem. I bent down and ran my fingers over the smooth berries, most of which were green, though I noticed that some had already ripened to a shiny black. I picked a handful and dropped them into my basket, then leaned closer to smell one of the bell-shaped purple flowers. Immediately, I was met with a bitter odor that threatened to unsettle my stomach.

Peter put down his basket and drew me back from the plant. "I'm not fond of their sharp, pungent scent. It makes my throat burn, as if I've stood too close to a fire."

I wrinkled my nose. "Still, they're quite lovely." I broke off several of the flowers and added them to the berries that rolled around in the bottom of the basket.

"The Countess told me that belladonna means 'beautiful woman'," he said, "and that on certain nights of the year the plant assumes the form of a gorgeous temptress who lures men to their deaths."

I broke off two more flowers and tucked one behind each ear. I spread my arms wide and spun around, looking up into the vast blue sky. I felt bold and powerful—like Scheherazade tricking the king to save her life in one of those ancient tales my father told me.

Peter plucked a berry off one of the shrubs and held it up, squeezing until the skin burst open and the juice ran down his fingers. "Lots of women use the oil to make eye drops. It dilates their pupils…makes them appear more seductive."

"Is that why the Countess wants us to gather them up?" I asked. "So she can crush all these little berries into a secret hypnotic love potion?" I snatched a handful of flowers and tossed them into my basket without even looking. "She certainly has an endless need to collect every beautiful object she can."

"True, she's very adamant in her pursuits," he said, "though I suspect they're hardly unique to just her. After all…" He kissed my cheek and flicked the flower behind my ear. "…what woman doesn't wish to be desirable?"

The servants were bustling about—harnessing a team of horses and loading cedar trunks into one of the three carriages—when Peter and I returned to the castle. Our faces were streaked with dirt and sweat, and the hem of my dress had been ripped by brambles and thorns. Our arms were sore from lugging wicker baskets which now overflowed with bell-shaped purple flowers and small black berries that glistened in the sunlight.

"How long will she be gone?" I asked him.

"Two weeks, most likely. She doesn't like to be away from the castle. She'll want to settle her affairs as quickly as possible."

We brought our baskets into the kitchen and left them on a table. After a quick drink of water we hurried back to the main hall where servants were still filing in and out of the entryway. Helen stood in the center of the foyer and ordered everyone about in an angry voice. She pointed inside and outside, and she kicked at several trunks that had yet to be loaded onto the carriages.

A group of five servants walked down the stairs in single file, each carrying a brown leather satchel.

"Those satchels..." I pointed to one that an older girl clutched in her hand. "What's in them?"

"Herbs and spices," Peter said. "Various remedies Anna has mixed together for the Countess. In case she suffers a fit or a seizure while she's away from the castle."

I was about to return to my room—so I could shut the door and shield myself in a tower of expensive fabrics—when I saw Sandra stagger down the stairs with the other servants. She joined the back of the line, wrestling with a burlap sack half her size and trying to prevent it from sliding out of her arms as she struggled to keep up with the rest of the group. Whenever she took a step, the burlap sack bulged out at awkward angles, emitting a muffled jingle.

I rushed over to the bottom of the stairs and grabbed her arm. "Where are you going?"

"With the Countess." She turned to me—her eyes bloodshot, her jaw swollen on the left side—and let the burlap sack slide out of her arms. It hit the floor with a loud clang.

"To Sárvár?"

"Yes," she said, "and wherever else the Countess decides to go."

I stood in front of her, my hands held out to keep her from walking any farther. "But...why?"

Peter stepped up beside me. "The Countess always brings servants with her when she travels, especially if she's gone for a few weeks." He reached down and hoisted Sandra's burlap sack onto his shoulders. "I'll carry this to the cart for you," he told her. "It's practically boiling outside, and you should probably conserve your strength."

I waited until he walked away—until the shimmering haze beyond had swallowed him up—and then I turned back to Sandra. "Why didn't you tell me you were going to Sárvár?"

"I only found out this morning," she said. "Helen came down to the kitchen right after you left and told me that the Countess wanted to see me."

I stared down at her hands. They were clenched from gripping the sack, her knuckles red and swollen from rubbing against the burlap. I glanced up at her bruised jaw. "Yes, but...why you?"

She reached out with a trembling hand to remove the flower that was tucked behind my ear. "Is this..." She spun it around by the stem, then sniffed the petals. Before I could say anything, she dropped the flower and crushed it under the heel of her foot. When there was nothing left but a few shredded petals, she pointed at the remains and said, "That's deadly nightshade, Maria."

"No, it's belladonna," I told her. "We were collecting it in the forest."

"Yes, but it's also known as deadly nightshade. It's one of the most poisonous flowers. The berries are toxic. Just eating a few can kill you."

"Peter told me that it means beautiful woman...that the oil can dilate a woman's pupils to make her appear more seductive."

"Yes, but it also causes hallucinations and blurred vision, sometimes even headaches and convulsions."

"But..." I gazed down at the shredded petals. "They look so delicate and innocent."

"That's what makes belladonna especially dangerous." Sandra stepped aside as another servant hurried past us. "In some villages they call it the devil's herb. They say he rises out of the ground at night to plant it in the deepest part of the forest, and that he waters it with blood."

"Those are just local superstitions."

"Perhaps, but if I were you I'd stay away from it." She edged closer and whispered, "There are enough ways to die in this castle without worrying about a small purple flower."

Just then, Peter returned to announce that the carriages were loaded. Sandra mumbled a quick thank you, and before I could say goodbye she had joined the other servants and disappeared outside.

"That sack looked terribly heavy," I said to him. "It sounded like pieces of metal knocking together."

He leaned against the oak bannister, glancing around the room as if figuring out the easiest path to escape.

"What was inside the sack?" I tapped my foot and waited for him to respond, but he just stood there and wiped the sweat out of his eyes. "Tell me," I demanded again in as strong a voice as I could collect.

"Locks and chains," he whispered, and then fell silent as the Countess descended the stairs.

Immediately, everyone in the foyer stepped out of her way and retreated to the walls on either side of the room like a parting of the Red Sea. She moved past the servants, her diamond necklace sparkling amidst the thin rays of dusty light that fell upon the darkened hall. Her fingers clutched a large silver flask, polished to a shine and emblazoned with the Báthory coat of arms, and the smile on her mouth was thin and cold.

Anna limped behind the Countess, a black cloak hugging her hunched shoulders. Tufts of white hair poked out from a shriveled bun, and her lips were wet with spittle, the blackened gums as thick as treacle. She was knotted and crooked, and when she looked at me her eyes were gray and milky.

The Countess stopped in front of me and held up her finger. "You collected the belladonna?"

"Yes, we brought it down to the kitchen."

"Excellent. And you'll complete your sewing while we're gone?"

"Yes, it should be done within the week."

Anna frowned. "You are a seamstress, not a dignitary. Don't presume that you have the luxury of setting your own deadlines." She turned to the Countess. "Perhaps Maria has been spending too much time with the rest of the louts and has forgotten her manners. That's what happens when someone lies down with dogs. They often get up with fleas."

The two women laughed at my expense—tittering in the shadows like cawing crows—and then they continued on to the entryway where, after speaking with Helen for several minutes, they proceeded outside to the waiting carriages.

I spun back around to face Peter. "What locks? What chains?"

"The Countess doesn't want servants escaping while they're away from the castle," he told me, "so she chains them together at night...all of them, however many there are...in the same room."

I ran outside, shielding my eyes from the sun as Anna and the Countess climbed up into the first carriage. The five servants had already been loaded into the second carriage, with the third one containing all of the cedar trunks. I saw Sandra pressed against the door, looking dazed and forlorn. She twisted her hands together and stared off into nothing. I moved closer and waved. She saw me and offered a timid smile. I opened my mouth—needing to scream and shout and hold her tight—but everything I wanted to tell her became lodged in the back of my throat.

The coachmen cracked their whips and the horses took off in a great commotion, their hooves pawing the ground in thunderous claps as they galloped down the winding hill toward Čachtice and the forest and whatever else lay beyond. I stood there watching until they rounded the bend by the oak trees, my hand still hanging in the air as Sandra's face disappeared in a cloud of red dust.

I never saw her again.

CHAPTER XV

I NEVER INTENDED TO disobey the Countess. Despite her wrath, she had warmed to me over the past few months, and I knew it would be foolish to squander such good fortune. I reminded myself that Peter was right, and that I should do exactly as he instructed—stop being wild, follow her commands, and act without hesitation—but try as I might I just couldn't sit in my room all day and stare at a covered-up mirror. I couldn't lie on my bed and think about Sandra and the other servants being chained up at night like wild animals.

Mornings, I pitched in with the chores, mostly chopping vegetables and washing out the pots and pans, but sometimes fetching water from the well or sweeping old hay out of the corridors. In the afternoons I trudged back up to my room where I sewed in silence until my stomach rumbled and sent me back downstairs for dinner. I ate whatever food was available—fruits and cheeses and crusts of bread dipped in grease—but I never sat with the other servants. They looked upon me as a complex puzzle, grateful I had stepped in to save my friend, but curious and suspicious of my growing connection to the Countess.

Helen was busy managing the castle—she had to supervise the kitchen, set up rooms for the etiquette academy, and ensure that the courtyard and surrounding grounds were kept in good condition—thus she had little time to hover over me and shout orders. After lunch she often withdrew to the library where she sipped red wine and wrote official letters. Sometimes, she and Peter roamed the fields behind the castle, while other times she rode a carriage into Čachtice to collect unpaid taxes on behalf of the Countess. Buoyed by an inflated sense of importance, Helen gave little thought to anyone else, and so I was free to explore the castle and its maze of twisting passageways.

The Countess had been gone for only a week when I stitched the last diamond onto the final gown. I presented it to Helen, who delivered some butchered version of a compliment. Then the sewing table, all of my needles and thread, a few rolls of fabric, a pair of scissors, and two rulers were all removed from my room. Henceforth, any small projects—such as mending holes in stockings and stitching patches onto ripped dresses— would be completed in the kitchen, where I was told to find a small table and make myself as invisible as possible.

Having completed the three gowns, I teetered on the edge of boredom, and with this newfound monotony I found myself assailed by a barrage of thoughts regarding Mama and Peter and all those girls who were now packing their finest clothes into small decorated trunks and heading to Čachtice to have their throats slit. It felt like I was tied to each of them by an invisible string, and any movement on my part—whether I spoke or sewed or took two steps forward—would disrupt their lives in varying degrees, like a wind that rustles the leaves one day and then rips off a thatched roof the next. In this way, I felt responsible for any pain they might suffer, and a heavy guilt gnawed away at my bones until I became sadder and more frustrated. I lashed out at servants who angered me, and I had difficulty breathing, as though someone were piling large stones atop my chest.

Night after night I dreamed of a long straight road in the country. Together, my father and I walked down it until the sky blackened and a heavy storm descended upon us. In the distance, through the wind and slashing rain, loomed a shadowy circle, a gaping mouth that spit out dozens of broken and bloodied bodies. Then Papa pitched forward and I screamed, and there he was, in a crumpled heap, lying dead by the side of the road. And I saw myself kneeling in the tall muddy grass to turn over his limp body, but every time I peered closer it was someone else's face staring up at me. And as I stumbled backward the corpse stood up and lumbered toward me, its face purple and bloated, the eyes rolled back to white—and then it pointed at me and asked, "Why?"

That dark entryway consumed my every thought, a deep obsession that crept around the outer edges of my mind like an itch I could never scratch. The Countess had warned me not to stray, but too often I found myself peeking around corners or tiptoeing down a narrow flight of stairs, inhaling the musty air as my callused fingers glided over cold stone walls. Several times I found myself lingering near the tapestry while my eyes darted in every direction, the voices from above a distant thrum as the flickering firelight threw misshapen shadows upon the ancient cloth.

For days I debated whether or not I should creep into the underground chamber. I feared that Helen might notice I'd gone missing and come looking for me. I worried that if I stepped inside that abysmal hole, I might become disoriented and lose my way, clawing at the walls until they caved in to suffocate me. But more than that, I was terrified of what I might discover. I'd heard screams emanating from somewhere beyond that entryway—had seen Benedict emerge from it with whips and chains, a devilish smile burned onto his face—and so I knew there were more secrets hidden away on the other side of all that blackness.

Still, despite the apprehensions that boiled inside of me, I finally found the courage to sneak away one afternoon while everyone busied themselves with final preparations for the etiquette academy. After confirming that Helen was occupied in the library, I stole a torch and crept along the winding corridors. I ducked behind the tapestry and inched my way down the crumbling steps, my eyes growing accustomed to the darkness as I hurried across the chamber. I hesitated for just a moment, my hands clenched into tight fists, and then I stepped forward to let that black void swallow me whole.

The ground was soft and damp, and the air smelled like fresh soil dug up after a rainstorm. The cavern was empty and silent. The only sounds were my footsteps sinking into the wet earth. I held the torch high in the air—stepping over broken jars and pieces of splintered wood—but stopped at the end of the tunnel when I came upon a wall of dirt and rock. I turned left and proceeded down an incline, my breaths less ragged as the tunnel widened out into a cavern filled with large curio chests and racks filled with dusty wine bottles. There were several torches mounted on the walls, but the light they cast was weak. Their feeble glare revealed old paintings in warped frames, the canvases ripped and faded, as well as a few rugs that someone had rolled up and shoved under a table, their intricate designs chewed through by mice and other rodents. I thrust my torch into a corner and jumped back when a spider crawled out from beneath a pile of yellowed documents. I knelt down and opened one of the smaller chests. It was filled with trinkets and heirlooms: letters from the Count and other dignitaries, a worn copy of the Bible, moth-eaten dresses and gowns, and a clay bowl filled with necklaces and rings.

The next cavern was even bigger, containing three cells dug into the walls, each space big enough for only two people to crouch inside. The cells had thick wooden doors with large iron locks, and a small hole near the top for air to pass through. I opened one of the doors and peered inside. There were leg shackles lying on the ground and brown patches smeared across the stone walls as if someone had tried to claw her way out. I took another step forward, then jumped back as several large rats darted through the thin puddles of light cast by my torch.

On the other side of the room was a table filled with torture instruments. There was a cat o' nine tails—a long whip with five leather claws at the end, the tips of which contained tiny metal balls studded with spikes. There were also thumbscrews and heretic forks, as well as a tongue tearer. I pictured all those girls fighting against their shackles while they thrashed about in a frenzy to escape, pleading to God while Benedict whipped and stabbed them.

I stumbled into the next cavern and found six sealed coffins. They leaned against a sloping wall that was green with the penetrating damp. I shuddered at the unbearable stench and swung my torch low to the ground, catching sight of dresses and trinkets that were strewn about in various stages of neglect and decay. Piled up in a far corner were several ornate mirrors, the glass cracked and covered with spider webs, and behind them, partially hidden, was a narrow opening.

Pushing aside the mirrors, I knelt in front of the crevice, holding the torch before me as I peered into nothingness. For a moment, I thought I detected a slight breeze tickling my face, but it might have been a stray cobweb. I crawled inside the passageway, coughing as the air thickened and grew colder. My shoulders brushed against the sides of the tunnel, scattering dirt and rocks onto the ground as I inched my way forward. Panicking, I rose up on my knees to hold the torch higher and my back scraped against the top. I couldn't turn my head to look behind me, and soon I felt claustrophobic. My free hand dug into the damp earth, and a fat worm wriggled through my fingers. The breeze I'd detected grew stronger. It was putrid and pungent with the scent of decaying plants, as if I'd fallen into a peat bog. A beetle crawled across the back of my neck, and I stifled a scream, thrashing around as bits of dirt fell onto my face. Distressed, I slipped and lost my balance, whereupon the torch struck the side of the wall and a shower of sparks erupted into the air with a sharp hissing sound. Attempting to right myself, I dropped the torch, cursing as it hit the ground with a dull thud. The dirt snuffed out the bright yellow flame and I was suddenly engulfed in total darkness.

I gripped the Celtic love knot between my fingers, treasuring the smoothness of the braided chain and reassured by the curving lines of the Irish silver. I placed it in my mouth and held it under my tongue, tasting the polished metal. Its bitterness helped to focus my attention. Within minutes, my breathing had slowed to a steady rhythm and I no longer felt as though I were trapped in a coffin.

Squinting into the vast emptiness before me, I lowered my head and crept forward. Soon, I detected a slight incline. The dirt below me grew finer and less rocky, and the stench I'd smelled earlier only intensified. I believed I might vomit at any moment and pressed my sleeve against my mouth to keep from gagging. I prayed to see a pinprick of sunlight or the shimmering haze of a distant fire, but the blackness stretched before me like an endless night. I pushed on—licking my dry lips and wishing I'd brought some water—when all of a sudden my hands reached out and found nothing but air. I somersaulted into the empty space and plummeted several feet before crashing onto a bank of hard earth. Upon impact, I tumbled down another incline, banged my head against a rock, and landed on my back with a painful groan.

I lay there until the dizziness passed, then I stood up and brushed the dirt from my dress. Without the torch I couldn't see anything, but I felt as if I were in a large cavern. I heard water dripping somewhere to my right and something small—a mouse?—scurried across what I now knew to be a stone floor. The air was so cold I could drink it. I choked down the panic in my throat and took a few steps forward, shuffling through the darkness with my hands spread out in front of me. I kicked another rock and noticed that it felt clunky against my foot. It made a strange hollow sound when it rolled across the ground. I bent down to pick it up, and as my fingers skimmed over the cracked surface—across the numerous grooves and pockmarks—I realized it wasn't a rock I was holding.

It was a human skull.

I screamed and tumbled backward, dropping the skull. Horrified, I raced up the incline, arms flailing as my fingers clawed at the walls. I found the opening through which I'd fallen and pulled myself up into the crevice, resting my cheek against the cool dirt as the darkness smothered me. Shivering, I lay there for several minutes until my breathing had slowed, at which point I plowed ahead on my hands and knees, wondering how I'd explain my disheveled appearance to Helen if she caught sight of me before I could change out of those filthy clothes.

I was almost to the other side—the light from one of the mounted torches barely a glint in the distance—when I heard the sounds behind me, faint at first and then growing louder. There was a heavy rustling, like dry leaves being scattered about. I heard clods of dirt fall to the ground, rocks and pebbles scraping together in a flurry of movement. And then, amidst the sensation of earth trembling, amidst the sound of my own terrified cries, there arose a spine-chilling moan.

Something else had crawled inside the tunnel.

Something was coming for me on its hands and knees.

I rushed ahead, zigzagging in a tumultuous fury, my fingers scratching at the hard dirt and flinging it behind me as fast as I could. My shoulders crashed into the sides of the tunnel and the back of my dress tore open when it grazed against the top. Any moment now I expected a hand to grasp my ankle and pull me back into that unholy lair where I would be killed and mutilated, or perhaps eaten alive.

Finally, bruised and winded, I spilled out of the crevice, coughing and sobbing and spitting pieces of dirt onto the ground. I stood up and rubbed my eyes—thankful for what little light washed across the cavern—then I doubled over and clutched a stitch in my side, gasping for breath. The skin on my knees was scraped raw, and my elbows were bleeding from where stone had cut into them.

I limped over to the nearest wall and removed one of the torches. I had just turned toward the entryway, ready to run back to the castle, when a small voice shouted, "Wait!"

As I whirled around, the sputtering flame held in front of me like a sword, I glimpsed someone crawl out of the crevice, coughing and wheezing.

It was Father Barosius.

He dusted off his green robe and came toward me. "I'm sorry I frightened you. I heard strange sounds from below while I was composing my letters."

I slumped against the wall, relieved. "I discovered a cavern…there was a pile of bones…there were skulls and…"

"You stumbled into the Báthory family crypt."

"Crypt?" I stared at him for several moments, still scared and confused. "In the church?"

"There are lots of underground tunnels connecting the castle and the church," he said. "They were constructed long ago should the Count and his family need to seek sanctuary in desperate times."

"Father, have you ever been down here?" I held the torch higher so he might better see all the horrors surrounding us.

"Many times, but only when the Countess is away from Čachtice." Father Barosius stepped closer and peered into my face. "Are you a servant?"

"My name is Maria. I'm a seamstress."

"How long have you lived in the castle?"

"Since the beginning of April."

"Many girls have died, Maria. And not all of them from cholera." He glanced around the room as if someone might be watching us. "I've seen their mutilated bodies."

"And I've watched them die, Father."

He grabbed my arm. "You must tell me what's happening inside these walls."

We sat on the ground, and I affirmed the priest's suspicions regarding the Countess and her treatment of the servants. My voice cracked and my eyes flooded with tears, but I clutched his hand and told him about her secret baths in the middle of the night. I told him how Benedict slit their throats, and how the blood rained down into the copper tub; I told him about punishments in the kitchen and bodies buried deep in the forest; I told him about the surprise visit from Count Thurzó and how he'd read the priest's letter aloud in the library; and I told him about her plan to open an etiquette academy so she could enhance her beauty by soaking in the blood of nobles.

"She's created a nest of iniquity," Father Barosius said. "And she must be stopped. Otherwise, hundreds will soon become thousands, and the land surrounding the castle will be filled with corpses."

"What if a villager found one of the bodies in the forest? Wouldn't a discovery like that provoke a reaction?"

"No one will dare to punish her for murdering peasants," he told me. "In many ways, the nobility might feel she is doing them a great favor. I would threaten to excommunicate her if I thought she might repent, but she believes herself to be one of the elect who are already destined for Heaven." He sighed and put his head in his hands. "I fear God will punish me for the part I have played in this deception."

"She isn't the only one who tortures and maims," I told him. "She has her loyal subjects who are equally guilty."

"Helen and Benedict?"

"Yes," I said, "and there is also Anna, a Croatian woman who supposedly lives in the forest." I looked over his shoulder at the crevice— a black fissure that once seemed deadly, but now seemed liberating. "Take me back to the church with you, Father. You can hide me somewhere until I'm able to return home."

He shook his head. "That I cannot do."

"But…why?"

"Because you would not be safe. The Countess will never allow you to leave here with her precious secrets bundled up in your arms. She will tear apart the village to reclaim you. She will scour the forest until she discovers where you're hiding, or until she trips over your broken bones."

Moments ago, my freedom had seemed so close and attainable, and now it had been snatched away. Still, I knew he was right. Where could I go? Mama and I would never leave our small cottage in Trenčín. Our lives were bound up in those mountains and valleys, tied to the shops and people we wound through on a daily basis. We were rooted in Trenčín and dependent on the comfort and stability it provided. More than that, I wasn't sure I could walk away from all my memories of Papa: his pipe still resting on the window ledge, his ax leaning against a wall in the corner, or those pieces of yellowed parchment bundled together with string inside his musty trunk.

Besides, even if we wanted to move away, we couldn't afford it. And I wasn't sure Mama was strong enough to pack up our valuables and flee across the countryside toward some distant speck on the horizon. How could we live a normal life if we spent every waking moment glancing over our shoulders, waiting for something to leap out of the shadows?

As long as the Countess was free to slaughter whomever she wanted, I would never be out of harm's way. I was trapped inside this castle, and trying to escape would only endanger those I loved. If I returned to Trenčín, the Countess would arrive there sooner or later and inflict a pain I could never imagine.

"I must find a way to avenge these crimes," Father Barosius said. "I've seen too many arrows drunk with blood. I have seen too many swords devouring innocent flesh. The Lord has given me a chance to make amends for my damaging silence, and I mustn't disappoint Him." He rubbed his hands together as if trying to spark a thought. "The Countess must answer for her crimes against the nobility. Unlike peasants, the nobles are far more vocal in their grievances, and they won't stand idle if they believe something terrible has happened to one of their daughters."

"She's much too clever to be caught in a trap, Father."

"Which is why you must remain in the castle and help me to end these dreaded attacks."

"Me?" I suddenly became aware that I'd been gone a long time, and that somewhere above me there might be people shouting my name, or sharpening knives in the kitchen so they could slice the flesh off my shoulders. "But what can I do? I'm hardly a soldier. Half the time I'm locked away in my room or being watched by suspicious eyes."

He leaned into me until the shadow of a flickering flame danced across his wrinkled face. "Can you read and write, Maria?"

"Yes."

"Then you must keep a record of all the girls the Countess lures into the castle. Who they are, where they're from. Thurzó and the king don't care about peasants, but, as I said, they'll snap to attention if the nobles begin to complain about their own daughters disappearing."

"How can we be assured Count Thurzó will return to the castle?" I asked him. "Especially if the Countess continues to justify her killing?"

"We must outwit her," he said. "Only by working together can we resist the devil."

"But...how do I record the names? And where should I hide the list?" I began to feel nervous again, as if I was back inside that narrow tunnel and the walls were closing in around me. "I've completed all her gowns. She has no reason to lend me paper and pencil."

He wiped the top of his bald head with the sagging sleeve of his robe. "I don't envy you this charge, but I know you'll never be safe while you remain inside this castle, not until her true intentions are discovered by those who have the authority to stop her."

"If she discovers I'm helping you, she'll hang me upside down and have Benedict slit my throat."

"The Countess seems to trust you, Maria." He smiled, but it was tinged with a deep sadness that filled his face with regret. "I can't force you to assist me in what I must now do, but please know that if you wish to return home someday and see your mother, you must exploit your relationship with the Countess, otherwise all those deaths will hang heavy on your conscience and you will never truly leave this terrible place, no matter how far you run."

I stood up. "I should return to my room before someone notices I'm missing."

Father Barosius grabbed my arm and pulled himself up off the floor. "Do you know where the chapel is located?"

"Yes, near the Great Hall."

"There is a passageway under the altar, a ladder that leads down to one of the tunnels connecting the castle to the church. I'll be there...waiting behind the altar...every Saturday afternoon between the hours of three and four o'clock. The Countess is usually in Čachtice at that time, and we shouldn't be disturbed."

"And...what if I'm unable to meet with you?"

"Then I'll recite the rosary and pray to God that I'll see you there the next time." He wrapped his arms around me, the smell of red wine still lingering on his breath, and suddenly I wanted to risk everything that was valuable to me and crawl back to the church with him.

"I'll do what I can to help you," I told him, "and I'll find a way to meet you in the chapel."

He smiled, but this time it was tougher and echoed a semblance of hope. "You are strong in body and pure in heart, Maria. But don't trust anyone." He gestured toward the three coffins propped against the wall. "Remember, you have no friends here in the castle."

CHAPTER XVI

THE COUNTESS RETURNED HOME at the beginning of September. The air was so muggy that the castle itself felt narrow and intruding, as if hundreds of people had been walled up in the same dark cell. Already, two girls had died in the courtyard of heatstroke, and four others had died of dehydration. The smell of manure had seeped into the castle—filling the leaden air with offensive fumes—and our arms were sore from swatting away those writhing black clouds that swarmed the corridors with their incessant buzzing.

On that Monday morning, every servant gathered in the foyer to greet the Countess. They lined up on either side of the room with their heads bowed and their hands folded. From my vantage point behind Helen, I watched the first carriage crest the hill and come to a stop. Benedict opened the small door and helped the Countess step out into the bright sunlight. Then he did the same for Anna. The other two carriages were packed with decadent girls who climbed down one at a time, treading with care through scattered mud puddles. They blinked up at the imposing castle, perhaps believing they were about to step into a fairy tale where their wildest dreams would come true.

Immediately, several servants rushed outside to collect every trunk, box, and chest from each of the three carriages. They hauled the baggage into the castle while Helen screamed at them to move faster. She kicked their shins and threatened to whip the meat off their bones. In the midst of this chaos, the nobles congregated in the center of the foyer, scolding the servants and complaining about the rough handling of their personal belongings.

I stepped off to the side and lingered beside a tall marble statue, watching Anna whisper something to the Countess. The old woman pointed her gnarled finger toward a grassy field in the distance and limped out the door. I crept over to the entryway, suddenly aware that while six servants had left with the Countess—Sandra included—only four had entered the castle. I waited, but no one else emerged from the carriages. Then Benedict waved Peter over and together they led the horses back to the stables.

The Countess shushed the girls and introduced each one to Helen, instructing them all to stand up straight—absolutely no slouching, no leaning to either side—and to look her in the eye whenever they said hello. She made several girls repeat this process and lectured them on the importance of greeting a stranger. She explained how they should never touch someone unless contact was initiated by a person of higher distinction, and how they should always remain two feet away so as to respect one's personal space.

Once the introductions were completed, Helen asked the girls to follow her toward the west wing of the castle where the servants had set up their living quarters. There, they could unpack, wash themselves, and rest before dinner. None of them spoke as they passed me. They were slow and sullen, and their cheeks—normally so white and smooth like a China doll—were flushed. They cooled themselves with handheld fans that looked to be made of silk.

I was so worried about Sandra that I almost didn't notice when the Countess stepped in front of me and asked, "Have you completed my gowns?"

"Yes. All three are now hanging in your bedchamber, just as Helen instructed."

"Excellent." She lifted her arm into a dusty ray of light and held it there for several seconds. "My skin is dry and flaky. I must attend to it soon."

I listened to the fading footsteps of twenty-five young women, trying to imagine their expressions when they found themselves hanging upside down in a dingy cavern and choking on their own blood.

"There will be a spectacular dinner tonight to welcome my new students," the Countess said, "and I would like for you to be there, Maria."

"I'm honored, thank you."

She stepped back and surveyed me. "I will provide you with a modest gown, which will save you the embarrassment of having to show up in these dull scraps of cloth."

"Thank you, Countess."

"And I will allow you to take a bath…with the help of some soap, of course. The ladies who sit near you will want to enjoy their meal and not gag on the smell of dirt and hay."

I bowed my head. "Your generosity is much appreciated."

She turned to leave, and in a moment of panic I reached out to touch her arm. "Excuse me, miss, but where is Sandra?"

"Who?"

"One of the girls who accompanied you on your trip? She wasn't among the other servants and…"

"Are you referring to that runt from the kitchen?"

I nodded.

"She's dead."

We stood there for a long moment, staring at each other in the hall.

"Dead?"

"Yes, Maria. The girl is dead. As dead as a dog run over by a coal cart."

I placed a hand over my heart, afraid it might shatter from the sheer force of her words, which she had delivered without the slightest bit of emotion, as if she were sharing something trivial. "But how can she…dead?"

"The word has a wonderful finality about it," the Countess said, annoyed by my stuttering. "It means your heart has stopped beating. It means your eyes have ceased to see, and your lungs no longer fill with air."

My knees felt like someone had kicked them out from under me. I leaned against the wall for fear I might crumble to the ground. "How did she…I don't understand…"

"The lazy grub would not stop complaining," the Countess said. "First she grumbled about the heat…then she droned on about the chain digging into her wrist every night…then she whined about her terrible thirst. I warned her that I was in far too good a mood to listen to her constant bleating, but the girl was simply insufferable, and a rat who gnaws at a cat's tail invites its own destruction."

"How did she…"

"The runt tried to escape one afternoon. Just flung open the door and jumped out of the carriage. She only made it about half a mile…running through some wheat field…before the other servants chased her down and brought her back, kicking and screaming."

I swallowed hard and held my breath, trying to stop the tears from running down my face. "What did you do?"

"I chose to be accommodating. I gave your friend exactly what she wanted. She asked for some water, and now she has more water than she ever dreamed possible. Unless, of course, the girl has somehow bobbed to the surface since we rode away, but that would be quite difficult given all the stones weighing her down."

The Countess turned away from me and strode up the stairs, humming a soft melody while I slid down the wall and pressed my cheek against the floor. I don't know how long I lay there. It seemed like hours, though it was likely only a matter of minutes. I watched a beam of sunlight slide across the floor, and several servants walked past me with hurried footsteps.

Eventually, I stopped crying. My head felt woozy—like I'd banged it against something heavy—but I managed to stagger up the stairs and back to my room. I collapsed on the bed and shut my eyes, my fists beating the mattress until my knuckles were sore. I raged inward, thinking about Sandra and the secrets I'd refused to share with her. I had been so firm and adamant in scolding her, thinking I was protecting her, but now I wondered if I'd been selfish in vowing to keep silent, afraid the Countess would discover my treachery and dismember me in her underground chamber.

Father Barosius had entrusted me with a plan to end these brutal killings. He'd asked me to help him defeat the Countess, to keep a record of all the noble girls who entered the castle. But how? I had no paper on which to write, no pencil with which to scribble that crucial information. Helen had removed everything from my room after I'd completed the last gown, and the only thing left, aside from the bed, was that awful mirror, which I now hated more than ever.

Soon I fell asleep, enveloped in the bliss of temporary solitude. I dreamt I was sitting in a small copper tub in the middle of the forest. A conspiracy of ravens soared through the pine trees, their black wings blocking out the sun, their shrill calls echoing across the wide green valley. The Countess floated above me in a web of chains, her throat impaled by a thin hazel branch. I stared up into a bronze sky while her blood drizzled down in misty sheets and dripped onto my naked body. But instead of recoiling from such horridness, I spread out my arms to invite it.

I awoke to a sharp noise somewhere in the castle—a servant dropping something on the staircase, perhaps—and opened my tired eyes with an exaggerated yawn. I glanced over at the blue linen cloth I'd flung over the mirror and felt a flash of anger burn my insides. I wanted to shatter the glass with my bare hands, punching and kicking and screaming until I was out of breath, until there was no one left to look at except a deformed outline. I wanted to see those sharp pieces flying across the room in a great sheet of sparkling dust, but I knew the Countess would become incensed if I destroyed one of her prized possessions. She wouldn't hesitate to throw me down and kick me in the ribs, to beat me with something as simple as a brass candlestick. And then, just when it seemed I might lose consciousness—or perhaps even die—she would grab the back of my neck and shove my face into every jagged shard. She would laugh when they sliced open my lips and cheeks, snickering when they slashed the tip of my nose to leave deep gashes, and she would continue her assault until long streaks of my blood crisscrossed the floor.

In that instant—like storm clouds parting to reveal a blistering sun— an idea ignited in my head. I knew how to record all those names, and I knew where I could hide them. I sat up in bed and considered every possible angle, working through each specific step and detail, over and over again, until I convinced myself the plan might actually work.

I needed only one small item, and with God's help I would steal it tonight during the feast.

Everyone assembled in the Great Hall at five o'clock. The Countess, dressed in a ruffled scarlet gown, entered the room and took her place at the head of the table. She sat on a raised wooden dais to accentuate her superiority, and behind her—clutching a long-handled Persian fan—a twelve-year-old girl cowered in the shadows. It was a known fact that Elizabeth Báthory did not like to sweat, and so this poor creature had been assigned the unpleasant job of making sure the Countess didn't become too hot during the evening. A small silver bell rested beside her plate, and next to it a tall crystal vase filled with purple tulips. There was also a shallow bowl filled with sweet lemons, and it was not uncommon to see the Countess throw fruit at someone's chest whenever she became bored with the dinner conversation.

Up in the Minstrel's Gallery, a young troubadour played the lute and sang a dreamy folk song about a woman who discovered true love and then vanished at sea during a storm; beside him, an older man danced and juggled wooden balls. The floor was covered with fresh straw and rushes, and I detected a hint of mint and lavender that someone had scattered to improve the smell. Large silk tapestries lined the gray stone walls—their intricate designs illuminated by the candles and oil lamps spread around the cavernous room—and the long banquet table was covered in white linen.

Helen sat next to the Countess, looking irritated and cheerless. She picked at her gums—trying to dislodge a fleck of food stuck between her two front teeth—and glared at me when I took my seat at the other end of the table. She had barely spoken to me during the past two weeks, preferring to point and grunt her instructions, and I didn't want tonight to be any different. The less I had to talk, and the less I had to listen, the more focused I could remain.

The twenty-five nobles, all adorned in shimmering ivory gowns, pranced into the Great Hall like they were princesses waiting to have untold wishes bestowed upon them by a fairy godmother. Each girl claimed her seat around the enormous table and sat rigid, hands folded and elbows off the table like the Countess had instructed. Entranced by the extravagance that surrounded them, they gazed upon the crystal goblets and stacked bottles of wine, marveling at the assortment of forks, knives, and spoons that stood guard over their gold plates.

When the troubadour finished his song, the Countess rang the bell and several servants hurried into the room. Some carried red jugs stamped with the Báthory coat of arms; others carried small white bowls. They walked around the table—beginning with the Countess before moving in a clockwise direction—and poured hot water into the bowls so we could wash our hands before eating.

More servants appeared, cradling large silver flasks, and they filled our goblets with a spicy red wine known as Bull's Blood. The Countess watched us swirl the deep ruby liquid, smiling as we held the crystal stems exactly as she instructed, and then she stood up to offer us a toast. "To your health, my little doves. Whenever I see thee, I thirst, and holding the cup, apply it to my lips more for thy sake than for drinking. May your arrival here in Čachtice be as advantageous to you as it is to me."

We drank the wine, careful not to let a single drop dribble down our chins, afraid it might stain the crisp white tablecloth. Yet another servant entered the hall, this time carrying an enormous basket of fresh rolls glazed with salted butter. She placed a glistening roll on the center of each plate, then disappeared again. I took my roll in both hands, dug into the firm crust, and pulled it apart until a blast of steam erupted from the center. The bread was soft and flaky in my mouth, and I savored every delicate bite, relishing the sweet buttery taste that lingered on my lips and paying no heed to the countless crumbs that tumbled down the front of my gown.

The Countess clapped her hands. "Don't cut your roll with a knife," she shouted. "Break it open with your fingers, and then tear off bite-size pieces. You must always be ready to engage in dinner conversation…preferably in a clear and loud voice…so never indulge in a mouthful of food that can't be chewed and swallowed in less than five seconds."

A fantastic aroma spread throughout the room as more servants brought in a vast collection of silver bowls, all polished to a shine and twinkling in the wavering candlelight, each of them a different shape and size and running the entire length of the table like stones in a river. There was wild mushroom soup; red fish soup with hot paprika; and goulash loaded with potatoes and carrots and chunks of beef. There were small dumplings stuffed with liptauer and goose liver, and deviled eggs stacked in pyramids on silver plates.

The servants ladled hot soup into everyone's bowl and refilled our wine glasses. The noise in the room quieted to a gentle hush as we dined on the rich food, trying to be as dainty as possible. The girls were eager and excited. They spoke of politics and religion, their smug words swaddled in wealth, and how they all hoped to someday live in a lavish castle. I made a concerted effort to remember as many names as I could, paying special attention whenever someone mentioned the small village she had left to seek greater opportunities here in Čachtice.

There was Agnes from Patvarc with wide eyes and a dazed look, and Brigitta from Koszeg who kept fidgeting with her hands; Felicia from Sima had red hair, and Giselle from Holloko had freckles splashed across her face; Violet from Alcsut was a tall girl who devoured food as though she had never eaten, while Irene from Tiszakurt did not speak a word the entire meal, choosing instead to stare down at her plate; Isabella from Rezi had chubby cheeks as red as embers; and Greta from Velem was so short she had to strain her arm forward to reach her goblet.

And on and on, a long list of blue-blooded names and unfamiliar places, too many to remember on a night when all I wanted was to forget.

No sooner had I scraped the bottom of my bowl—the taste of cod and sweet onion still circling my tongue—than more servants appeared carrying large cutting boards loaded with half a dozen pork tenderloins, each as thick as a man's arm, filled with spinach and tomato puree, and nestled in a bed of white rice mixed with green peas. The pork was sliced into thin strips, the clear juice dripping down the crusted sides, and the moist meat was transferred to our waiting plates. I minded each piece of silverware—watching the other girls to see whether they selected a fork or a spoon, and which size—and I made sure not to chew with my mouth open, especially because I was sitting in view of the Countess, and I didn't want to embarrass either her or myself.

Agnes, who sat beside me, speared a dumpling on the end of her fork and whispered, "What's your name?"

"Maria," I told her. "I'm a seamstress. From Trenčín."

Her eyes grew as large as the plate in front of her. "Your village is on the Vah River?"

"Yes," I said.

"Have you seen the ghost of Elisa Day?"

I heard several forks and spoons clink on the edges of plates and bowls, the other conversations tapering off one by one like a dying echo, and then each girl looked straight at me for the first time that evening.

"Who is Elisa Day?" Violet asked from farther down the table.

"A girl as beautiful as the wild roses that grow along the riverbank," I said. "Legend has it that a handsome young man walked into her village one day and fell in love with Elisa as soon as he saw her."

"And they dated for three days." Agnes held up three fingers, and I noticed a large signet ring on the index finger of her left hand. The band was thin and made of gold while the top was square and inset with a large chunk of malachite. The stone was vibrant green, and from where I sat it looked like a tiny forest was nestled against her pale knuckle.

I nodded toward the rest of the girls. "On the first day, he visited her house and they talked by the fireside…on the second day, he brought her a single red rose, and he asked her to meet him in the forest where all the wild roses grew…on the third day, he brought her down to the river and killed her. He waited until her back was turned…then picked up a large rock and whispered, 'Beauty must die.' With one swift blow he struck her on the back of the head and she died instantly. He put a fresh rose between her teeth and pushed her lifeless body into the water. To this day, people who live along the Vah River claim to see her ghost wandering the forest, blood running down the side of her head while she clutches a red rose in her hand."

Some of the girls looked shocked; others giggled. Soon, though, the conversation shifted. The Countess explained at length the rules of the castle—even cautioning the girls not to enter the forest lest they fall prey to the wolves—and then she discussed the main parts of their forthcoming training: how to sit and stand like proper ladies; how to walk with finesse; how to get in and out of a carriage with graceful elegance; and how to take a turn about the room so as to flaunt one's beauty.

While the Countess was addressing everyone in the Great Hall—while their eyes were fixated on her commanding presence at the other end of the banquet table—I lifted the napkin from my lap and calmly placed it atop the dinner knife that lay to the right of my plate. I glanced at Helen to make sure her attention was focused elsewhere, then I waited until all the servants had left the room. I sipped some water, whispered a quick prayer, and willed my hand to steady itself, terrified that any erratic movements would arouse suspicion.

As the Countess was gesturing toward the silk tapestries and boasting that they were woven by the Byzantines, I took a slice of the tender pork and chewed it slowly, allowing the juices to drip down my chin. Leaning forward, smiling at their frivolous conversation, I reached down and grasped the napkin, making sure to wrap my fingers around the knife to conceal the glinting blade. I brought the napkin to my face and dabbed both sides of my mouth, then rested the napkin on my lap, balancing the knife on both knees as I scooted forward in my chair.

The evening continued with no other disruptions. I ate until I felt sick, and when I finally sat back, my eyes fluttering in a drowsy ecstasy, Viktoriya and another servant approached the banquet table holding silver platters that overflowed with assorted desserts: sponge cakes glazed with caramel and nuts; red currant and almond pies; and crepes filled with raisins and strawberry jam and then baked with a coating of meringue.

We picked at our plates for the next hour, only stopping when our mouths were full of yawns and our bones were full of sleep. The sun had moved farther west, sinking lower in the sky until it became a fiery ball in the stained-glass window, exploding yellow and red across the table. Bursts of light twinkled off the plates and bathed the entire room in an orange sheen. Minutes later, a strong wind gusted in through the door leading to the kitchen; it shook the tapestries and ruffled the linen tablecloth, bending the high flames that flickered above us in their crooked torches.

"Do you think the castle is haunted?" Greta asked.

Isabella clapped her hands. "How marvelous it would be to see a ghost floating through the corridor in the middle of the night."

They chattered on for several minutes, spooking each other with embellished tales of ghouls and goblins. They wanted to know if the castle was keeping its own grisly secrets, if there were bodies hidden behind the walls, and if there were restless spirits seeking retribution.

I kept silent, watching and remembering, angry at all that had happened, and terrified of everything that was yet to come. My left hand gripped the edge of the table while my right hand clutched the dinner knife. Trembling, I removed it from the napkin and slid it beneath my gown, its sharpened edge nestled against my ribcage.

CHAPTER XVII

THE COUNTESS DIDN'T WAIT long to begin murdering her prized students, and on their second night in the castle—as they drifted in and out of sleep, their bellies full of rich food and their heads dizzy with wine—I was shaken awake by Helen and brought down to the chamber.

She chose Violet from Alcsut as the first victim, most likely because the girl was tall and strong, her cheeks a healthy pink, her step a bit more lively than the others, and thus the girl was seasoned and ripe, brimming with that rejuvenating liquid the Countess valued above all else.

Benedict woke the doomed girl, careful not to disturb the others, and told her the Countess wished to see her. Violet was still confused and half-asleep when she stumbled into the cavern, barefoot and shivering, rubbing her eyes as they adjusted to the grimy light. Each lingering blink revealed to her the white tub and the spiked cage, and the rusted chains that hung down from an iron ring in the ceiling.

The Countess sat in the empty tub, lamenting the dryness of her skin as though she might crumble into dust at the slightest touch. Helen hovered near the entrance to the underground tunnels, barely visible in the weak shadows that limped across the room. And Anna seemed to be everywhere and nowhere at the same time. One moment, her breath was on the back of my neck, and then—what seemed to me only seconds later—I would hear her steady footsteps echo back to me from deep inside some distant cavern.

Violet had just enough time to utter a shout of surprise before Benedict pushed her to the ground. He pressed his hand into the small of her back and sat atop the horrified girl, pinning her down while she kicked and screamed. After tearing off her thin nightdress, he used a pair of pliers to rip the skin from just below her shoulder, leaving a jagged gash as large as my fist. He then handed me the chunk of flesh. It was warm and soft, the edges tattered and dripping with blood. He ordered me to wash the Countess, to rub the moist flesh all over her body in the same way one might use an ordinary cloth.

I screamed inside, a long painful howl that convulsed my entire body. I reached out and took it with both hands, picturing Sandra's face as I knelt beside the tub. I locked eyes with the Countess and ran that soft flesh down the entire length of her back and across her breasts, my fingers digging into the sinewy tissue as I gripped harder to keep it from slipping out of my trembling hands.

Violet crawled along the floor until Benedict lifted her up and carried her over to the chains. I refused to look up at her, though I felt compelled to. Instead, I remembered Sandra chopping vegetables in the kitchen; I remembered her writing ashen words on the floor, her once silvery voice now drowning out those horrific shrieks that pricked my skin.

"You appear queasy," the Countess said to me. "Perhaps you believe we should have shown this poor girl some mercy and cut her elegant throat as soon as she stumbled into the room?"

"I wasn't brought here to think," I whispered, "and it's not my place to question your grand design."

"Pain quickens the heart," she said, "which forces the blood to surge through those delicate veins and arteries. They say it flows inside us in a circle, with no beginning or end. But here, in this very room, there is an end with a purpose." She smiled and touched a thin stream of blood that ran down her leg. "The only lasting beauty is the beauty of the heart, Maria, and I will drain as many as I must for the sake of my longevity."

Helen stepped forward and together she and Benedict attached Violet's ankles to the chains. I moved away from the Countess and dropped the chunk of flesh on the floor, staring at my bloodied hands until my eyes hurt, aware that Violet's throat had been slit only when the screams finally ceased. I glanced up to see the Countess stretch out her arms, rejoicing as drops of red rained down on her in feverish splashes. She lifted her hands and feet into the firelight, arching her back so she could watch the blood seep into her skin. "It feels fresher," she said, "more silky and pure."

Benedict gestured toward the tub, which was mostly empty. "Would you like me to fetch another girl?"

"No," she said. "This is an exceptional stock…the perfect vintage, really…and I mustn't be wasteful. One girl every few days should suffice."

Anna materialized out of the darkness like a ghost rising up from the mist. She picked up the flesh I had dropped, wiped off the dirt and dust, and handed it back to me with a disapproving look. "Attend to the

Countess while this is still warm, otherwise I'll tear a sizable chunk from the tenderest part of your own body."

I took several wobbly steps forward and swept Violet's flesh through the thickening puddle on the bottom of the tub. Using large broad strokes, I covered the Countess's entire body with blood—soaking the frayed flesh again and again, and squeezing it in my fist to watch deep red trails cascade down her neck and chest—until she looked absolutely frightening in the glittering firelight.

"Are you afraid, Maria?" Her hands grasped both sides of the tub. A small drop of blood was smeared across her left cheek.

"Yes, Countess."

"If you embrace a spirit of timidity," she told me, "then you'll wilt like a neglected flower. But if you want your name chiseled in stone…if you wish to be admired for all your accomplishments…you must begin each day with conviction."

I scrubbed her arms and legs, trying not to stare at the flesh in my hand.

The Countess dipped her fingers into the pool of blood and held them up to my face. I detected a strong metallic odor. "You believe I'm taking life," she said, "when all I'm doing is merely transferring it."

I wiped away a trickle of cold sweat that dripped down the side of my face, my hands shaking with anger at the thought of Sandra and Violet and the countless other girls who had died inside this chamber, remembering that their bloated bodies had been loaded onto a cart and wheeled deep inside the forest, their remains dumped onto the ground for the wolves to feast upon.

Above me, the chains creaked with the weight of the body, which swayed back and forth in an eerie rhythm, casting such deep shadows into the tub that for a brief moment it appeared to be bottomless, and I believed that if I leaned too far over I would fall into that blackness and plunge straight to hell.

The next morning, the Countess informed everyone that Violet had grown tired of decadence and affluence, and had left the castle to return home. The Countess revealed this during breakfast while the girls were indulging in cold meats and assorted cheeses, chewing puff pastries and cutting into thick cuts of bacon, and then washing it all down with steaming pots of green tea. Her sharp voice rose above the tinkling of glasses and the resounding clang of forks scraping against silver plates. When the Countess had finished speaking, she dabbed the corners of her mouth with a white linen cloth and asked if they had slept well.

"The beds are most comfortable." Isabella looked down at her plate, then glanced over at the others. "Though…sometime in the middle of the night…I was awakened by screams coming from somewhere inside the castle."

"What you heard were servants being punished for their incompetence," the Countess told her. "If they misbehave like children, they are castigated like children. The Bible tells us not to spare the rod, and I'm happy to oblige the Lord in his infinite wisdom."

The girls laughed, commenting on the laziness of servants, and continued eating their breakfast. None of them exhibited even a little surprise that Violet had departed and, indeed, they didn't seem disappointed. It occurred to me that many of them probably welcomed Violet's sudden absence, as it increased their own chances of ingratiating themselves with the Countess, which they believed would propel them further into high society. They wanted to receive private lessons and tailored compliments. I could see it in the way they interrupted each other during meals—glaring with suspicious eyes while they feigned sweetness with their light touches and syrupy words—and how they jostled one another as they pushed their way to the front of the group whenever the Countess entered the room.

After breakfast, Helen brought me outside. She pointed toward the grassy field behind the castle. "The harvest festival is only a few weeks away, and we still have much to do. While we can't help losing daylight, we mustn't lose our focus."

Since completing the last gown, I'd been tasked with helping other servants prepare for the harvest festival. Coming from Trenčín, I understood the importance of plucking crops and storing them for the cold winter months—of acknowledging the dying soil by celebrating everything the Lord had been gracious enough to provide—but never before had I seen such grandeur and diligence applied to what I'd always known to be a simple and humble event.

The Countess wanted a huge bonfire as the centerpiece for the night's festivities, and so I'd begun carrying armfuls of wood into the field so Benedict could construct an altar and foundation. I'd begun assembling baskets filled with winter squash and ears of dried corn, and the pantry was overflowing with pumpkins and bottles of red wine. Every morning the kitchen staff heated pots of apple cider spiced with cinnamon, and the entire first floor of the castle now smelled like juniper and nutmeg.

In Trenčín, most families celebrated the harvest by sitting around a crackling fire in their cottage—eating almond cakes and singing songs and telling stories—but here at the castle I couldn't think of anything worth celebrating. I hated that all the spices and foods I'd grown to love over the years were being used to honor and make merry, covering up the carnage underground like flowers planted over a shallow grave.

Helen gave me a tattered pair of brown pants and a red hemp shirt. "Peter is out in the field with a bale of hay. The Countess wants you to set up a scarecrow so the birds will stop pecking away at the food."

I trudged out to the field—the tall blades of grass swishing against my legs, the ground still crunchy from an early-morning frost—and walked around the makeshift altar until I spotted Peter. He was crouching down on the ground with a burlap sack, which he stuffed full of straw, hay, and leaves. I peered over his shoulder, then immediately shrank back as a hideous face stared back at me. The eyes were two black buttons of differing sizes that someone had sewn on in a haphazard fashion, and there was no nose, just a wide empty space above a mouth that was nothing more than a narrow slit cut into the fabric.

"Do you think this will scare away the birds?" he asked.

"Only too well." I knelt down beside him. "They might never come back."

Together, we stuffed the scarecrow's shirt and pants, stopping to laugh when Peter tossed straw into my hair. He scooted backward to avoid my playful swipe, then leaned closer to remove the straw with the tips of his fingers, stealing a kiss on my neck as he did so.

When the scarecrow was bulging and misshapen, we assembled it by sliding the clothes onto a long wooden pole. Peter secured the shirt and pants with some string, then plunged the sharp end of the pole deep into the ground, twisting and grunting until he was sure the pole was firm in the soil and wouldn't topple over in the wind. Finally, he reached up with both hands and put the burlap sack on the very top, tying the base of it tight against the rough wood so the face took on a pinched and even more grotesque appearance.

Peter took my hand and led me toward the wooden foundation where someone had scattered cloves and sandalwood amid clusters of fresh green ivy. We sat down and I leaned my head against his shoulder. He pressed my palm against his cheek and rubbed my fingers, massaging the skin with a fierce concentration until he stopped at my thumb and held it up in the bright sunlight.

"That's a nasty wound," he said. "You should wrap that with a bandage before it gets infected."

I looked at the half-moon gash—swollen and purpled, the edges crusted over with dried blood—and shrugged. "The Countess has me running in so many directions that suffering cuts and bruises has become as commonplace as receiving insults from Helen."

"You should be more careful," he said, "or you're likely to injure more than just your pretty little thumb."

I pulled my hand away. "I thought you were supposed to protect me."

"My sincerest apologies." He made a half-hearted attempt at a bow. "It seems I've forgotten my duties."

"Perhaps you've been distracted by all that extra baggage the Countess brought back from her trip."

"You're far prettier than any of those other girls," Peter told me. "The Countess plucked them from the countryside like weeds in a garden. But you…" He stared into my eyes and ran a finger over my chapped lips. "…you were a much more difficult prize to secure, Maria."

"Me…but…why? I'm just a peasant."

"When it comes to beauty," he said, "the Countess is not concerned with authority or ancestry."

"A wise choice," I said, "because I have neither."

"I'm sure there are many seamstresses who can stitch and sew and cobble together a fancy dress," he said, "but the Countess was quite adamant that only the most lovely and virtuous girl be entrusted with fabric that was destined to touch her skin."

I felt a surge of pride, remembering the care and precision I'd demonstrated when measuring and cutting the three gowns. I remembered the soft, airy feel of the lace cuffs and how the necklines sparkled with diamonds when I'd completed each one and held it up to the light.

"Elizabeth Báthory is a superstitious woman," Peter said. "She believes the most beautiful woman will craft the most beautiful clothes. That's why she obsessed over finding you for almost a year, why she sent Anna to investigate hundreds of possible girls and to inquire about their skin tone and complexion, demanding that she inspect every stitch and seam."

I shook my head in disbelief. "What compels someone to scour the ends of the earth just to enhance her beauty?"

He grabbed a fistful of ivy from the base of the altar, shredded it into tiny pieces, and tossed them into the air. He watched the leaves and stems swirl above our heads, then cast me a sideways glance. "Look in the mirror when you're fifty," he said, "when you're old and gray and full of aches, and see if you can ask that question with less contempt."

I lay back on the soft grass, hands behind my head, and stared up at the clear blue sky. My long black hair was spread out around me, floating in the gentle breeze as though I were adrift in a vast green sea. I could have closed my eyes and fallen asleep right then and there, wishing that when I opened them again my mother would shake me awake from the nightmare I'd been living.

Peter rolled onto his side and tried to kiss my cheek, but I pulled away and sat up. I was moody and not afraid to show it.

"You're quite the riddle," he said. "Flirtatious one moment and cagey the next."

I was tired and sore, and even when I wasn't moving I still felt like I was rushing through the castle with someplace to be and something to do. If I wasn't with the Countess, then I was helping to prepare for the harvest festival; and if I wasn't preparing for the harvest festival, then I was alone in my room, listening for sudden footsteps as I created the secret list for Father Barosius, inscribing every name and detail I could possibly remember.

The main problem was Peter. He was always lurking in the corridor. At first I enjoyed his constant attention, craving the closeness he wrapped around me like a blanket, but after my meeting with Father Barosius I felt that I was in constant danger, and I didn't want Peter to stumble after me like a lovesick boy and then find himself in trouble with the Countess.

In the past few weeks he had become my shadow. He helped me with the chores, carrying baskets and pieces of wood; he brought me clothes to mend and lingered in the doorway while I threaded the needle; or he decided he was hungry and joined me in the kitchen for a quick meal. Mornings, he waited outside of my room with a smug look on his face. Nights, he escorted me back upstairs and tried to worm his way into the darkness with awkward kisses.

And then there was the guilt, heavy in my stomach like molten lead, sometimes reducing me to tears or doubling me over in the middle of the night. Down in that hellish chamber, I thought about Sandra and her small vegetable garden, and how she'd been weighted down at the bottom of a lake. But above ground, where the air should have been cleaner, I could only think of twenty-four girls—young and pretty and bursting with inherited dreams—who were dazzled by large shiny objects in their constant eagerness to please the Countess. In their quest to be seen and heard, they remained oblivious to the profound terror that poured forth from those ancient walls like a pall of black smoke billowing up into a fiery sky.

CHAPTER XVIII

TWO DAYS LATER, THE Countess received an official letter from Count Nicholas Zrínyi. He was married to her eldest daughter, Ursula; he was also a distant cousin of Count Thurzó. His letter announced that he would arrive at the castle on Friday afternoon, and that he wished to speak with the Countess regarding a matter of extreme importance.

She was sitting in the library, drinking a glass of red wine and reading *The Faerie Queene*, when Helen entered and gave her the letter. After reading it over several times—during which she cursed at the ceiling and slapped at the paper with the palm of her hand—she crumpled it up and threw it against the wall.

"I will not allow myself to be dominated by men," she said.

The Countess thumbed through a few more pages, trying to exude a sense of calmness, then slammed the book shut and left the library, returning to her bedchamber where she remained for the rest of the day. Once there, she refused to sit still. She hovered around the room like a moth. She lay on the bed, her pale feet draped over the edge, and picked at a sprig of grapes. She stood by the window and watched fat raindrops splash against the glass. Later, she sat in front of a tall mirror while I brushed the knots out of her thinning hair. She didn't speak to me, but several times she leaned forward to address her own reflection. Her words were quick and terse—laced with anger and suspicion—and through clenched teeth she stared hard into the polished mirror and questioned why her son-in-law should choose this time to visit with her.

I nodded when appropriate and kept my head lowered, though inside I couldn't help but rejoice. I reveled in her uncertainty and discomfort, and every time she squirmed in her seat I felt like hugging myself and dancing around the room. Ever since the Countess had returned from her trip and informed me of Sandra's murder, an insatiable thirst for revenge had bubbled up inside of me, and now it erupted like a boiling geyser. Perhaps it was because she seemed so vulnerable—or because she lacked the poise that normally defined her—but what I wanted most was to grip her hair in my hands and wind it around her throat three times, squeezing until the last breath expired from her lungs.

At five o'clock, Anna swept through the door. "Is it true that Count Zrínyi will arrive tomorrow?"

"Yes," the Countess said. "And already I wish he would go away and leave me alone."

Anna shuffled across the room and put two firm hands on her shoulders. "He's a meddlesome fool, groveling to Thurzó and the king in the hope of securing more lands and titles."

"He's always been rebellious," the Countess said, "but his timing unsettles me. Especially this close to the harvest."

"There are means to render you unseen," Anna said, one eyebrow arching up. "Let me take care of Count Zrínyi, and I can assure you that whatever concerns and accusations he drags into this castle won't be multiplied."

The Countess walked over to her writing desk. "You have the necessary ingredients?"

Anna nodded. "Everything except for the water. If you wish, I can begin the preparations immediately."

She pushed away a stack of letters and drummed her fingers on the smooth oak, gazing up at the red and white Báthory family crest. "It must be done tonight, when it's dark and we can be assured of privacy. I want no more distractions."

Anna left soon after, and from the tall window I watched her hurry across the castle grounds and disappear into the forest. Half an hour later, several servants knocked on the door and trudged into the room hauling buckets of hot water. The Countess said nothing, but pointed toward a bronze tub that was tucked away in a small corner, nestled between two cedar bookshelves and positioned beneath a dramatic portrait of her husband. He appeared stoic and rigid as he stood in the middle of a crowded battlefield.

"Maria, come bathe me," she demanded after the servants had left the room.

I shuddered for a moment, but calmed myself with the knowledge that there'd be no screaming or slashing. There would be no clanking chains or water turning red with spilt blood. And since sunlight still shone through the windows, I wouldn't be surrounded by a myriad of shadows that slithered along the floor to coil around my thin body.

The Countess removed her clothes. I folded them and laid them on the bed. I took her hand and held it tight as she stepped over the high rim of the tub and lowered herself into the thick white steam. She leaned forward to let me sponge her back, and I knelt on the soft rug, happy to hear birds chirping outside as they flitted among the trees. I was happy to look up at a carved white ceiling instead of shielding my eyes from a carved-up body.

When I finished washing the Countess, she splashed water onto her face and ordered me to scrub harder on the back of her neck and on the soles of her feet. By the time Helen entered the room—clutching a towel in one hand and a small silver cup in the other—her skin looked fresh and glowing.

The Countess stood up and took hold of my outstretched hand. When she had planted both her feet on the rug, I dried off her body as best I could, then spread open the towel and wrapped it around her wet frame. She didn't move toward the bed to retrieve her clothes, but stood there waiting as Helen pushed past me to dip the cup into the tub. I gave a small shout of surprise, but the Countess didn't seem fazed by this strange turn of events. On the contrary, she watched with a keen fascination as Helen filled the cup with the grimy and oily water.

As the rest of the night unfolded, I learned that Anna was preparing a soul cake for Count Zrínyi. Down in the kitchen—once the servants had been locked away in their rooms—I gathered the necessary ingredients and laid them out on the counter while Anna whispered to herself in a language I didn't recognize.

She mixed flour, salt, and yeast into a small clay bowl. Next, she added an assortment of herbs she'd collected in the forest. To this concoction she stirred in the dirty bath water, kneaded the dough with her hands, and let it rest on the counter until it rose up like a small mountain. She then pierced the grayish dough with a knife, kneaded it several more times, and baked it in the oven.

Once the small round cake had cooled on a metal rack, Anna placed it on a silver plate and surrounded it with five lit candles. Bending forward, she whispered the following words: "Leaves fall and the days grow cold. The Goddess pulls her mantle of the Earth around her, wrapped in the coolness of night. O, gracious Goddess of all fertility, we have sown and reaped the fruits of our actions, good and bane. Grant us the courage to plant seeds of joy in the coming year, banishing misery and hate. Teach us the secrets of wise existence upon this planet, and render us invisible from our attackers."

I stood in the entryway, watching Anna repeat those strange words over and over again until their rhythm began lulling me to sleep. After several minutes, she picked up the plate, blew out the candles, and melted into the darkness without a word. Her footsteps moved through the kitchen and into the pantry, and then the postern gate creaked open and a cold breeze chilled my skin. I hurried forward, banging my arms and legs against the assorted tables and chairs, until I stumbled outside into the frigid air, engulfed by the smell of hay and honeysuckle. As my eyes adjusted to the deepening night, I watched Anna's small black figure hobble across the moonlit field and disappear into the thick forest. And as I pulled shut the heavy postern gate—wanting nothing more than to collapse on my bed and fall asleep—I prayed she would veer off the path and be torn apart by wolves.

On Friday afternoon, Count Zrínyi arrived. I wondered what business he wished to discuss, and if or when he would eat the soul cake. I was tired and sore, for the Countess had bathed in the blood of another girl the night before—Agnes from Patvarc—and in her overexcitement she demanded several vigorous scrubbings that had stiffened my back and peeled the skin off my fingertips.

Having risen late, I spent most of the morning in my room, sewing cloth-covered buttons onto old shirts, until the Countess called me down to the foyer. She stood in the open doorway, wearing a red dress inlaid with gold threads. A pearl necklace hung around her neck—each shiny white orb as large as one of my knuckles—and her hair was pulled back in a tight bun except for two small curls draped over each side of her forehead, framing the anger she sought to contain as Count Zrínyi rode up to the castle and dismounted.

He was in his early twenties, a short and muscular man, clean shaven with green eyes and brown hair cropped short. Upon entering the castle, he removed his black broad-brimmed hat and thrust it into my hands.

"How is Ursula?" the Countess asked, kissing him on the cheek.

"Your daughter is well and sends her respects." His voice was warm and husky, as though the words had been forced up from the back of his throat. "She wishes to see you at Christmas. Perhaps you'll consider traveling to Vienna to grace us with your presence."

"I appreciate your invitation, Nicholas." And with that, the Countess took his arm and led him down the hall toward the library.

I stood there with a confused look on my face, shifting from one foot to the other and thinking I should head back upstairs to continue my sewing. Suddenly, the Countess snapped her fingers and said, "Did I dismiss you, Maria, or have you risen in rank since breakfast and now possess the authority to make your own decisions?"

"Apologies, Countess." I followed behind at a languid pace, allowing them enough room to talk and gossip in private, but when we reached the library she let him enter the room and then held back to speak with me.

"I may have use for you, Maria, depending on his intentions." She put her hand on my shoulder and leaned in closer. "Stay with us while we conduct our business. Sit in the corner and remain silent unless I address you. Is that understood?"

"Yes, Countess."

We stepped inside the library. I sat near the door while she and Count Zrínyi gathered by the window, shrouded together in the dusty sunlight.

"To what do I owe the honor of this visit?" she asked him.

He glanced over at me. "I hesitate to discuss this matter while…"

"Maria is one of my most trusted servants," the Countess said. "I'm not bothered with words falling into her lap. I can assure you she won't carry them out of this room."

The Count poured himself a small glass of whiskey and drank half of it. "There are many stories piling up around the countryside. Dreadful stories about torture and murder. And there are reports that…" Again, he glanced over at me and frowned.

"I'm not a mind reader, Nicholas. Please finish your thought before it blows away."

"That these killings are sanctioned by your Ladyship."

She laughed. "Those with power will always acquire two things in great abundance. Wealth and stories. You can't amass one without the other."

"So these ramblings are nothing more than outrageous rumors?" he asked her.

She turned to me. "Maria, you have been living in the castle since April. Have you witnessed any bloodthirsty deeds?"

"No, Countess."

"Have you seen anyone hung, drawn, and quartered? Or stretched on the rack?"

"No, Countess."

"Have you been treated unfairly in any way?" she asked me.

"No, Countess."

"Have you seen innocence punished for the sake of brutality?"

"No, Countess."

"And are you happy working here with the other servants?"

"Yes, Countess."

She smiled. "You see, Nicholas. This castle is hardly the deathtrap you suggest it to be."

Before he could respond, Helen entered the room carrying a silver plate. On it sat a small fork and the soul cake. She handed Count Zrínyi the plate and then bowed, saying, "You must be hungry after your long journey."

"Thank you." He picked up the fork, cut into a corner of the cake, and began to eat. I watched him chew and swallow. My stomach churned at the thought of that grimy water—teeming with bits of dirt and flecks of skin—being poured into the batter and stirred with a warped wooden spoon, one that Anna had found on the floor, the handle coated with dust, the backside crusted over with dried chunks of meat.

For the next several minutes, Count Zrínyi alternated between pieces of cake and sips of whiskey until the plate was empty save for a few crumbs. He waited until Helen had left the room before turning once more to the Countess, his hands folded neatly in his lap. "The nobles are deeply concerned about these allegations. They believe you're blackening the aristocracy."

"Their apprehensions are unfounded." She offered him more whiskey, then poured some for herself, sipping it in silence while she watched him over the rim of her glass.

"Still, these repugnant accounts are bleeding into the political arena and clouding the Báthory name," he said. "The king has reason to see you punished for these crimes, whether or not they're genuine. If Matthias prosecutes you, he'll void the debt he owes to you. He can claim all your titles…seize all your lands."

"Are you worried about your inheritance?"

Count Zrínyi swirled the whiskey in his glass. "I'm worried about Gregory Thurzó. He's now second in command to the king."

"He is also kin to us."

"True. And now he finds himself in a precarious position. He's well aware that your own cousin, Gabriel, is rousing anti-Hapsburg sentiment on the other side of the border."

The Countess scoffed. "The Hapsburgs are no friends of mine. Were Gabriel to rally troops against the king I would certainly support such a revolt."

"I wouldn't declare such loyalty beyond these walls," he said, "especially if Thurzó feels it's in the best interest of Hungary to stifle your power and authority. Yes, he is kin, but he may feel pressured by Matthias to protect the crown."

"Thurzó has already visited me to express his concerns, and to offer his unyielding support."

"I know," said Count Zrínyi. "I spoke with him in Vienna last week."

"Then you must know that he left here feeling quite contented?"

"True, but he also advised you to be cautious and quiet. And now you've created more unwanted attention by inviting young girls here with the promise of teaching them decorum and respectability."

She drummed her fingers against the side of her glass. "There's no crime in wanting to provide the nobility with a bit of demureness."

"And what of your four children?" he asked her. "Have you given any thought as to how your actions might affect them?"

"My children no longer require parental guidance," she told him. "I've supplied them with assiduous care and motherly love, and I make no apologies for their upbringing."

Count Zrínyi finished his drink and placed the empty glass on the table beside him. He frowned and stared out the window, watching a withered branch scratch at the glass. "Perhaps you are expending your energies on too many duties, and now the strain…"

"I'm quite capable of keeping my affairs in order, Nicholas. I feel neither exhausted nor troubled, unless I happen to be suffering through an absurd conversation in which someone is foolhardy enough to suggest that I'm being careless and incompetent."

"I meant no disrespect, but…" He picked up his empty glass, stared at it for a few seconds, and then put it back down. "Ursula and I are concerned that…well, you're almost fifty years old and…you can't possibly manage all of these estates by yourself." He glanced again at his empty glass, perhaps hoping that someone might fill it with whiskey so he could drink away the uncomfortable moment.

She leaned forward, her jaw set tight. Her eyes pinned him down until he wriggled in his seat like a boy caught misbehaving. "You believe I'm too old to be useful?"

MICHAEL HOWARTH

"No, I just meant…"

"You believe that I should be folded up and shoved into the back of some closet like a crumbling antique?"

"Of course not," he said. "I'm merely suggesting that perhaps you have too many obligations."

The Countess smacked her hand against the arm of the chair, and a great cloud of dust rose into the air. "I've been carrying this family's name upon my back since Francis died…entertaining the nobles and attending to the peasants, as well as overseeing my castles and finances and…"

"But you rarely visit your estate at Sárvár." Frustrated, he reached for the decanter and poured himself another half glass. "Or the one at Ecsed, for that matter. And whenever you do leave this gloomy castle, it's only to collect taxes from griping landowners. It's clear that your seclusion has fueled these wild stories, and now it's alienating you from those who wish to protect you most."

She sipped her whiskey in silence, and the tension in the room became so unbearable that I shifted around in my seat, crossing and uncrossing my legs, turning my head to read all the gold-printed titles on the shelf behind me.

Count Zrínyi cleared his throat. "Your family is worried about these rumors and we intend to suppress them."

"I'm in full control of my faculties, Nicholas. I will address these rumors, and those who continue to spread them, as I see fit."

"It's not healthy for a woman your age to carry this burden alone," he said. "I daresay you appear much more haggard than in times past."

The Countess leapt up—spilling what little whiskey remained in her glass—and raised both hands to her pale face. She patted her cheeks and forehead in frenzied concern, pressing both thumbs against the loose skin on her neck as if feeling for a pulse. Just when I thought she might calm down and regain her composure, she picked up the empty glass and hurled it against the wall where it shattered into pieces.

As these outrageous events unfolded, Count Zrínyi watched me from across the room. Even when the Countess shouted for a servant to come and clean up the broken glass, his eyes never moved from my corner of the library; even when she walked past his chair to stand in front of the window; even when she molded her hands into tight fists and stared up at a gray sky smeared with wispy white clouds.

"I can't help you if I'm kept in the dark," he said.

The Countess, still refusing to look at him, exhaled a long breath.

"Have servants been tortured and killed here?" he asked, raising his voice.

She said nothing.

"And is it true that the priest was asked to dispose of hundreds of bodies that were mutilated beyond recognition?"

Still, she said not a word.

But it didn't matter. For it was only when Count Zrínyi leaned forward—his eyes still set upon me as he swirled the whiskey in his glass—that I realized it wasn't the Countess he'd been addressing.

And I don't know why—perhaps I was remembering the last time I saw Sandra, her small frame lugging a burlap sack full of chains; or perhaps I was tired of always wondering if I would live to see another morning—but I sat up straight in my cushiony chair, palms flat on my knees, and caught my breath in my throat. With shaking hands, I brushed away a curl of hair that had fallen across my forehead. I remembered what the Countess had told me about spurning timidity, and that one must act with conviction.

Steeling myself, I swallowed hard—fighting back the urge to look away from the intense gaze of Count Zrínyi—and then I stared into his eyes with all the courage I could gather, terrified of the future but knowing I must act now if I was to have one at all.

I nodded my head yes.

CHAPTER XIX

THE COUNTESS WASN'T EXPECTING her son-in-law to spend the night at the castle, but when he became ill there was no other option. I'm sure she wanted to throw him on his horse and send him straight into that violent thunderstorm barreling in from the west, but to display a further lack of emotion might have prompted even more questions, and she was already juggling more distractions than she could handle.

After affirming Count Zrínyi's suspicions, I left the library and returned to my room. I shook all over, and I kept rolling my neck and shoulders, trying to stop the headache that rose up from the pit of my stomach. I ran my hands through my hair and stopped for a moment to steady myself against the wall, excited by my boldness but also fearful of the consequences it might bring. I felt as if I were walking through a tunnel that became more narrow and twisted the farther along I walked, and that it would eventually crush me from all sides.

But more than that, I didn't want to be anywhere near the Countess, for she was incensed at the manner in which Count Zrínyi had disparaged her appearance, and her anger swept through the halls like a tornado, leaving behind a trail of bloodied servants for the rest of the afternoon. I sat on my bed surrounded by a mountain of musty shirts and a small pile of cloth-covered buttons, and I sewed for several hours until my fingers throbbed, at which point I heard two sets of footsteps ascend the staircase and enter the Countess's bedchamber.

For a moment all was quiet, but seconds later a great cry of anguish rose up to pierce the silence. I leapt off the bed and removed my shoes, then tiptoed barefoot into the dim hallway. Trying to avoid creaks in the old wooden floor, I crept along a stone wall until I reached her door, which was slightly ajar. I turned my body toward the staircase so I could watch for anyone coming and pressed my ear against the open space, concentrating as hard as I could to hear the conversation.

"…dare he accuse me of damaging the aristocracy," the Countess was saying. "…a whimpering nobody…more concerned with power and position than family and honor…"

"Drink this, Elizabeth." I recognized Anna's voice, rough and hard like cracked leaves scraping across flagstones in a courtyard.

There was silence again for several moments, a long exhale, and then a sharp clang as something heavy was placed upon the bedside table.

"…embarrassment to his class," the Countess said. "…leave Čachtice at first light…"

"…prudent to execute restraint," Anna told her.

Their tones became more hushed, the pauses less frequent. Outside, the sky broke open and sheets of rain beat against the windows, obscuring their words even further. I pressed my ear closer to the open space, unsure if they were arguing or deliberating, and then cringed as something struck the other side of the door and shattered into pieces.

I made to return to my room—worried they might catch me eavesdropping, or that Peter might sneak up behind me—when Helen's voice slithered into the squabble, low at first and then louder. "…mustn't expend your energy," she said. "…continue our preparations…"

"…circle of stones," Anna interrupted, at which point the Countess offered a noncommittal grunt.

"…demonstrate patience," Helen said. "…just a bit longer…" And then a clap of thunder shook the castle and the rest of her words were drowned out by the storm.

"…blessing must be protected…" The Countess raised her voice, and I could tell she was standing in front of her window.

"…harvest festival soon," Anna said. "…pass through the fire…"

I was about to pull away from the door when the Countess spoke my name. I jumped back in horror, expecting the door to be thrown wide open—whereupon I'd be dragged into the room and beaten—but then Helen and Anna began to talk all at once and their words became so entangled that I soon lost focus.

Beneath me, the floorboard creaked. I took a step toward my room, and the bravery that had surged through me earlier now began to ebb. My knees buckled, and I heard the Countess speak my name a second time, more deliberate and cagey. And then Anna laughed in such a way that my shoulders tightened and beads of sweat dotted my forehead. I pressed my elbows into my sides, trying to make myself as small as possible, and craned my head forward to catch snippets of their whispered conversation.

Their words wound together in a snarling knot of names and phrases, but through the jumbled undergrowth—through the rain and the wind and the rumbling thunder—I caught two words that the three of them continued to repeat, over and over again, until their incessant babble sounded like some hideous chant.

"Alban Elfed."

The following afternoon I planned to meet with Father Barosius in the chapel, sometime after three o'clock when I could sneak away without being noticed. The Countess was still in her room, transfixed by her reflection in the mirror, and Count Zrínyi was sick in bed, having spent the previous night vomiting and running a high fever. I had worked in the kitchen for most of the morning, sweeping and washing pots, and it was clear that everyone was on edge because of the Count's visit, and now his subsequent setback in returning to Vienna. Normally, the Countess dealt with any displeasure by slaughtering as many servants as she could afford to lose in as many ingenious ways as she could imagine, but since Count Zrínyi was laid up in bed—and within earshot of any bloodcurdling screams—she was forced to deliver insults instead of blows.

Despite this lull in savagery, the servants were still petrified, for we all knew this reprieve would be short-lived. Instead of being rescued from despair, we found ourselves caught in the eye of a terrible storm that showed no signs of ending. All I could think about was meeting with Father Barosius and staring into his crinkly eyes. He was the only force of good that shone up from this deep pit of evil, and I needed to describe to him the sequence of strange and horrific events that had transpired during the past few days: the rawness of Sandra's death, my decision to affirm Count Zrínyi's suspicions, and the strange conversation I'd overheard the night before in her Ladyship's bedchamber. I needed to speak the words aloud, to release them into the open air before they lodged in my throat like a pile of small bones.

I kept to myself all morning, wrapped up in the shadows and counting the hours as they crept by. I knew Peter would find me again once I left the kitchen, and I agonized over how to evade him so I could escape to the chapel. He found me in the hallway as I was heading back to my room. I tried walking faster when I heard his footsteps—and even ignored him when he shouted my name—but before I could turn around and feign surprise, he gripped my shoulders and steered me behind a tall marble statue of Ares.

"Where are you rushing off to, Maria?"

"Nowhere," I stuttered.

"I swore to protect you, but instead of being a gallant knight I'm chasing after you like a spurned lover." He moved closer, his lips twitching in a crooked smile, his breath hot and sweet. "Why do you evade me?"

I sucked in a great breath of air and steadied myself against the statue. "Perhaps you've been looking in the wrong places. I've been rushing around like a fly in a bottle, helping to prepare for the harvest festival."

"Should I follow you upstairs and inspect your room?" he asked. "Just to make sure there are no monsters lurking beside your bed?"

I was desperate and scared—needing to speak with Father Barosius before I went mad—and I knew the longer I stayed in the hallway with Peter, the greater the chance that the priest would grow weary of waiting. I clicked my fingernails against the wall and fiddled with my Celtic love knot, wishing Helen would appear and send Peter on an errand. When it became clear he had no intention of leaving me alone, I kissed him on the lips with as much passion as I could rally.

"Meet me by the tapestry at three o'clock," I told him.

His eyes flashed for a moment and an ecstatic moan rose up from his chest. He wrapped his arms around me, his fingers wandering up and down my back as he pressed his knee between my legs. His barbarity shocked me. There was a wildness in his eyes and a roughness to his movements, and I was surprised at how easy it was to manipulate his feelings. I had never seen him so willing and eager, so determined and yet so unfocused, and I reveled in this power I held over him.

"We must be discreet," I whispered. "The Countess is in a rotten mood, and it wouldn't be good for her to find us sneaking off together when there's still so much work to be done."

He grabbed my arm. "Let's go right now."

I drew away and shook my head. "I've been down in the kitchen all morning, chopping vegetables, and now I smell like turnips and cabbages. Give me time to change my clothes."

Peter nodded, bits of spittle clinging to his lower lip, and hurried down the stairs like an animal released from a cage. I wondered how long he would wait for me beside the tapestry, and what excuses I might offer when he confronted me later.

Father Barosius crouched behind the altar, whispering prayers and clutching his rosary. Upon seeing me, he jumped up and gave thanks to God.

"We need to hurry," I told him. "Peter has become suspicious. He'll come looking for me."

"And what of the Countess?" he asked. "Has she continued her ferocious acts?"

I nodded.

"Are you keeping a record of all the victims?"

"As best I can. Their names are safely hidden."

He peered into my face, then reached out to touch my cheek. "Your eyes are bloodshot and your skin feels clammy. Are you ill, child?"

I grabbed the edge of the altar as a wave of hysteria crashed over me. "I'm suffocating under a pile of corpses, and the harder I claw my way out, the more they press down on me. The smell of death is everywhere…it's seeped into my clothes and my skin…instead of thinking about my mother and our cottage, I keep wondering if I'll die in the kitchen…surrounded by other servants…or maybe in my room when my back is turned and I least expect it…I wonder if God will grant me a painless death…other times, I wonder if I even deserve one."

He sat cross-legged on the cold stone floor and pulled me down beside him. "Don't lose hope, Maria. I know you want to run away from here and never look back, but you mustn't do so blindly, otherwise you may find yourself running in circles."

"I already feel that way, Father." My voice was small and weak. "Nights, if I'm lucky, I sit alone in my room and patch old clothes. Sometimes I'm pulled out of bed to assist the Countess with her baths, listening to girls cry and beg for their lives while I plunge my hands into their warm blood. I ache inside and out, every hour of every day, but I'm so afraid to fall asleep because all I see when I close my eyes are corpses strung up on chains, judging me with their lifeless eyes.

"And my days are just as dark. Mornings, I rise early and trudge down to the kitchen, chopping and scrubbing and sweeping up the trash. Afternoons, I'm sent outside to help the other servants prepare for the festival."

Father Barosius cocked his head. "And what festival is this?"

"The harvest festival," I told him. "For the past few weeks the castle has been a flurry of commotion, and now that the nobles have arrived it's become even crazier. We've been moving bales of hay and collecting firewood from the edge of the forest...we've been constructing a large foundation for the bonfire...setting up a small altar on one side...and filling baskets with squash and pumpkins and dried corn."

"I've lived in Čachtice for over forty years," he said, "and I've never heard of such a festival taking place at the castle."

The hair stood up on my arms. I felt like I'd been dropped from a great height. "But the autumn equinox..."

"...Is important, yes, but mostly as a time of great reflection. We acknowledge that the earth is dying a little more each day and so we pray for a healthy winter, but the Lord demands that we be humble, Maria, and he requires no pomp or spectacle to renew each season."

Panic and desperation rose up within me. "But the cooks and servants have been preparing for weeks, and..."

Father Barosius shook his head. "The Countess must have some diabolical plan, otherwise she wouldn't expend such energies on a mere reaping. It's clear we're losing time, and that our only hope is to appeal to the nobles. But you must bring me some proof that I can present to them when the time comes. We can't offer the names you've collected unless we give them a reason to search the castle."

"How?" I asked. "The Countess is growing more suspicious, and she hasn't let me roam very far since her return."

"I'm sorry, but my hands are bound," he said. "Count Thurzó was quite adamant that were I to speak ill of the Countess again, or to dispatch more letters to the king, I would be punished severely. And if I'm arrested, or simply forced to leave Čachtice, there will be no one left to help you."

I told Father Barosius about Count Zrínyi's visit the day before, and how the Countess became angered by his pointed accusations. I told him how I'd validated the Count's suspicions by nodding my head when he turned to look at me, and how the Countess became incensed when her son-in-law commented on her haggard appearance.

I revealed the strange bath the Countess had taken in her bedchamber and how Anna had used the dirty water to bake a soul cake. I explained how Count Zrínyi became sick hours later and was still too weak to get out of bed, and how he wished to speak with me, but had been denied by the Countess.

By the time I finished speaking I was sweating and out of breath, my knuckles raw and white from clutching the hem of my dress. Though still terrified, I felt lighter than I had in days, as if great blocks of stone had been lifted off my chest.

Father Barosius stood up and smoothed out his robe. He paced back and forth, his brow furrowed. "You must find a way to speak with Count Zrínyi. He may be our only hope of securing an end to these killings."

"The Countess will never allow it." I rose and laid a trembling hand on his shoulder. "I'm already risking my life by meeting you here, Father. Were anyone to find me in Count Zrínyi's room I would surely have the flesh ripped from my body. I can't draw more attention to myself, which is why you must be the one to meet with him."

"Me?"

"Yes. You must wait until he leaves the castle and then intercept him somewhere on the road. Tell him everything I've revealed to you, and impress upon him that we must act fast lest more noblemen lose their daughters to that bestial woman."

He considered this for a moment. "Very well. I'll find a way to apprehend him in the village without the Countess finding out, otherwise it will spell doom for the both of us."

I turned to leave, and it was only then that I remembered the cryptic conversation I'd overheard the night before. "Father, do the words 'alban elfed' mean anything to you?"

He shuddered and wheezed, grasping my arm as he pitched forward. The color drained from his wrinkled face as if I'd shot two arrows into his chest. "Alban Elfed?"

I nodded.

"It means 'the light of the water' and…" He licked his dry lips and wiped a fine sheen of sweat from his forehead. "It's an ancient tradition that references the coming of winter when the balance of day and night begins to shift, when darkness takes over the land."

"A spiritual belief?" I asked. "Like All Souls Day?"

"No," he said, "it's much older than Christ, and far more sinister. Alban Elfed is a pagan ritual celebrating the autumn equinox, a time to give thanks to the Goddess and God for the previous year's bounty, and to secure their favor and blessings for the coming months."

Confused, I looked down at the half-moon gash on my thumb—still sore and purpled—and tried to remember more. "There was also some mention of stones. And a circle."

"Those are necessary for the offering that is made to the God and Goddess," he said. "To invoke the spirits, one must recite the blessing in front of a pyre, which is constructed out of oak and decorated with baskets of fruit and dried leaves. And then four candles are lit and placed within a small circle of stones."

"Why four?"

"Because four symbolizes the natural elements," he said. "Earth, air, fire, and water. As well as the four seasons."

"How do you know this?"

Father Barosius glanced up at a mural of the crucifixion. He made the sign of the cross. "One can't properly appreciate the wonders of the light unless he fully comprehends the mysteries of the dark."

I fumbled for the right words. "But…what's so sinister about gathering food and wood…about offering thanks for our provisions?"

"Because the offering is not an animal," he said. "The spirits will only listen to a fire kindled upon human bones."

My thoughts were drawn to that enormous altar and foundation being constructed outside, and how the Countess demanded its completion by the autumn equinox. Just last week I had commented on its size, ignorant of its true purpose and expecting it to be fueled by logs and bark and handfuls of dried grass, not a living soul consumed by flames and then shriveled into hot ash.

"I fear you've been misled, Maria, and that there's more to this harvest festival than a few bottles of wine and some yellow sparks shooting into the night sky." Father Barosius laid a hand on my shoulder. "It seems the Countess is preparing for an unholy sacrifice, though I must admit I'm unclear about what she hopes to gain by making such an offering."

"The Countess has more food and clothes and priceless treasures than even the king himself," I said. "She's rich and powerful, ruthless and cunning, and…"

He peered into my face. "Can you think of nothing she desires?"

And then—as if someone had lit a candle in my mind—I pictured the Countess standing in front of her mirror for hours at a time, obsessing over her age and fearful of turning fifty; applying herbs and lotions to her pale skin every morning; and lowering her naked body into a smooth white tub filled with blood and shadows.

I remembered the day she held a lock of my hair in her hand, when she leaned close to me and whispered, "I would claim your beauty as my own if I could."

Or the day I convinced her to bathe in noble blood, how she smiled at me and said, "You will prove to be even more valuable once autumn arrives."

And then there was Peter, always watching me and knowing my whereabouts, eager to shield me from harm and promising that if I behaved myself I would live long enough to watch the leaves change colors.

I had come to the castle as her special guest—welcomed into her own private circle—and now I understood why I had never been struck or beaten, and why the Countess didn't want me damaged in any way.

Father Barosius grabbed my arms and shook me. "The equinox is only a few weeks away, Maria. Perhaps she wishes to sacrifice one of the young ladies she's lured to the castle. We must discover which one and warn her before it's too late."

The room spun around me, and the floor seemed to disappear below my feet. I turned away and reached for something solid to grab onto, my entire body shaking as tears spilled down my dirty cheeks. "There's no need, Father. I already know who the Countess has chosen."

CHAPTER XX

IT SEEMS STRANGE, BUT knowing her Ladyship's monstrous intentions somehow lessened the dread and paranoia I'd been experiencing. I knew I wouldn't be harmed until the twenty-first of September, and this understanding afforded me a small sense of hope that I might somehow find a way to survive. As well, I felt a surge of power in having unlocked their wicked secret, for it meant that the imminence of my death—while terrifying and real and only a few weeks away—forced me to focus on a plan to escape, which I began formulating as soon as I left the chapel that afternoon.

Count Zrínyi recovered from his sudden illness and departed the castle three days later, still asking to speak with me and still being handed flimsy excuses by the Countess. I stood by the window for a long time, staring at the crooked trail that led down to the village, my stomach twisting into knots. As I watched him ride out of sight—a bit pale and fatigued, and slumped over his saddle—I prayed that Father Barosius would find a way to meet with him and to convey all we had discussed in the chapel, that Count Zrínyi would expose her true nature to Thurzó and King Matthias, and that he would do so before the sun rose on the morning of the harvest festival.

To complicate matters, Peter was furious at me. He had stood by himself in front of the tapestry for forty-five minutes, agitated and brooding, his anticipation of our rendezvous replaced by a bitterness that he spat into my face later that night with a vehemence I had never seen in him. I'd avoided him as best I could upon leaving the chapel, sneaking through the hallways like a thief and listening for his heavy footsteps, but he cornered me at the top of the stairs several hours later, demanding to know why I'd made him look like a fool.

"I suddenly felt ill," I said. "I was afraid I'd caught whatever sickness has been throttling the Count."

"You seemed healthy enough when we last spoke." He put his hand on my forehead, searching for a fever. "Perhaps some properly planted kisses will hasten your recovery."

"Or perhaps a good night's sleep." I wrapped my arms around him, hoping to numb his anger. "Would you rather I was rundown or wound up?"

He pushed me away with a frown. "Where were you? I looked for you in your room, and then down in the kitchen."

"I stepped outside for some fresh air. I thought the breeze might restore my color." I touched his arm. "Surely, you wouldn't want me looking a fright."

Peter swung his next words like a mace. "When you offer to meet a man alone, Maria, you shouldn't be concerned with how you look, but with how you act."

I stepped back and crossed my arms, staring at his face—so contorted and angry and hurt—until it grew soft and hazy and blurred into the surrounding darkness. Here before me was a boy who believed he had everything when in fact he had nothing; he thought he wielded power when in truth he was only borrowing it from those who understood best how to brandish it.

Once upon a time I'd wanted to trust him. But now he was cloaked in a shroud of uncertainty. His mannerisms, usually so flirtatious, seemed manipulative and conniving. His laugh was hollow, as if someone had wrung all the joy out of it. Even his smile looked like it had been dipped in poison.

"Your relentless prancing exhausts me to no end," he said. "I protect you from Helen and the Countess and I lavish you with attention, slipping you extra food when no one is looking, and all I ask is that you stand perfectly still for a few measly minutes so I can have my way with you."

"I have no desire to be someone's table scraps," I told him. "If that's all you want, then I suggest you rummage through the garbage."

He glowered and clenched his fist, as if wanting to strike me. Then he leaned forward to kiss my cheek. "Be bold," he said, and brushed away a hair that had strayed to my lips. "But not too bold."

For days, I agonized over how to collect proof of the Countess's crimes. Regardless of which path I might choose, I needed to give Father Barosius enough time to show my proof to Count Zrínyi. And I needed to give Count Zrínyi enough time to act on it, otherwise I might never return to Trenčín and, instead, my charred bones would lie forgotten in some field behind the castle.

But my options were limited, and as the days grew shorter and the air became colder I became more and more nervous, cringing every time the Countess commented on my beautiful skin, petrified when she selected another girl for her washing, and knowing that every time I stared up at that girl I would see my own face shrouded in flames. Each writhing body was a wall of ferocious heat that rose up to crisp my skin, every jangle of chain another hissing ember.

Despite my having dined with the students on their first night in the castle, they didn't go out of their way to speak with me, no doubt repulsed by my simple smile and rustic clothes. The most I merited was an acceptable nod as we passed each other in the corridor, though a few of them—Brigitta from Koszeg and Felicia from Sima—sometimes smiled and engaged me in idle banter.

Mornings, we breakfasted together in the Great Hall. Afterwards, I went about my duties while they met in the ballroom to begin their daily lessons: how to bow and curtsy; how to talk to a gentleman; and how to initiate and participate in conversations with princes and kings and dukes and duchesses. Sometimes they read etiquette manuals on fashion, discussing the advantages of silk and wool; other times, the Countess lectured them on proper hygiene, urging each girl to trim her nails once a month, to brush her hair before going to sleep, and to wash her hands before every meal. After lunch they rode horses through the countryside, learning how to sit and hold the reins so as to impress potential suitors. They took long walks through the meadow at the bottom of the hill, picking various blossoms and sprigs and chatting about the importance of each flower and how it relayed a certain message from God: a lilac conveying splendor, a blue poppy suggesting chastity, or a peony denoting potency.

The Countess injected every lesson and outing with a heightened sense of importance that befitted those spoiled highborns, convincing them that their being away from home was not merely a waste of time and gold coins, but a transitory phase in their lives that would propel them onto thrones and parapets, and would adorn them with sartorial eloquence worthy of their ancestral bloodlines.

While the girls attended to their fancy meals and privileged instruction, I sat in my room and brooded over how best to proceed with Father Barosius and Count Zrínyi. My first plan was to smuggle one of the corpses out of the underground chamber, but I was too weak to sling one over my shoulder and carry it into the chapel, nor could I drag it through the tunnels and into the crypt beneath the church. Given my size, it would take me hours to complete such an arduous task, not to mention the enormous risk involved. If anyone caught me, there'd be no way to explain myself. Besides, even if I mustered the strength and confidence to execute such a plan, there would be no time to collect one of the bodies, as Peter often brought them into the forest while they were still warm.

I considered asking Father Barosius to escort Count Zrínyi into the forest so he could see the bodies for himself, but I couldn't remember which route Peter and I had taken the day we collected the belladonna, and I didn't know the exact spot where he disposed of each girl. Besides, there might not be any bodies left once the wolves had finished stripping away the flesh.

After struggling with various scenarios, it became clear that to shock the royalty into taking action against the Countess I needed something personal and distinct to offer as proof, and a ravaged skeleton wouldn't reveal many secrets. So I wandered the castle in a nervous daze, my mind alight with images of rusted chains and bloody knives and yellow flames stretching high into a starry sky. I paced up and down the corridors, whispering impulsive ideas and searching for some means of securing the coveted evidence. But it wasn't until three days later, while I was outside tending to the animals, that an idea appeared right in front of my face, dazzling me with its brilliance and simplicity.

It was late morning and the air was balmy. A cloudless sky spread above me, and some of the leaves were already beginning to turn red and orange and yellow. The smell of nut breads wafted out of the kitchen in a thin trail of steam, and I knelt down in the dirt, laughing as one of the goats nibbled grass from the palm of my hand. I had just flexed my thumb—which was still throbbing and enflamed, though the deep red scab had since crusted over—when I heard footsteps approaching from the courtyard.

A shadow descended upon me, and a sharp voice cracked the unspoiled silence. "Hasn't anyone ever told you not to play with your food, Maria?"

I stood up, brushing dirt from my knees. The Countess looked even paler in direct sunlight, the lines in her face deeper and more pronounced, gray wisps of hair gusting around her face like Medusa's venomous snakes.

"That goat is born so it can die," she said. "There is nothing profound or heroic in its existence. Its only purpose is to provide sustenance, and only by being slaughtered and skinned and tossed onto a plate can it achieve that desired end."

I stroked it under the chin, whereupon it bleated and nuzzled my hand.

"You have been quite the busy little bee," the Countess said. "Buzz, buzz, buzzing around." She took my arm and together we walked across the field toward the pyre.

My skin tingled and the hair stiffened on the back of my neck. I swallowed the excess saliva collecting in my mouth. If she had pulled out a knife and slid it across my throat, I wouldn't have been shocked.

The Countess pointed to the tall wooden structure rising up in front of us. She motioned toward the baskets filled with squash and corn, at the pumpkins scattered around the base and encircled by coils of bright green ivy. "Your hard work has brought you much profit, Maria. You are stronger than when you first arrived, less skittish and more emphatic."

I curtsied. "Thank you."

"Helen tells me you've committed many long hours to preparing for the harvest festival, which is why you deserve to be here when we light the fire."

My body went cold, and my knees crumpled beneath me. I tried not to imagine how it must feel to be burned alive, to be bound hand and foot and tossed into a thundering hellhole. I forced a smile and looked up at the trees, envious of all those birds that could fly away at the first sign of trouble.

"Do you know why fire is so important?" she asked me.

My mind was foggy, and my lips felt numb, stung by the force of her words. "To cook food...for warmth...protection?"

"A fire purifies, Maria. It provides an opportunity to make something sacred by reducing it to its very core. And then, through the power of embers and smoke, it sends all those bits and pieces back into nature, into every rock and tree and river, so the cycle can start anew, much like the Phoenix that rises up from its own ashes."

She released my arm, stepped over a gourd, and patted the rough wood with the palm of her hand. "When I was a child, we gathered coals from the harvest fire and carried them to our hearths inside the castle. My parents believed that doing so would bring good fortune."

I thought about all those girls who would continue to die if I burned up in a cloud of smoke, and I thought about all those bodies— throats slashed, bones broken, abandoned deep in the forest—that had stained my memory forever.

The Countess rapped the wood with her knuckles—snapping me back to attention—and as she did so, the bright sunlight gleamed off a thick bracelet that hung around her wrist, shooting golden sparkles across my line of vision.

I pictured the nobles walking around the Great Hall, laughing and gossiping with an air of superiority, weighed down with rings and necklaces, each precious heirloom encrusted with diamonds and rubies and emeralds. And I saw their bodies—lifeless and bruised and naked—being carried out of that bloody chamber, loaded onto a cart, and wheeled into the forest while blades of grass glistened with dew.

Watching those golden sparkles, I wondered if there was a hidden room somewhere in the castle, filled from floor to ceiling with clothes and jewels and tumbledown trunks—all that remained of those wretched souls the Countess had ensnared as unwilling pawns in her Dionysian pursuit of Apollonian beauty.

That evening, I sought out Peter. He was in the Great Hall, stacking wood near the hearth. He seemed surprised to see me. A combination of contempt and excitement passed over his face, but instead of greeting me in his customary manner, he brushed bits of dirt and shavings from his wrinkled shirt.

I sidled up beside him and placed my hand on his chest. "Do you find me rotten to the core?"

A faint smile played at the corners of his mouth. "You have the mind of a toad, the heart of a fox, and the look of a dove," he said.

"I don't wish to be difficult," I told him, "but I feel as if my skin is speckled with big ugly warts, especially when I pass all those posh ladies strutting down the hallway with their coifed hair and their silk dresses."

"Is that the source of your recent sulkiness?" he asked, his voice tinged with genuine surprise. "You aspire to be a siren instead of a servant?"

I turned away and wrung my hands, trying to appear frustrated and confused. I needed him to see me as vulnerable. The more I pretended to rely on him, the more he'd embrace his coveted role as protector. "Why do you needle me for wanting to look attractive, for desiring nice clothes and jewels?" I asked. "All I want is something with a bit more shine so you can see me glinting in a darkened hallway."

Peter skimmed his sooty fingers down the side of my face, leaving a thin trail of black dust. He held up my Celtic love knot. "Is this so repulsive that you'd trade it for something with more esteem?"

I sat in front of the hearth and put my head in my hands. "I don't apologize for being moody. I'm not so naïve to think that if I toss a coin into a well, some handsome prince will whisk me away to his castle in a horse-drawn carriage, or host a fancy ball so the two of us can dance in circles until the sun comes up."

His eyes narrowed. "It's not like you to be insecure, Maria."

I stared out the window and slumped my shoulders. I prayed he would pity me, that he would grow cocky and offer to rescue me from this sudden malaise.

"Isn't it every girl's wish to play the part of an alluring debutante?" I asked him. "My mother says it's far better to collect dreams than it is to collect troubles."

He laughed then, a bellowing of disapproval that resounded throughout the hall. "I much prefer having ambitions. Dreams are just the froth that's left over from a fervid imagination."

"Still…" I kissed the rough stubble on his face, tempting him with those very things the Countess herself most desired: youth and vitality. "I don't suppose you could snap your fingers and present me with a stunning bracelet?"

"Perhaps I might…" He knelt down beside me. "I don't profess to be a magician, but I suppose I could rummage through some drawers, dig deep in a few corners…"

My hand found his knee, whereupon I gave it a light squeeze. "The harder you poke, the happier I'll be."

Again, there was a wildness in his eyes. He pushed aside a lock of my hair and caressed the nape of my neck. "What wishes would you grant me if, indeed, I acquired such a treasure for you?"

Before I could answer, his left arm slithered over my shoulder and across my back, pulling me toward him until our lips touched. He pressed his tongue into my mouth; it tasted sour, like a grape picked too early from the vine. I knew he wanted to run off somewhere quiet and hidden, groping for clips and clasps, my burnished hair tumbling about while his hands ventured under my dress, searching for pockets of warmth.

I let his fingers wander for a few minutes, and then I drew away with a blush and stared into his eyes. We sat inside the Great Hall, concealed in the encroaching night, our faces inches apart, and I seized that moment until I thought my heart would burst, until Peter seemed ready to pounce.

Later—after I massaged his ego with sweet words, after I rested my lips against his ear and breathed a long husky sigh—Peter walked me to my room. His body was loose and warm, all the anger and frustration having melted away. He appeared giddy and lightheaded, reduced to a stammering smile.

When we reached my door, I offered him one more kiss on the lips. "Something big and bright and shiny," I told him.

He nodded. "I'll have it for you tomorrow."

I slipped into my bedroom and closed the door, then pressed my ear to the wood, listening to Peter's footsteps fade away. I knew he wouldn't wait until the morning to fetch my prize. I'd spent a considerable amount of time baiting him, and his eagerness had risen to such a fevered pitch that he wouldn't sleep until he was assured of the means to possess me.

Moments later, I opened the door and crept out into the hallway. I remained close to the wall, hiding in the shadows as I tiptoed down the wide stairs, stopping every so often to follow the sound of Peter's heavy footsteps as they echoed off the stone floor. I heard him walk past the corridor that led to the tapestry, and I realized he was heading toward the east tower. It was the part of Cachtice Castle that sat closest to the forest, and the darkness in the woods seemed to seep through those very walls. Overgrown trees, thick with foliage, wrapped their gnarled branches around the turrets and spires, crowding the narrow windows and shrouding the entire area in perpetual gloom.

I stayed close enough behind to catch fleeting glimpses of Peter as he rounded corners, always conscious of his movements and the general direction he was heading, but far enough behind so as not to be noticed. Eventually, he opened a small door on the left side of the hall and disappeared inside. I waited for a couple of minutes—glancing behind me in case anyone should approach—and then I inched my way forward, my feet heavy as lead. I walked past the door to the end of the corridor and turned left, crouching down behind an alabaster statue of Aphrodite.

I hid for what seemed like hours. I heard servants moving around in other parts of the castle—their footsteps thin, their voices fragmented—and somewhere outside a dog barked. Finally, Peter exited the room, whistling to himself as he stared down at something gold and glittering in the palm of his hand.

I watched him round the corner and stood up to flex my sore legs. I edged my way down the narrow corridor, wondering what sort of treasures the Countess had been amassing, and for how long. My hands shook as I gripped the latch, but I managed to wrestle open the door and peek inside the room, praying it would somehow provide the means of my salvation.

The space into which I now stared was dark and small, shaped like an oval with a rickety spiral staircase in the center. Bright moonlight streamed in through two large windows high above me, and as my eyes adjusted to the silvery beams I saw that the entire room was filled with crooked shelves stacked from floor to ceiling, on which rested various types of clothing and jewelry. Dozens of trunks lay scattered throughout, and there was so much dust in the room that I could reach out my hands and brush it away like a thin curtain.

I navigated the area around me, stepping over shoes and burlap sacks and winding through the assortment of small trunks. I glanced across the room, scanning the shelves until I spotted a jumble of rings and earrings and necklaces all lined up on a bottom shelf. Hurrying over, I rummaged through the collection, searching for the malachite ring that Agnes had worn, pushing aside a clutter of earrings and pricking my finger on the tiny rusted posts.

Ten minutes later—having pored over several shelves and peeked under layers of musty dresses and gowns—I found the ring and slipped it onto the forefinger of my right hand. If I clasped both hands together, and pressed them tight against my chest, no one would notice the ring as I walked through the dark passageways. Then, once I returned to my room, I only needed to hide it somewhere until my next meeting with Father Barosius.

I made to leave, but as I passed the spiral staircase I glanced up at the slants of moonlight that pierced the muggy air like so many arrows. I needed to see what existed in that room at the top of the stairs, so with my hand on the unsteady railing I climbed through the sparkling dust until I stepped into an even smaller room encircled with windows. There was a rocking chair and a small table, more trunks resting under piles of moldy gowns, and a dressing screen in the corner whose wood had warped over time. I walked toward one of the windows and looked out onto the field behind the castle, trembling as the pyre loomed up from the invading night, waiting there with inhuman patience to sear the flesh from my bones.

Looking around the rest of the room, I spotted nothing of interest save a stack of leather-bound books, among which were copies of Ovid's *Metamorphoses* and Dante's *Divine Comedy*. I considered tucking one under my dress to bring back to my room, but the risk was too great. Instead, I flipped through a few brittle pages, remembering those days when Papa would read to me in the meadow behind our cottage.

Suddenly, I heard the door swing open below me. Dropping the book, I ducked behind the dressing screen and crouched down with my back to the window. Someone entered the room. There was a large shadow, a faint smell of musk, and then Benedict's voice rose up in a sharp burst. "These aren't your personal belongings that you can just take whenever you please."

For a moment I was certain I'd been caught, and that Benedict would drag me down those winding stairs and lead me back to the Countess. But then, just as I was trying to decide where to hide Agnes's ring, I heard another person trudge into the room and emit a long, drawn-out sigh.

"If the room is to be treated like a vault, then why isn't it bolted shut?" Peter's voice drifted up to me, angry and judgmental.

"Fear works better than a lock," Benedict said. "No servant would dare to enter this part of the castle. Now put it back. Right now. And don't ever presume that her Ladyship's property can be so easily divided."

"It's only a necklace. I was going to return it."

"That girl has addled your brain with her pining requests and blushing glances, and now she has you acting like a damn fool."

"I deserve to be rewarded." Peter's voice shifted from a whimper to a growl. "Why can't I have my way with her before..."

"Because the Countess has spent a year preparing for this, and if you jeopardize her plans she'll throw us all to the wolves."

"Maria is weak and lonely," Peter said, "and much too scared to run away. Besides, she trusts me completely."

"Perhaps, but she's cleverer than you think," Benedict told him. "Not to mention obstinate."

"But what harm is there in showering her with some attention?"

"Maria will receive plenty of attention when I light a roaring fire beneath her. Until then, you are not to deviate from the plan."

"I'm tired of guarding a beautiful chest that I'm not allowed to open," Peter said, and I heard his fist slam against a wall.

"Your anger is justified," Benedict said, "and you'll have your revenge, but if you give the Devil a foothold he'll drag you down into the deepest pits of hell."

Peter grumbled some more and scuffed his feet on the floor. Then I heard a clamorous clinking.

"Now put it back," Benedict said, this time louder and more fierce.

There was a soft cascade of slithering chains as Peter added his necklace to one of the towering piles that littered the wobbly shelves.

"Your main task is to watch over the girl," Benedict told him. "Not to stroke her hair and charm her with expensive jewelry."

Without another word, the two of them left the room. The door closed, and the latch slid into place. I listened as they walked down the corridor, fearful they might return, and then I sat in silence for several minutes, picking at my scabbed thumb until I gathered enough courage to stand up. I lunged at the pile of books and knocked them to the floor, my hands shaking as angry tears spilled down my cheeks and tightened my face into a snarl. I cursed myself for being so naïve, for misjudging Peter's plotted betrayal as nothing more than the capricious whims of an adolescent boy who'd been scarred by a deranged upbringing.

I turned toward the window and gazed out at the forest. My eyes raced across the tops of the trees, following that green canvas until I could just make out the foggy outline of the Little Carpathians way off in the distance. I rested my forehead against the glass and shut my eyes, aware that Agnes's ring was squeezing my finger, and knowing that, one way or another, my time at Čachtice Castle was coming to an end.

CHAPTER XXI

WITH EACH PASSING DAY, the remaining girls in the etiquette academy grew more arrogant, parading around the castle as if they were treasures to be adored. There were now fifteen of them—each one learning manners and customs she would never have the opportunity to enjoy—and every empty space at the banquet table was met with celebration rather than suspicion. Given their bouts of boastfulness, I avoided the girls whenever possible, which proved difficult given that the Countess wanted me near her at all times.

And then there was Peter. I despised him with a vehemence I had never known, and his failed attempt to procure a necklace only intensified his shameless urges. I always wondered where he might be lurking, and I feared being alone with him. Fortunately, Benedict watched over him to ensure there were no more blunders, which meant we saw little of each other save for a quick kiss at the end of the night, or some hurried whispers as we passed each other in the kitchen. I continued my charade of teasing him. I tossed out worthless compliments and appeased him with lingering stares. I basked in his frustrations, and relished how his eyes ached when they wandered across my lips and down the curve of my neck, the way his hands reached out to touch my cheek, only to find empty air when I turned away and withdrew into the darkness.

Peter's treachery was a white-hot ember that I clutched tight in both hands, pressing it against my body until vengeance burned a hole in my chest. And it was this searing pain—along with Agnes's ring—that I brought into the chapel for my final meeting with Father Barosius.

As usual, he was crouched behind the altar, muttering prayers while his thick fingers skimmed over the wooden rosary that was draped around his neck.

I closed the door and approached him. "I can spare only minutes. Helen thinks I'm outside fetching wood for the fire. Is there any news from Count Zrínyi?"

"He's issued a formal complaint with the Hungarian Parliament, but..."

The priest's look distressed me. "Have I been abandoned?"

"No, but he warned me that the word of a servant carries little heft among the nobles."

Kneeling down beside him, I slipped the ring off my finger and handed it to Father Barosius. "This belonged to Agnes from Patvarc. She was short with brown eyes...raven-haired with dimples on both cheeks."

"I'll deliver it to Count Thurzó personally."

"Thurzó?"

"Yes, the king has put him in charge of investigating the Countess. Now that he believes she is murdering young girls from the aristocracy, he's ordered Count Thurzó to collect evidence, as well as signed testimonies from priests and noblemen."

"But the festival begins a week from tomorrow." My voice rose as panic uncoiled within me.

He took my hand. "The festival will last for three days, and I believe you'll be safe until the second night...on the solstice...when there exists the proper balance between light and dark."

A sharp clang resounded from somewhere outside at the end of the corridor. We shrank back and stared at the chapel door, waiting for it to swing open, our chests heaving.

Father Barosius leaned closer. "Everything laid out in that field...the arrangement of the squash and pumpkins, the clothing, the autumn colors, even the people who are present...it must all be used to heighten the spiritual connection. Only when the Countess has established a divine essence...at the heart of which is the fire...will she have honored the gods with her offering."

I thought about the Countess and her meticulous nature, how she organized everything in her life with a determination that bordered on fanaticism. "How many people need to be present?"

"In most Pagan ceremonies, three is considered the magic number...much like our reverence for the holy trinity...but the number four is also important because it corresponds to..."

"The seasons?"

"Yes, as well as the four natural elements...earth, air, fire, and water."

I bristled again in thinking of how I'd been a pawn in her devilish game, of how I'd been woven into the fabric of her detailed preparations, many of which she'd set into motion long before I arrived at the castle. And then—just as Father Barosius glanced again toward the chapel door—something he said flashed in my mind like sunlight glinting through a crack in the clouds.

"What colors?" I asked him.

"Ones distinctive to autumn…red, orange, yellow."

Three colors. Three dresses. One red, one orange, and one yellow. All made of silk with lace cuffs and a V-shaped collar, the necklines stitched with four…

"And what of diamonds, Father?"

He considered this for a moment. "Besides symbolizing wealth and power, they're vessels of positive energy, strengthening the bond between two worlds, one physical and one spiritual."

Three dresses. Each studded with four diamonds. One dress for the Countess, one for Helen, and one for Anna.

I stared at the wooden cross above the altar, scraping my knuckles against the flagstones as if I might rub away the shame that was rising up inside of me, enraged that my own fingers had played such an intricate part in stitching together the means of my own destruction.

"You must convince Count Thurzó to arrest her before the festival begins." Again, I felt myself on the verge of screaming.

"I'll do everything in my power to save you." He held up Agnes's ring. "If no one decides to act, then we'll smuggle you out through the underground tunnels and hide you in the church."

"I fear there won't be time, Father."

"We're not yet crushed. Hard-pressed perhaps, but not destroyed. In the meantime, you must not draw attention to yourself, Maria. You must not stray from your daily activities. If you arouse suspicion…if the Countess senses even the slightest wrinkle in your behavior…she'll imprison you in the deepest hole she can find."

Days and nights washed over me in rapid succession. I stumbled around the castle like one paralyzed in a dream, exhausted from sheer terror and fearful that no one would arrive in time to save me. Every morning I awoke with anticipation, hoping this would be the day when Count Thurzó rode up the winding hill with the king's soldiers. But as the sun continued to rise and set, the atmosphere grew more dismal and somber, as if the castle had been shut off from the outside world. I found myself staring out the windows and lurking near the gatehouse. I prayed for a galloping cloud of dust, but no man or beast crested the horizon.

The Countess summoned me to her bedchamber several times that week, ordering me to brush her hair and to rub Greek lotion made with honey extract into her skin. Anticipating her desired prize, she kept to the upper floor of the castle, content to eat her food off silver trays, and if she ventured into the lower depths it was only to soak in blood.

Peter continued to prowl after me, and the more I pulled away the more frustrated he became. He shed his caring demeanor like a snakeskin until he was reduced to a sniveling husk, and the only compliments he offered were toward the Countess, whose joyous mood he knew better than to disturb.

One afternoon—as I was heading toward the kitchen for a piece of fruit and a crust of bread—he surprised me at the bottom of the stairs and pulled me into the Great Hall.

"Have you forgotten all your promises, Maria?" His rough hands hung loose around my neck.

I forced a smile, conscious of his thumb pressing into my collarbone. "I've neither neglected nor misplaced them."

"Then why am I not feasting on them, one at a time?"

"Because they were subject to certain rewards, which I've yet to receive."

"Yes, though not for lack of effort."

"Surely you can filch something as small as a ring...concealed neatly in your pocket?" I raised my voice, aware that he was moving closer and pinning me against the wall.

"You might be leaving here soon," he told me. "Shouldn't we make the best use of our time together?"

I took his hand and placed it against my cheek. "Perhaps when the festival is over...when we can steal more time alone...maybe then we can sneak away to a dark corner and dust off those promises...one at a time."

His face softened, but only for an instant. "I'll find you a ring," he said, though his words were shaded with menace instead of compassion. "And I'll do so before the beginning of the festival."

Mindful of Peter's constant rage, I avoided those darker recesses and moved through corridors where I was assured of less violent company. This proved easier than expected, for as the festival loomed closer, Helen watched my every move, and no sooner did I leave one room than I would hear her footsteps treading behind me. She followed me into the kitchen when I ate my meals; she stepped outside when I gathered wood in the courtyard or tended to the chickens. No matter where I journeyed—both in and around the castle—I felt as if a chain had been manacled to my ankle, and that someone was constantly pulling on it to ensure I didn't run off into the woods.

Two days before the festival was to begin, Helen brought a white dress into my room and held it up to the candlelight. It was plain and ordinary, a piece of gossamer with long, frilly sleeves that resembled a monk's robe. Given the splendor and radiance of the gowns I had sewn for the Countess, I was surprised at the simplicity of the fabric until I realized it was disposable and would soon be reduced to cinders.

Helen tossed the dress into my arms. "You will wear this during the festival."

I smoothed out the flimsy material and pressed it against my body. "Thank you, miss…but…"

She frowned. "You do know how to put on a dress, don't you? Surely, there have been times in your life when you were required to bathe and look presentable."

"Yes, it's just…" I brought the dress to my nose and inhaled. It smelled musty, as if it had been locked away in a trunk. "I only worry that it might become ruined in the midst of so much smoke and ash."

Helen cast me a disparaging look, though it was etched with a wry smile. "The dress will serve its purpose, Maria, of that I have no doubt."

Then she turned and shut the door, leaving me alone in my room. For the next several hours I sat on my lumpy bed, praying and shuddering in the impending gloom as I listened through stone walls for the distant sound of salvation.

The harvest festival began on the evening of September twenty-first. I was ordered to bathe and change into the white dress, and then I was borne away by the Countess and Helen. Neither one wore the special gowns I had stitched and sewn. Instead, they appeared in simple ivory dresses. They escorted me down the grand staircase and led me through the curving corridors until the three of us stepped outside, dazzled by a bright orange sun that slipped below the horizon.

They walked on either side of me, clutching my arms as though I sensed their evil plot and might try to escape. The hem of my dress brushed against the ground, and without thinking I hiked it up so as not to dirty it. The cold air swirled around me—smelling of grass and newly turned earth—and I heard the steady hum of crickets. Overhead, the wind gusted through the branches, and through the tops of the trees I watched dark clouds slither across the sky, revealing a cluster of stars that shone bright in the gathering darkness.

The servants had been locked away in their shabby quarters, and in front of me stood the remaining nobles, dressed in their fancy gowns. They milled around in idle chatter, nibbling sugar cakes and dried cinnamon sticks. I marched forward, aware that all eyes were now turned toward me, and as I drew nearer to the pyre I was aware of how high it towered above me, stretching into the sky like some grotesque hand reaching out from the grave.

I had imagined a private ceremony with the Countess and Helen and Anna, but instead of cauldrons and hooded figures, there were crisp autumn leaves and the sweet smells of nutmeg and juniper. I anticipated everyone bent low and whispering secret prayers, but instead there was laughter and singing. Fat acorns decorated the base of the altar, and strewn around the rest of the pyre were flasks of red wine, ears of corn bundled together with twine, and several large pumpkins that were already turning moldy.

The nobles seemed oblivious to my ragged breaths and trembling footsteps, and their presence unnerved me. Were they aware of her Ladyship's plan? Was this execution meant to be a public celebration? Surely, the Countess, given her penchant for privacy, wouldn't want to circulate knowledge of her unholy deeds, especially amongst a gaggle of giggling girls.

Benedict approached the pyre with a large torch. He threw it into the pyramid of kindling and dried leaves, which flared up in a quick burst of heat. I stepped back, watching as the fire rose higher into the night sky, the flames dancing and leaping as the wood hissed and popped. Someone handed me a cup of hot apple cider, and I drank it in a trance, my eyes transfixed on the roaring inferno before me.

After several minutes, Anna appeared in the midst of the revelry, holding two large candles. One was black and the other was white. Leaning forward, she placed the candles on the pyre, securing each one in a bowl of sand, and then she lit the wicks with a small hazel twig she pressed against a burning ember.

"Maria." Peter tapped me on the shoulder, and when I said nothing he spun me around and took my hand, his eyes gleaming as if consumed with fever. "I have some news that should please you."

I flung off his hand. "Nothing could please me except to awaken from this nightmare."

Peter made to grab me, but his lunge was impeded by Benedict, who grabbed him by the scruff of the neck, whispered into his ear, and dragged him away toward the edge of the crowd.

A wall of heat prickled my face as drops of sweat collected on my forehead. Wisps of smoke curled around my arms and legs. I stood rooted to the ground while those around me continued to eat and drink, congregating in their own private clusters while they laughed and sang songs. They danced barefoot around the leaping blaze and watched thick streams of smoke billow into the vast night sky.

The Countess remained silent—her arms folded, her cheeks reddened from the intensity of the fire—but no sooner did thick lines of wax drip down the sides of each candle than she stepped forth and held up her hands.

The crowd hushed, and everyone gathered around the base of the pyre in a tight circle.

"Tonight, we celebrate the equinox," she said. "We acknowledge that there is harmony and order in the universe, that there is a balance of night and day. And tonight, in giving thanks for the crops we have reaped, and for the good fortune we have received, we also seek balance in our own lives." The Countess wrapped her left hand around the white candle, then her right hand around the black one. Hot wax spilled onto her fingers and dripped down her slender wrist, hardening into long jagged streaks that rose up in the flickering light like bulging veins pressing against her translucent skin.

"This black candle symbolizes the darkness…" she said, "…the pain and hardships we hope to eliminate from our lives during the winter. While this white candle symbolizes the light…the joys and accomplishments we wish to bring forth in abundance so as to ensure a healthy and productive spring."

Everyone raised their glasses and drank to God and his blessings, then the songs started up again and more sugar cakes were passed around along with baskets of fresh fruit. I wandered the field, clutching an apple in my hand, biting into it every now and then when I felt on the verge of collapse, relishing the way my teeth cut into that hard red skin to pierce the soft white flesh.

My shivering increased the farther I strayed from the fire, so I lingered near the edge of the crowd. On the other side of the pyre, through writhing flames, I caught sight of Peter watching me. His features were hazy in the wavering space between us, his smile distorted in the smoky air that rippled outward in blistering waves, and it was only when he raised his hand high above his head that I realized what he'd wanted to tell me, for when he stepped closer I could see—quite visible in the blinding light—a small silver ring on the pinky finger of his left hand.

CHAPTER XXII

I AWOKE THE NEXT morning in a state of panic—restless and petrified—not even sure if I had ever fallen asleep. I opened my eyes to find my nightgown drenched in sweat, the blanket strewn across the floor, and a pillow clutched tight in my arms as though it might protect me from the evil that was coming soon to take me away.

Next to the blanket, crumpled in a ball, was my white dress. The bottom edges were tinged green from the wet grass, and there was a faint brown stain from where I'd spilled a bit of cider when someone knocked into me. I grabbed the dress off the floor and held it to my nose. It smelled of smoke, an earthy blend of charred oak and apples and nutmeg. I laid it on the bed and looked away, dreading the moment when I would have to slip it back on and trudge outside toward the waiting fire.

I had stayed close to the Countess for most of the night, especially after it became clear that Peter had fulfilled his promise and expected me to slink off into the woods so he could claim his prize. However, he dared not approach me while the Countess was in such a jovial mood, for while she kept a casual watch on me it was clear that Benedict was keeping a strict watch on Peter, and thus his movements were limited to circling the pyre like a prowling cat.

I put on some clothes and crept out of my room. It was still early, the sun just risen in the sky. The castle was quiet. Despite my inner turmoil, I was famished, so I tiptoed down the grand staircase toward the kitchen. As I rounded the corner, someone snuck up behind me and clamped a hand over my mouth. I clawed and thrashed like a wild animal. An arm wrapped around my waist and lifted me off my feet, and then I was swept away down a side corridor. My assailant dragged me into the cold damp shadows, and then my body went limp when we passed behind the tapestry and I realized we were descending into the underground chamber.

We proceeded through the main room and entered the cavern filled with curio chests and towering racks of wine bottles. But instead of pulling me into the next chamber with the three barred cells, we turned into a side tunnel, passing beneath a stone archway. Several minutes later the path ended in a small cavity that contained only a large armoire and a torch set into a wall sconce. A putrid smell hung in the air. I was thrown to the ground, and when I looked up—peering into the murky light—I saw Peter smiling down at me.

"I appreciate your willingness to join me, Maria. I promise I'll make it worth your while."

I stood up, brushing dirt off my knees, and backed away until I collided with the armoire. "When a man wishes to romance a lady, he shouldn't drag her off into hidden corners."

"Then she should surrender herself when asked." Peter held out his hand, revealing the ring I'd glimpsed the night before; it was an orange moonstone encircled by four yellow sapphires. He slid it off his pinky and handed it to me. "Put it on."

The ring was a bit small, but I twisted it onto my index finger, managing a weak smile as I glanced around the room so as to take in my surroundings. The cavity in which I now found myself was low and narrow, the floor rocky and uneven. Peter stood between me and the tunnel, so escape was impossible. And I was buried too far underground for anyone to hear my screams.

"Do you feel beautiful?" He stepped closer and exhaled a long breath, licking his lips as he took my trembling hand in his. "You're exquisite…even in this cruel darkness…a bottle of wine that has yet to be uncorked."

I pushed him away. "You swore to protect me once, and now you accost me like some thief."

"A thief steals what doesn't belong to him. You belong to the Countess, and are therefore mine by association." He stroked my cheek. "And as for protecting you, I've done that admirably. You're still alive, are you not?"

I spat in his face. "Your smugness repulses me."

He laughed. It was a loud boisterous chuckle that echoed inside the tiny chamber. "And your naiveté amuses me, Maria. You still believe I wish to bury you in my arms like a passionate lover, but what I wish most of all is to bury you...and every last peasant...deep in the cold hard ground."

His candor, and the blunt manner in which he delivered it, shocked me. "It's the Countess, isn't it? She's perverted your mind with her own delusions."

Peter kissed my forehead. "You're lucky to have known your parents. It's a blessing I was never afforded. I can't recall much about mine...only muddled glimpses of my mother holding me in her lap, or my father driving the horses at the front of the wagon." He took a step back and looked at me with disgust. "But my most vivid memory is of the night they died. How the murderers tied their hands and arms with cord...how they were beaten with clubs...whipped until their skin was slashed and torn...how my mother suffered more than two hundred blows before dying."

"The Turks—"

"Did not kill my parents," he shouted.

I recoiled as specks of spittle dotted my face. "But you said..."

"I never said the Turks were responsible for my parents dying. You assumed as much in your profound ignorance." Peter grabbed a fistful of my hair and jerked me toward him. "One doesn't easily forget the sight of peasants in the midst of a revolt, burning and looting and murdering innocent people as they slither across the countryside."

"Terrible manners, indeed," I said. "A few of which you seem to have picked up yourself with relative ease." I fought to stand straight and tall, and to look him in the eye, though my knees shook and my lips trembled.

"Retribution must be dealt in absolutes, Maria." Then, pushing me aside, he wrenched open the armoire door.

From out of the darkness tumbled a corpse. It was bloated and swollen, covered with large blisters, several of which had burst open to reveal a thick yellow pus. Clear fluid leaked out of the eyes and nose and ears, dribbling out of the corners of the mouth. I could see several places where bone had started to tear through the cracked skin. The eyes had sunk into the skull, and the gums had peeled back to reveal blackened teeth. But the long hair—now stringy and matted with dried blood—as well as the tattered remains of a simple dress, suggested it was one of the servants who lay before me.

"Most bodies I dump for the wolves," he said, "but every now and then I like to keep one for myself."

I staggered backward, gagging on the smell of rancid flesh.

Peter laughed. "I suppose you find this revolting, but it provides a great comfort to see them suffer as I've suffered. It invigorates me, watching all these peasants putrefy until they become so rotted that pieces of them slide through my fingers whenever I bend down to pick them up."

Suddenly I felt short of breath, certain I would pass out if I didn't run outside and inhale the fresh air. "Who...who is she?"

He sat down beside me and brushed the hair from my eyes. "She's like all the others who came before her. Nobody of importance, and nobody who will be missed."

I turned away and folded my arms across my chest, trying to squeeze myself into a tight ball.

"But you, Maria, are important," he said. "And you will certainly be missed, which is why we must say our goodbyes now before the Countess takes you away from me forever."

Before I could respond, he climbed on top of me, pinning my legs with the weight of his body. I thrashed around and screamed, trying to kick him off me, but in my weakened state I was no match for his aggression. He clutched one of my hands and held it over my head. With his free hand he grabbed the front of my dress, trying to rip it off my wriggling body. He wedged his knees between my legs, pressing them apart as he reached for my face with his coarse lips.

I squirmed underneath him, rejecting his harsh kisses. Cursing, he slapped me with the back of his hand, then glanced down to wrestle with the sweat-soaked fabric. His attention diverted, I lunged forward and bit his ear with all the force I could muster. He reared up and howled in pain—his weight shifting off my legs—and that's when I ripped my Celtic love knot off the chain and plunged it as deep as I could into the side of his neck. As soon as it punctured the skin, I twisted the cross with my remaining strength, yanking downward in a diagonal line until a jagged gash opened up and a thick stream of blood erupted all over me.

Peter's eyes widened. He grasped at his throat, trying to squeeze shut the enormous wound, but the gushing only intensified as warm blood poured down the front of his shirt. I pushed him off me, still clutching my cross, and scooted backward, colliding with the armoire. He gurgled one final insult, the words bubbling out of his mouth in a red froth, and then he toppled over with a heavy thud.

I stared at his body for several minutes, trying to catch my breath. I was uncertain about what to do next. I knew I should return to my room as soon as possible before someone came looking for me, but I was covered in blood and needed to wash it away. The only place with that much water was outside at the well. Then there was the matter of Peter's body. I didn't have time to haul it into the woods, but I couldn't leave it there on the ground where someone might stumble upon it. And the Countess was sure to notice he was missing—especially tonight during the harvest festival—which meant there would be lots of probing questions and even fewer answers.

After careful consideration, I slipped the Celtic love knot into a pocket on my dress, then I grabbed Peter's hands and dragged his body toward me, lifting him up as best I could and shoving him inside the armoire, whereupon I closed the door and secured the latch. That being done, I picked up the corpse, cradling it in my arms like a newborn baby, and carried it through the tunnel where I deposited the crumbling remains in one of the cells, propping it up against the back wall. Finally, I pulled the moonstone ring from my own finger and secured it onto one of the corpse's, cringing as her loose skin peeled away in mushy layers.

I found a large piece of fabric in one of the trunks and returned to the alcove, wiping away as much blood as I could. This soiled piece of cloth I then deposited in the armoire before returning to the main foyer, grateful that the castle was quiet save for a few servants attending to their morning chores. I hid among the shadows and snuck up to my room. I grabbed a clean dress out of the trunk, stole downstairs once again, and rushed outside through the entry door, choosing to walk the long way around in case anyone should be positioned in or around the kitchen.

Approaching the back side of the castle with extreme caution, I ran over to the stone well and pulled up a large bucket of water. I crouched low in the grass, hiding myself from view, and removed my bloody clothes, remembering to take the Celtic love knot out of my pocket. I scrubbed it hard with my fingers until most of the blood had disappeared and only a thin trace of red tinged the silver edges. Then I tied my bloody clothes into a small bundle and tossed them down the well into that black abyss.

I washed myself all over, shivering in the frigid air until my skin was rubbed raw. Satisfied, I put on the clean dress, careful not to soil it with dirt or grass stains. I was about to stand up when a sharp noise alerted me to two servants walking across the courtyard. One of them had kicked over a rusted pail and was now bending down to retrieve it. I squatted behind the well with my knees tucked under my chin and held my breath, glancing up every few seconds to see them swatting at flies and kicking at mushroom caps. I waited while they passed by me on their way to the pasture. Soon, the two figures crested a small hill and their voices faded into the wind as they disappeared from sight.

I returned to the castle by way of the postern gate, creeping into the kitchen like one of the field mice. None of the servants noticed as I sat down at a large table near the fire. I spread out my hair and let the bellowing heat warm me, my arms and legs still trembling.

Though I wasn't hungry, I nibbled on a small crust of bread and drank a glass of ale in the hope that it might soothe my clattered nerves. For the next half hour, I remained silent with my back against the wall, staring down at the grooves cut into the table, knowing I had only hours left to live and that I must soon devise a plan or be engulfed in flames.

It was during this time that Helen slammed her fist on the table, rousing me from my reverie. "Snap to attention, Maria. There's work to be done and here you are looking ill and confused."

"Apologies, miss." I clasped my hands together and thrust them farther under the table, pressing them against the underside so as to stop my entire body from shaking. I hoped she wouldn't notice my wet hair and bloodshot eyes, and I hoped she wouldn't detect the panic in my voice. Taking another generous sip of ale, I slunk lower in my chair and burrowed into the shadows, praying I'd washed away all traces of blood.

Helen leaned forward and wrinkled her nose. "You smell like a fleapit. Worse, you look like you've slept on the hearth all night."

When I didn't respond, she knocked my crust of bread off the table. "The Countess doesn't want you attending tonight's festivities looking like a vagrant. As soon as you're finished pecking at your bread, you'll go upstairs and bathe. Then you can assist me with tonight's preparations."

"But…my sewing…I have clothes to mend, and…"

"I'm sure we can find someone in this great land to sew a button onto a shirt," she said. "It's more important that you appear presentable."

"Yes, miss."

"The Countess is especially cheerful this morning, and she'd like you to remain by her side throughout the day. In her graciousness, she's allowed you the use of her bedchamber so you can bathe in private and not be disturbed."

I offered a smile to show my gratitude, though inside I was screaming. I would have much preferred to bathe in one of the dirty troughs that sat in the pasture, crusted with filth and swarming with mosquitos.

After Helen left, I drank another glass of ale and stared at the roaring fire. Feeling nauseous, I tossed my crust of bread to a scrawny dog that was sniffing around the table. Servants rushed past me with their arms full of pewter plates and cast-iron pots; they carried bottles of sweet wine and bronze trays loaded with chopped vegetables. I ignored them all, though not a single one approached me, perhaps sensing my heightened state of despair. When the kitchen became too crowded, I stood up and made my way toward the main foyer.

Hurrying through the Great Hall, I passed Viktoriya walking in the opposite direction. She glanced over at me and our eyes met for a brief second. Her hair was disheveled, and a thin layer of dirt encircled her ashen face, but I noticed a sense of pride in the way she thrust out her chest, and how she bared her teeth as if she were ready to fight at a moment's whim. I thought back to that terrible day in the kitchen when she and Sandra had pressed me for information, and how I'd swatted away their mounting concerns, believing I was shielding them from further harm.

Without thinking, I grasped Viktoriya's arm and led her down a side hallway. She didn't object, only raised her eyebrows while uttering a small cry of surprise. When we reached the tapestry, I broke down and confessed everything I'd seen and heard since my arrival at the castle, including Sandra's murder and the true reason for the creation of the etiquette academy. I revealed how Peter carted the bodies into the forest, and I told her about the recent visits by Count Thurzó and Count Zrínyi. Finally, I divulged where exactly in my room I'd been hiding the names of all those girls who had fallen prey to her Ladyship's perverse desires.

Viktoriya became still, one hand covering her mouth. She sucked in a quick breath, then shuffled back against the wall. "Why?" she asked me. "Why now…after all this time…are you telling me these horrible things?"

"Because if anything should happen to me…if I'm led to that pyre tonight with no hope of deliverance…you must escape through the tunnel and find the priest."

She placed her hand on the tapestry. "I don't want to go down there, Maria."

"I know, and I pray you never have to." I kissed her cheek. "Hide yourself when Helen locks up the servants. Once we're all outside, the castle will be deserted and you'll be free to sneak away."

She continued to pester me with questions—her voice rising and falling as her emotions swung between anger and desperation—but as the minutes passed I became more and more fearful of Helen, worried she might come looking for me if I didn't appear in the Countess's bedchamber as she had instructed.

Silencing Viktoriya, I drew her away from the tapestry and again reiterated the location of the secret tunnel leading to the church. I begged her to be cautious, and to waste no time in seeking out Father Barosius if any harm should befall me. I pulled the Celtic love knot out of my pocket and pressed it into her hand, imploring her to keep it safe until I could collect it again at a later time. Then, taking her arm, I guided her back to the main foyer where I bid her goodbye, praying that—unlike Sandra—I would somehow see her again.

The Countess sat in her chair by the window, sipping a cup of tea mixed with honey and cinnamon. Next to her lay a silver plate piled high with smoked sausage, goat cheese, and sweet bread. She smiled when I entered the room and beckoned me toward her.

"Maria, you look absolutely dreadful. I want you to appear lovely tonight, and instead you show up mangy and unkempt, as if you'd just crawled out of a potato sack." She pointed at the small bronze tub, which sat behind a folding screen on the other side of the room. "The water is still hot, though not scalding."

I thanked the Countess and walked over to the tub. Slipping off my shoes, I knelt down and dipped my fingers in the water. The temperature was warm and inviting. I removed the rest of my clothes and dropped them in a heap on the floor, then eased myself into the tub, groaning as my sore muscles loosened and a wave of drowsiness swept over me. I inhaled the steamy air and detected a faint hint of chamomile.

Closing my eyes, I let my entire body slide under the water, and I remained there for as long as my lungs would allow, savoring that small bit of solitude. I wondered what it must feel like to drown, and if Sandra had felt any pain when she'd sunk to the bottom of the lake. Gazing up at the rippled surface—mesmerized by flashes of distorted light—I felt an overwhelming desire to stay on the bottom of the tub where my entire world was quiet and safe, to empty out my lungs until I lost consciousness and drifted to a place where the Countess could never find me.

When my chest began to burn, I broke through the surface with a loud cough, gripping the curved sides while I fought to regain my breath.

The Countess loomed over me—looking as cold and impassive as always—sprinkling herbs and rosemary oil into the water and swirling them around with the tip of her finger. She picked up a coarse linen cloth that was draped over the edge of the tub and ordered me to lean forward. I sat up straighter and hugged my knees, gazing out the window as she began washing my back in long, rhythmic strokes.

"Your skin is absolutely flawless," she said. "One doesn't often find such magnificence beyond a castle wall." She scrubbed my ears and down the base of my neck, then wrung the dirt out of my hair. "Did you know that the Greeks would apply honey to their skin to prevent aging, and sometimes olive oil to make it shine? Or that the Egyptians would use the dye from plants and berries to mask their gray hair?"

"No, Countess."

She washed my arms, then moved around to the front of my body. "Holy men like to preach the importance of preserving our soul, but they neglect to honor that which is visible. If our soul is like a butterfly, isn't our skin the cocoon that nurtures and protects it?"

"Yes, Countess." I scooted back and raised my legs into the air, one at a time so I wouldn't slide under the water. She dripped rosemary oil onto the cloth, wrapped it around my feet, and scrubbed the soles until they glistened. Afterward, she washed my legs until they were pink from the heat.

"I've taken much pleasure in our time together," she told me. "And although we both know you must leave here eventually, please take comfort in knowing you've served a special purpose, and that my gratitude...which isn't so easily awarded...you have certainly earned."

"Thank you, Countess."

She traced her finger along the length of my neck, in much the same way I'd seen Benedict use a sharpened knife to open a girl's throat. "You seem particularly naked today, Maria. What's happened to your precious love knot?"

"The chain...it broke this morning..." The words wedged themselves to the roof of my mouth. "...while I was dressing...I put the pieces in my trunk."

The Countess laughed. "Some believe that wearing silver will keep evil spirits from entering the body. I hope your little mishap hasn't extended an invitation to the devil."

I grasped the sides of the tub and stood up, letting the water drip off my body. She handed me a towel and I stepped onto the ivory rug, shivering as the cool air caressed my skin.

"Your dress is being cleaned in preparation for tonight," she told me. "In the meantime, you'll stay with me for the remainder of the day. I'll have some food brought up if you're hungry, and if you wish to sew, you may do so by the window where you can be assured of adequate light."

"I would hate to invade your privacy," I said, "especially on a day when there are speeches to be made and ceremonies to be honored."

She handed me a woolen robe and watched as I put it on. "Surely, you don't consider me terrible company?"

Her bedchamber, which I'd once found so luxurious and breathtaking, had now transformed itself into a lavish prison. Hidden away from the rest of the castle, I had no means of contacting Father Barosius, or of sneaking away on my own. And if Count Thurzó did arrive before nightfall, how could I show myself in his presence and disclose all that I knew? My freedom was now stripped away, and under the watchful eye of the Countess it seemed I would remain trapped in that room until the fire was ready to receive me.

CHAPTER XXIII

MORNING TURNED INTO AFTERNOON, and the sky grew ominous as massive black clouds soared over the Carpathian Mountains. A chill crept into the air, stirred by a gusting wind. I nestled inside the soft woolen robe, wrapped in the lingering scents of rosemary and lavender. For over an hour, I paced back and forth—fidgeting with my damp hair and chewing on my fingernails—until the Countess ordered me to lie down. She said I looked weary, and she didn't want me fatigued for the evening's celebration. I pretended to be thankful and rested my head on one of her satin pillows, trying to forget how Peter had torn at my dress with such viciousness, and how I'd ripped open his throat with the same degree of vengeance.

Helen brought me a glass of red wine and a bowl of goulash. Despite my growing consternation, I drank and ate for the sake of conserving my strength. After lunch, I sat by one of the windows in a plush velvet chair, peering through the red damask curtain at that infernal pyre. Servants walked back and forth from the kitchen to the field, adorning the structure with crisp autumn leaves and fresh piles of kindling. Pumpkins and apples and squash—having grown moldy and misshapen from direct contact with the wind and rain—were replaced with their fresher and sturdier brethren.

The Countess sat at her desk, composing letters and writing in her journal, and the furious scribbling of her quill was the only sound in the room. Sometimes, she would rise and sashay in front of the tall mirror, caressing her cheeks or pinching the folds of skin beneath her chin. During these brief moments she would glance over at me, and though she remained silent, her leering unsettled me. If she could have peeled off my skin with her bare hands, I believe she would have done so.

Sometime after five o'clock, Helen came into the room—her face knotted up in concern—and murmured a few words to the Countess. They conversed for several minutes, stealing glances at me while they whispered into each other's ears, and then the question I'd been dreading shot across the room like a thunderbolt.

"Maria, have you seen Peter?"

"Not since last night…at the festival."

The Countess advanced upon me, her eyes reproachful. "Not even this morning?"

"No. I went straight to the kitchen as soon as I woke up."

"By yourself?"

"Yes."

"You saw no one in the corridor?" she asked. "You spoke to no one while you ate?"

"No, Countess."

She knelt in front of me. Her hands gripped my knees. "How strange. He fawns over you at sunrise…he lusts after you at sunset…and yet he's neglected you since yesterday?"

I cleared my throat. "It appears so, yes."

"And where do you think he might have run off to?"

"I don't know. He spends a lot of time in the forest…it's possible he got lost, or…maybe he met with an accident…perhaps a wolf attacked him…"

The Countess frowned, her pale lips pressed together in an ugly slash. "I've never had cause to question his loyalty…and he would never abandon me. He knows how important today is."

"Perhaps Benedict will know what's become of him," I said.

Helen hovered over me, blocking out what little sunlight filtered into the room. "Benedict is engrossed in his own preparations, Maria. He has neither the time nor the inclination to keep track of everyone who marches in and out of the castle."

The Countess turned to Helen and said, "If something has happened to Peter, I expect it was sudden and serious. Find Benedict and tell him to search the castle. And if he still can't locate the boy, have him search the forest. And ask the servants if any of them saw or spoke with Maria this morning. Peasants are often forgetful, and it's possible our little seamstress has misplaced some of her memories."

I was brought to my room and instructed to remain there until someone came to fetch me. Once the door closed, I broke out in a sweat and my heart seemed to freeze in my chest. Would Benedict conduct a thorough search of the underground tunnels? And what would happen if he discovered Peter's body?

I sat on the edge of my bed until well past dinner, dozing off several times only to be jolted awake by the rush of a chilling nightmare. I stared at the door until it became a large brown blur, and when it finally creaked open there was an explosion of white as the Countess unfurled the white dress and placed it in my arms. In that instant, all hope drained out of me, and I felt like a hollowed-out version of my former self.

She watched as I took off her robe, and it was only then that I noticed she was wearing the red silk gown I had sewn for her, complete with the lace cuffs and the V-shaped collar, the neckline studded with four sparkling diamonds. She waited until after I'd changed into the dress and slipped on my brown sandals—which proved difficult given my locked legs and trembling hands—before saying, "You look as radiant as ever, Maria, but something appears to be missing."

I stared at her, confused.

"Your Celtic love knot," she said. "Give it to me. Perhaps it can be repaired for tonight's ceremony."

My knees bent, and I seized the edge of the bed so I wouldn't pitch forward. "I'm not sure where…I looked for it earlier, but…"

The Countess opened my trunk and threw out its contents—dresses, shifts, tunics, a pair of leather shoes, a gray coat, and the faded green hood my mother had given to me. When there was nothing left inside, she slammed it shut and said, "How tragic. I suppose it just fell out of your pocket, rolled down the stairs, and continued on its merry way?"

"I don't know…I seem to have mislaid it."

Without another word, she grabbed my arm and hauled me out of the room. We proceeded down the grand staircase. I noticed the sun had set long ago, and in its place the night had spread out its darkness like a thick blanket.

When we reached the main foyer, Benedict stood there waiting. His boots were muddy and his hair was wild. His forearms were dotted in blood, as if they'd been nicked by branches and brambles.

"He's not in the forest," he told the Countess. "Nor have I found any evidence to suggest he's even left the castle. The boy seems to have vanished."

She made a sweeping gesture with her arm. "Lock up the servants straightaway, and then bring our guests into the village. Make sure they're entertained and well-fed. Apologize for my absence and explain that I've been detained, but I'll rejoin them tomorrow once I've settled my affairs."

"Everything has been arranged exactly as you requested," he told her. "The other two are dressed and waiting."

The Countess grabbed my arm, but instead of leading me outside toward the field, we turned down a side corridor, heading in the opposite direction of the pyre. I wanted to ask where we were going, but my tongue sat in my mouth like a heavy stone. I stumbled forward—my eyes darting in every direction as if expecting a monster to leap out of the shadows—and with each new corridor we entered, my apprehension mounted and I became more despondent.

We snuck behind the tapestry and proceeded down that dark passage. Up ahead, I heard scattered whispers and saw orbs of flickering light. The air smelled of ginger and cloves, not of blood and decay.

I entered the chamber to find Helen and Anna standing next to the copper tub. Helen wore yellow while Anna wore orange, each gown a splash of bright color like small dabs of paint on a gloomy canvas.

Behind them stood a wide table fitted with rusty manacles, and underneath it sat two small cages. One cage was empty; the other contained three rats. Beside the empty cage rested two thick coils of chain.

Surrounding the center of the room was a small ring of white candles, and it was into this fiery circle that I was now thrown.

Horrified, I stayed on the floor, shaking and choking back sobs while the Countess removed a torch from the wall. Anna and Helen reached under my arms and yanked me up. They heaved me onto the table, cursing when I kicked and scratched at them like a madwoman. Despite my hysterical lunges, they held me down with their weight. They shackled my hands and feet.

I screamed until my lungs burned. The Countess clamped her hand over my mouth and waited until my cries for help tapered off into muffled pleas. After thrashing around for several more minutes, I crumpled into exhaustion and fought to control my breathing, which was harsh and ragged.

The Countess leaned over me and said, "I'll remove my hand, and in return you will not speak unless you are answering a direct question. If you disobey, I'll burn your hands and you will never sew again."

She withdrew her hand. I remained silent.

"Where is Peter?" she asked me.

"I swear I don't know."

"You're a poor liar, Maria. I believe you know where he is, just as I believe that misplacing your love knot on the same day is not a coincidence."

"The chain broke this morning."

"Whether he tried to steal it from you isn't my concern. I only wish to know his whereabouts, which you'll divulge without further delay."

The iron shackles cut into my wrists and ankles, and the more I tried to move the harder they scraped against my skin. "I saw him last night, at the festival."

"When did you see him today?"

"Only yesterday," I told her. "Not since then, I swear."

"Is he here in the castle?" she asked.

"Please. I don't know."

Helen picked up the empty cage, one side of which was open, and placed it atop my chest. Then she and Anna stood on either side of me and pulled tight the attached leather straps, hooking them under the edges of the table as if I was a patient being strapped down for an operation. The cage bore down on my chest, crushing my ribs, and I struggled to suck in even a single breath of the musty air.

"If you don't tell me what happened to Peter," the Countess said, "Anna will place those rats into this small cage. And then I'll hold this torch against the bars. Have you ever seen rats scramble to escape, how they screech and claw and whip themselves into a frenzy?"

Anna bent down. I heard the cage door screech open, followed by a loud squeal. I turned my head to find her stroking one of the rats, which squirmed in her bony hands, its long whiskers twitching.

"There will be nowhere for the rats to go," the Countess said, "and in their panicked attempts to avoid the scorching heat, they'll be forced to burrow into you."

When I struggled once more against the heavy chains—shouting for help as my wrists began to bleed—she gave an exasperated sigh. "All I want is an honest answer. Is that really so difficult, Maria?"

"A torn dress can always be mended," Helen said, "but a ripped-open stomach won't fare so well."

I looked over at the rat, its pink nose sniffing the air, its black beady eyes gleaming in the sparse light, and at that moment I knew I'd been abandoned. I grew frantic and tried to sit up. I thrashed and screamed as if possessed by a demon. I caught sight of blood dripping down my ankle, and I imagined each rat eating me alive from the inside.

But there still existed—somewhere within my wounded body—a glint of reason, and as I gazed at the streams of blood flowing from my wrists and ankles, I remembered that the Countess needed me alive. She wouldn't have spent months arranging this particular night, or being meticulous in harboring her secrets, only to watch me die in the bowels of the castle.

She had stripped away everything important in my life. She had let those around her scavenge whatever happiness I might have clung to, and now she demanded to know what had become of Peter. Not knowing his fate, and being powerless to help him, had deprived her of the control she coveted. But, unbeknownst to her, I knew when and how my time in Čachtice would end, and that empowerment now weakened the authority she demanded.

"Tell me where he is," she said, "and I'll remove these shackles. We'll meet the others at the festival, and tomorrow we'll laugh over this silly quarrel."

I stopped resisting and let my body relax. Immediately, the chains felt lighter, and the tightness in my chest dissipated.

"Maria, you will answer me!"

I turned toward the Countess. Her face looked coarse and splintered in the unsteady glow of a quivering flame. "No," I said.

She blinked several times, her mouth slack. Then she handed the torch to Helen and told Anna to unstrap the cage. As soon as it was removed, I inhaled a large breath of air, coughing as the dust and smoke invaded my aching lungs.

The Countess grabbed my face and dug her nails into my skin, squeezing with such force that I feared she might crush my jaw. Only when I cried out in pain did she bend down and whisper into my ear.

"I will enjoy making a spectacle of you, Maria. You've insulted my generosity, and you've desecrated my home, and for that I will reduce you to ashes. It will give me great pleasure to hear your skin crackle, to see your shriveled heart lying amid a pile of your smoldering bones."

With the sleeve of her gown, she wiped away the tears streaming down my face. "And after I've thrown what's left of you to the wolves, I'll bring your mother to the castle so I can introduce her to the rats."

She glanced up at Anna, who stood across from her on the other side of the table. "Bring our guest something to drink. She must be thirsty after her valiant struggles."

Anna hobbled across the room and picked up a large crystal goblet set atop a slab of carved stone. Clutching the goblet in both crooked hands, she ambled back—careful not to knock over the burning candles—and handed it to the Countess.

"My dear, it's only a bit of wine," Helen said as I fought against the chains. "With a pinch of dried belladonna stirred into it."

Anna stood behind me, one hand pinching my nose, the other gripping my chin. The Countess pried open my mouth, thrust the goblet against my lips, and poured the sweet wine until it spilled down the sides of my face. I gagged and tried to spit it out, but Anna held my mouth shut until I was forced to swallow the poison.

"When this mixture takes effect," Helen said, "she'll be docile enough to carry outside."

I closed my eyes, wondering how many seconds or minutes would pass before I sank into oblivion, until the world I knew became a horrifying parade of bizarre hallucinations.

The women gathered around me. They watched. They waited.

My heart beat faster and my mouth became dry. The air grew heavy and settled on top of me like the lid of a coffin. The noises in the chamber, once so deep and echoing, now became faint and muffled.

Soon a sporadic clack—sharp and rhythmic—rose up from the deadened space around me. I turned my head toward the passageway and fought to open my eyes. The candleflames were soft and splotchy, just flecks of yellow light smeared across my line of vision.

The three women stood silent. They watched. They waited.

My legs began to spasm. My skin started to burn. I listened as the clacking became more pronounced, wondering if something evil was rising up from the earth below me. It lengthened into a steady procession of clanks and thuds, each one swelling in volume until I realized that someone was approaching the chamber with hurried footsteps.

From the darkness appeared a pinpoint of light. A torch held by a shaky hand stepped out of the passageway, and a face emerged from the orange glow like a bird unfurling its wings.

It was Viktoriya.

I struggled to throw off my chains, to warn her against coming any closer.

And then she moved aside, and from out of the tunnel came Count Thurzó and Count Zrínyi. They were accompanied by six armed guards.

"What is this intrusion?" the Countess yelled.

Count Thurzó pointed to Anna and Helen. "Secure these women," he told the guards, "and then search the rest of the castle."

Two guards placed them in chains and escorted them out of the chamber. Count Zrínyi rushed over to unshackle my hands and feet. Though I could no longer feel the table beneath me, I managed to sit up and fall into his arms.

Count Thurzó, seeing me freed, now turned to the Countess and said, "In the name of the king, you are under arrest."

"On what grounds?" she asked. "Interrogating this servant who's conspired against me, and who's now implicated in the disappearance of a young boy?"

"For the torture and killing of highborn ladies," he said. "You, Elizabeth, have shamed the aristocracy and tainted the respect of all who would serve you."

She scoffed. "And where is your evidence?"

"I have signed testimonies from several priests, as well as from various members of the gentry."

"Many of my servants have succumbed to cholera," the Countess told him, "and several of those highborn ladies have left here of their own accord. I will not be held responsible for sickness or cowardice."

"There are enough speculations to warrant an investigation," he told her, "and I suspect we'll find more damning proof once my guards have explored the castle."

"I will not admit to anything," she told him.

"The cells…" I pointed behind me at the dark entryway. "She keeps the bodies there…until the forest…for the wolves…"

The Countess laughed. "The girl is delirious, Gregory. You're more likely to find heirlooms than horrors, but if you feel inclined to rummage through chests of drawers and trip over broken bottles, then so be it."

Count Thurzó instructed Count Zrínyi to remain in the chamber, then he led two of the guards deeper into the underground tunnels.

I sat on the floor, my head resting against the leg of the table. Viktoriya ripped off the hem of my dress and tore it into strips. She bandaged my wrists and ankles. I tried telling her all that had happened, but the exertion ravaged my body even further and I became lightheaded and queasy.

The Countess stood tall and resolute, her fists clenched. She didn't look at me once during their prolonged absence. Instead, she gazed up at the ceiling, fuming.

When they finally returned from their search, Count Thurzó was the first to speak. He thrust out his chest, his square jaw set firm, and announced that a body had been found in one of the cells. "It's badly decomposed," he said, "but it's definitely the body of a young woman. And she's wearing a jeweled ring, so she must be nobility."

"Impossible," the Countess said, concern now worming its way into her steely voice. "Someone must have snuck down here and hidden the body." She pointed at me. "This little whore is to blame, and I want her arrested."

Count Thurzó knelt down beside me. "You are Maria?"

I nodded.

"Father Barosius tells us you can provide evidence to support these grim accusations?"

"The east tower…" I reached up to grip the edge of the table. "The entire room…clothes and jewels and necklaces…"

Count Zrínyi helped me to my feet, and when I began to slump over he put his arm around me. He rested his other hand on my forehead, which was drenched in sweat, the skin turning red and blotchy. "What have they done to you?"

"Belladonna," I whispered.

Count Thurzó motioned to one of his guards. "Go and find the physician. Bring him here immediately. Meet us in the main foyer."

Without a word, the guard dashed into the passageway.

"My room…" I grabbed onto the collar of Count Zrínyi's cloak. "We need to go there…written down names…"

Both Counts stood on either side of me, gripping my loose arms, and together they escorted me out of the chamber. Behind us trailed Viktoriya, followed by the Countess who was flanked by three guards, their swords at the ready should she attempt to flee.

I don't remember walking through the narrow passageway, or the Countess hurling insults at my back. I don't remember the rank smell of the tapestry or being guided up the grand staircase.

Instead, I remember staring down at my sandals and my ripped dress, watching my feet shuffle along the floor and not recognizing them as my own. I remember collapsing when we entered my room, and how Count Zrínyi picked me up and laid me on my bed.

I felt myself sinking into a black pool of nothingness. Summoning my last bit of strength, I pointed to the full-length mirror, still covered with the blue linen cloth. Count Thurzó tore off the sheet, and in its reflection I saw the Countess glare at me with intense hatred.

And before I lost consciousness, I heard her utter a gasp of surprise as he pulled the mirror away from the wall and turned it around, revealing not just the solid oak veneer, but the dozens of names and villages I had scrawled across the wood in my own blood.

EPILOGUE

FOR THE NEXT FEW days, I lay shut up in a darkened room, swooning with hallucinations as a raging fever withered my body. I drifted somewhere between lucidity and delirium, tormented with spasms and bouts of nausea, the blackness around me peeling back, layer after layer, until time became a circle and all I knew was a constant throbbing in my skull. Each ragged breath was met with distant whispers as servants wiped my forehead with cold rags. They pried open my mouth to spoon in water and tea, and honey mixed with apple cider.

When I finally opened my eyes, I found myself in one of the guest rooms, the satin pillows rising up around me like a fortress, the black sheet twisted around my legs and soaked through with sweat. My wounds had been rubbed with salve and covered with fresh bandages, and though I still ached—my ribs were bruised, and my legs were an ugly mess of cuts and bruises—my thoughts were no longer in disarray.

Immediately, a search was begun to locate Peter. It was believed that, fearing he might be caught, he'd run off into the forest where he was killed by wolves. When Count Thurzó questioned me about his whereabouts, I shook my head in ignorance, refusing to divulge what had transpired between us that morning. Despite my heroics, I was still a peasant, and I didn't want to admit I had killed him for fear I'd be arrested.

Still, no matter how many times I tried to forget about Peter, I kept picturing his stiffened corpse lying inside that armoire, his body bloated and leaking, his flesh being gnawed on by a legion of rats.

The Countess, I learned, was under house arrest. Count Thurzó mandated that she be kept below the castle in her secret chamber, and that all tunnels leading into it should be barricaded with iron bars. Several armed guards were now posted at each gate, and she was denied any visitors save for dignitaries—whom she welcomed—and priests—whom she abhorred. In addition to a trunk filled with her dresses and gowns, she was given a dilapidated desk, some blank sheets of paper, and her ink quill.

Benedict had been captured while returning to the castle that night. Count Thurzó placed him in chains—along with Anna and Helen—and ordered his guards to bring the three of them to Vienna. Once there, they were jailed as accomplices of the Countess and tortured for information. Rumors persisted that they were beaten with wooden clubs, pressed with heavy weights, and subjected to thumbscrews until they passed out from the pain.

As for the remaining students, they were shocked when five guards appeared out of the fog and knocked Benedict from his horse. And they were more appalled when those same guards then shackled the injured man and led him down the hill. Amidst a flurry of speculation, the girls were escorted back to the castle and ordered to pack up their belongings. The next morning, Count Zrínyi announced that the etiquette academy had officially closed. Stunned, the bewildered girls were then placed into waiting carriages for safe return to their families.

Most of this information I gathered from Viktoriya, who brought me food and drink every morning and afternoon. She sat on the edge of my bed, sharing news and gossip while I slurped hot soup and ate an assortment of jarred fruits and vegetables. She told me how Count Zrínyi had stayed in the castle to restore order. Outside, the altar and foundation were torn down, and the wood—most of it warped and charred—was stacked next to the storehouse to use as kindling during the long winter months.

Several days later, Count Zrínyi assembled all the servants in the Great Hall and announced that everyone would be provided with new clothes and given three meals a day, including small rations of pork and salted fish. No longer was starvation a form of discipline; no longer would servants be beaten for knocking a bowl of lentils onto the floor. Finally, he announced that the servants' quarters would no longer be locked at night.

While Count Zrínyi seemed a decent man, there were rumors that he planned to move his family into the castle, and that his niceties were performed not out of respect for the servants, but in the hope that his good will would persuade us to testify against the Countess. If—as the Countess herself had suggested that day in the library—Count Zrínyi was concerned about the Báthory family's rights and titles, then perhaps his seizure of the castle suggested a strategy to retain her Ladyship's money and estates should King Matthias ever attempt to claim them as his own.

Within a couple of weeks, my wounds had healed and I was able to move around for long stretches without becoming sore or dizzy. At Count Zrínyi's request, I moved my belongings into the servants' quarters, overjoyed to have a window once again so I could gaze outside at the sun, admiring how the mountaintops in the distance seemed to puncture those feathery clouds drifting high above the forest. Below, the field looked barren without the pyre and all its embellishments, though the emptiness was a welcome change, like a dark stain scrubbed clean from a white cloth.

Most days, I sat alone in my room amid a towering pile of clothes. I couldn't bear the prolonged stares and accusatory whispers—all fed by wild stories and outlandish assumptions—so I avoided questions and company, preferring to mend a ripped seam, or to sew large black buttons onto a woolen shirt. I tended to the animals in the pasture and fetched buckets of water from the well. Other times, I assisted Viktoriya with the cooking, especially if Count Zrínyi was entertaining visitors in the Great Hall, or meeting in the library with witnesses who journeyed into Čachtice from neighboring villages to provide damning testimony against the Countess.

From the beginning of October until the end of December, Countess Báthory spent her days writing long and detailed letters to the aristocracy. She proclaimed her innocence and reminded the nobles that her husband was a national war hero who had donated his money to crown and country. She demanded to see her children; to visit her other castles so she could conduct public and private business affairs; and to meet with King Matthias at his palace in Vienna to discuss matters of extreme importance. Each request, however, was denied by Count Thurzó. In retaliation, the Countess accused him of not defending her honor and, instead, of choosing to place his misguided faith in the random scribbles of a deceitful peasant.

More than ever, I wanted to return home to that small cottage in Trenčín. I wanted to tell Mama everything I had seen and heard; and as each word sailed out of my mouth, I wanted to bury it deep in the ground and pack the dirt under my feet. But I had been witness to so many atrocities, and Count Thurzó needed me to provide a detailed account of which girls had been murdered, as well as when and where and how. Every few weeks, he returned to the castle to meet with Count Zrínyi and to apprise him of the ongoing investigation. By overhearing several of their conversations, I discovered that Benedict and Anna and Helen had all sworn their innocence, concocting ridiculous lies so as to ingratiate themselves with the king and thus escape being sentenced to death. They blamed the murders on jealous servants, ghostly apparitions, and even on Peter, claiming the boy was unbalanced and immature, a wild gypsy her Ladyship had adopted out of kindness who could never control his bestial tendencies.

One afternoon, as I walked past the library, I heard Count Thurzó say, "The king wishes for the trial to be public and quick, and for it to be held at the court in Bratislava. He's most insistent."

"He's vengeful and vindictive," Count Zrínyi replied. "And while his actions might be warranted, you shouldn't agree to this, Gregory. We can't allow all of Hungary to learn of these murders. The Báthory family has won high honors on the battlefield and its name shouldn't be disgraced in the eyes of the nation. I refuse to have our legacy thrust into the murky shadow of this degrading woman."

"Agreed," Count Thurzó said. "In the interest of future generations, everything should be done in secret. If a court were to try her, it would infringe upon our laws to spare her life, and despite having seen her crimes with my own eyes, she shouldn't be executed by virtue of her nobility. To do so would set a dangerous precedent."

Furious, I fled to my room and beat the pillow with my fists, thinking of Sandra and Violet and Agnes, and the horrible means by which they had all died. How could the Countess escape death when there was a bloody trail winding behind her, hundreds of bodies long? She had torn apart families and abused her power, had reveled in the torment she inflicted upon others, and instead of suffering retribution she was now cowering behind the Báthory coat of arms, using her birthright as a protective shield.

I was accustomed to ache and regret—to being mocked and ignored by those who rang silver bells, and whose deep pockets jingled with shiny gold coins—but I raged at this injustice, remembering how my father always swore that peasants were still being punished for the uprising of 1514. Tired of famine and plague, and a declining income that widened the gap between rich and poor, the peasantry had formed an enormous army and burned manor houses and castles. Their leader, Gregory Dózsa, rallied them to loot churches and kill priests, and they roamed the countryside for months, evading the government until Dózsa was captured and a red-hot metal crown was placed atop his head. He was burned alive at the stake, and his followers were forced to eat his flesh. Those peasants had died for someone else's sins, and now the Countess would live in spite of hers.

I pushed a pile of clothes off my bed and lay down, embracing the anger that flourished within me and knowing that without its strength I would have broken apart months ago, abandoning my resolve when I needed it most. Perhaps I should have felt more forgiving or compassionate—clinging to scripture and reciting prayers like a pious peasant—but I had learned long ago that hard living produces hard feelings.

The trial began in the middle of January, though the Countess was not present, for by law she wasn't allowed to be tried. Instead, Benedict and Anna and Helen were brought to Čachtice—chained and emaciated—to answer for their crimes. Peter, his body still missing, was declared dead, and thus unable to provide additional testimony or defend himself against their pointed accusations.

Hundreds of noblemen descended upon the small church where judgment would be delivered, each one sharing outrageous stories about the shocking brutalities. There were rumors that the girls' flesh was roasted over a fire and fed to the servants, and that the priest had brought the Countess a Holy Bible and asked her to read it, whereupon she threw it to the ground. There were even reports that she drank the blood of her victims out of a golden chalice, and that sometimes she drank directly from the hot stream as it gushed from their slit throats.

Count Thurzó presided over the two-day trial—assisted by several of the king's representatives—and he began the proceedings by announcing that through the grace of his Royal Majesty, he hoped to protect the good and innocent, and to punish the guilty. "Elizabeth Báthory is charged with committing outrageous and inhuman acts," he told the spectators, "and for performing satanic cruelty against Christian blood. According to my own estimation, she has murdered approximately six hundred and fifty women during the past ten years. These bodies were disposed of in many ways. They were placed into coffins, they were left in the forest for wolves to eat, and some were even left in underground cells to rot."

There were gasps and murmurs, a crescendo of anxious prayers, and then Count Thurzó summoned Father Barosius to appear before the court. Hands folded before him, the priest described his frequent meetings with the Countess. He revealed how he had traveled to the castle several times a week to load stacks of coffins onto his wagon, and that he was ordered by Helen to bury them in the churchyard as soon as possible under the false pretense that cholera might spread to the rest of the village.

After the priest related his tale, Count Thurzó praised him for composing a poignant letter to King Matthias, reiterating how such correspondence was crucial in initiating the investigation into her Ladyship's nocturnal activities. Other representatives then commended Father Barosius for his persistent bravery, after which Count Thurzó revealed that, by order of the king, hundreds of bodies had been dug up in the churchyard, and that the girls had not died of cholera, but of severe beatings and lacerations. Many of the bodies revealed broken bones, prominent bite marks, and blackened skin from severe burns. As a final piece of evidence, Count Thurzó noted that almost every girl had been found naked and with her throat slashed.

Later in the afternoon, Benedict sat in front of the panel, his wrists and ankles manacled, his large frame hunched over the table as though he might become sick at any moment.

Count Thurzó asked him, "How many women and young girls has the Countess killed?"

"I don't know about any women," he said, "but I was present for the killing of at least one hundred girls. Most of the bodies were brought into the forest, but I know that four girls were burned in a pit by the side of the road, and three are buried in a garden near the courtyard."

"And how were these girls tortured and killed?"

Benedict glanced over at Helen and Anna, his once rugged face now thin and sallow. "They were whipped, sometimes as many as five-hundred lashes in a row, until their bodies burst. Sometimes Anna Darvolia cut off their hands with scissors. Other times, Helen Szentes stabbed them with needles if their work wasn't done well. If they couldn't start a fire, or if they didn't lay an apron straight, they were taken down to the chamber and tortured to death."

Helen was summoned soon after. She sat with her hands in her lap, the manacles scraping against the bottom of the table whenever she shifted her weight. Her long blonde hair had grown whiter during her imprisonment, and she appeared dirty and broken, not unlike one of the servants she'd often scolded or beaten.

"Who assisted the Countess with these tortures?" Count Thurzó asked her.

"Benedict Deseo often burned them with a fire iron and stuck pins in their mouths, or sometimes the nose and chin. One girl was killed because she stole an apple. When the girls shamed themselves in front of royal visitors, he locked them in the underground cells for a week and allowed them to starve."

"And what of Anna Darvolia?"

"She instructed the Countess in cruelty and was her confidante. She knew that sometimes the Countess enjoying burning the genitals of naked girls with a blazing torch. And she, herself, would pry off pieces of their bodies with red-hot tongs. Often, I saw her sitting alone in a darkened room, muttering sacred chants and spells. When Count Zrínyi visited the castle a few months ago, she put a curse on him and he was weakened for days."

The room settled into an eerie silence, save for the guttering flames that bent and twisted whenever a blast of wind shook the holy walls. Then—in the midst of collective shudders and shocked faces—Helen licked her lips and leaned toward her inquisitors, pronouncing in a loud voice, "Anna Darvolia has always lived in the forest. She is very knowledgeable in magic and the art of poisoning."

On the second day, several servants were summoned to the church and asked to reveal the horrors they had witnessed. Viktoriya said, "The Countess was very particular about what she wanted. If a girl didn't move fast enough, or if she didn't speak in the proper tone of voice, then the Countess and the others would stick pins in her mouth or chin, or they'd beat a girl on the palms of her hands and the soles of her feet until she passed out."

Another servant, Izabella, related the following: "One day the Countess was so sick she couldn't get out of bed, and when the goblet of wine she asked for wasn't filled to the top, she demanded that the girl be brought to her bedchamber so she could punish her. While Helen taunted the girl and held her down, the Countess bit her on the cheek and burned her arms and legs with red-hot spoons."

Throughout this testimony, I sat in the last row of pews, studying the stained-glass windows, my mind lost in the birth of Christ and the wedding at Cana so I wouldn't have to relive each terrible moment as it was spread open like a treasure map and brandished in front of an eager and vindictive public. Occasionally, I glanced over at the assembly to find Helen glaring at me, or Benedict tugging at his beard, that horrid scar seeming to rise and fall with each nervous pull. Anna, who had fallen ill with headaches and shivers, sat crumpled in a chair near the fire, her voice a low rasp that betrayed her delirious state. In her weakened condition, she wasn't permitted to testify before the court.

Whenever I became nervous—fearing someone might discover Peter's body, or perhaps accuse me of being a willing participant in the murders—I had only to touch the Celtic love knot that hung around my neck. Viktoriya had replaced the chain and polished it to a shine, and when my fever broke she had presented it to me, beaming with pride at having saved my life. During those long, miserable days inside the cramped church, I cherished the cold silver trailing through my fingers, feeling its strong connection to home. I took solace in knowing my prolonged nightmare would soon be over, and that, unlike most of Countess Báthory's victims, I was fortunate enough to even have a future.

By mid-morning the parade of servants had ended, and I stood before the court to explain how I'd been brought to Čachtice as a seamstress, and that I soon became privy to her Ladyship's secrets. The court expressed great interest in my detailed account, for not only was I an intended sacrifice, but I had shed my own blood to collect information about each of the victims. For the next few hours, I answered each and every question with as much confidence and memory as I could rally.

Clutching a cup of water, I told Count Thurzó that I'd seen a girl stabbed with scissors and later murdered; I recounted my secret meetings with Father Barosius in the chapel, and I described the room in the east tower filled with dresses and gowns and discarded jewels. I spoke of collecting belladonna in the forest, and how I'd watched Anna prepare the soul cake for Count Zrínyi. And then, just when I felt as though I would collapse from exhaustion, I revealed to the court how the Countess had bathed in the blood of her victims, and how Benedict had dragged the girls into the underground chamber and hung them on chains so Helen could cut their throats.

Given my damning testimony, the court didn't wait long to find the torturers guilty. Count Thurzó rose before the onlookers and declared the condemned to be, "murderers of innocent people, henchmen in this terrible execution, and in need of fair punishment for your horrible and nefarious crimes." He spread his arms wide and stared down at each cowering shape. "Because it's the sacred course of justice, I must send a warning and an example to all those who have acted, or plan to act, in a similar way. For you three, however, who have perpetrated such monstrous deeds, you shall receive the sharpest punishment and eternal shame."

Benedict, Helen, and Anna were sentenced to die on the morning of the third day. Benedict was beheaded, still maintaining his innocence like a coward, and his head was placed on a pike at the entrance to the castle. Helen and Anna, having stained their hands with the blood of Christians, had their fingers torn out one at a time with red-hot iron tongs. They were then burned alive, and their charred remains were placed on pikes to the east and west of the castle.

That afternoon, the court convened and declared Countess Báthory to be insane and unfit for society. The king's guards led her into the church at dusk, whereupon Count Thurzó handed down her punishment.

"You, Elizabeth, are like a wild animal," he said. "You have brought a paralyzing fear into our hearts by slaughtering many innocent women, of both noble and lower levels. You don't deserve to breathe the air on this earth, or to see the light of the Lord. You shall disappear from this world, and you shall never reappear in it again. As the shadows envelop you, may you find the time to repent your cruel life. I hereby condemn you to lifelong imprisonment in your own castle."

The Countess never showed one trace of remorse. She stood tall in her red gown and scowled at each of the king's representatives, marching up to their long table without first asking permission. "You have angered me with this trial," she told them, her voice still harsh and unbending after so many months underground. "Others have provided false testimony against me, and you've accepted it as gospel. I have been a mistress and a mother to all of my servants, and I've never been treated right, whether in small or large matters. Today is an affront to the nobility, and I promise that you and your children will regret my fate."

Immediately, the Countess was taken to the west tower and walled up inside her bedchamber. All of the mirrors were removed, as were most of the rugs and furniture, including her private tub. She had the luxury of a bed and a large trunk full of dresses and gowns. She was allowed a desk and a chair, and the privilege of writing letters to her children. Many of her books were brought up from the library so she could read in solitude by candlelight. The windows were replaced with blocks of stone and her only contact with the outside world was a small hole in the door through which servants passed her food and water.

Before returning to Vienna, Count Thurzó issued a decree that—by order of King Matthias—Elizabeth Báthory's name would never be spoken again in polite society.

I left Čachtice a few days after her imprisonment. For my troubles, I was given thirty gold pieces, fifteen pounds of wheat, and deep white scars on the top of each thumb.

Father Barosius offered to escort me back to Trenčín, but I declined. Instead, I asked him to provide me with only a strong horse and a day's supply of food and water. He appeared hesitant, staring off into the woods, until I clasped his hand and said, "You mustn't worry about me. I know the way home."

As I passed through the gatehouse that cold morning, I looked up at the tower and imagined Countess Báthory peering into the murky shadows, cursing the wrinkles that stretched across her cracked skin, and bemoaning the mottled spots that marked her complexion. She was living between stone now, searching in vain for a reflection that would never appear, and I smiled to think how she would sit alone in that darkened room, shrinking into a dusty red gown she would probably wear until the day she died.

ACKNOWLEDGMENTS

MANY PEOPLE JOURNEYED BESIDE me as I braved my way toward Countess Báthory's castle, and I'm grateful for not only their company, but also for their unwavering support.

As with all historical novels, the research process is both invaluable and necessary. I read many books detailing the life of Elizabeth Báthory, including letters and court documents. In researching the early 1600s, I studied clothing, language, cuisine, landscape, and other pertinent details that enhanced the gothic flavor of the novel while presenting a realistic depiction of life at Cachtice Castle. Of particular importance were several visits to the Natural Portrait Gallery and the Victoria and Albert museum to study their artwork and exhibits. The primary and secondary sources available to me were vital in crafting this particular story.

My wife, Joey, is not a fan of horror, but she agreed to read an early draft of the novel. She did peek through her hands while reading the more grisly parts, but she lived to tell the tale. As always, her suggestions were helpful in completing the final draft.

My good friend Matt Keating also read one of the first drafts. I appreciate him donating his spare time, as well as his insightful comments, which helped to shade in several historical details.

I'd like to thank Christopher Payne, President of JournalStone Publishing, for giving this novel a good home, as well as my editor, Scarlett R. Algee, for her notes and suggestions.

A huge thanks to my agent, Anne Tibbets, for believing in this book and for championing it with the same intensity the Countess exhibits toward preserving her own beauty. Anne's feedback was instrumental in strengthening the story and mood. Her ideas helped to further develop

Maria and the Countess while also accentuating the suspenseful atmosphere.

Finally, I'd like to thank everyone who loves this genre as much as I do. Your excitement is infectious and continues to send me into the woods, steering me through the dark underbrush so I can creep among the ruins and explore hidden paths.

ABOUT THE AUTHOR

MICHAEL HOWARTH was born in Hyannis, Massachusetts. He is the author of two critical texts, *Under the Bed, Creeping: Psychoanalyzing the Gothic in Children's Literature* and *Movies to See before You Graduate from High School* as well as a young adult novel, *Fair Weather Ninjas*. A Professor of English at Missouri Southern State University, he teaches Children's Literature and Film Studies in addition to directing the Honors Program. He currently lives in Joplin, Missouri with his wife, the poet Joey Brown.

CPSIA information can be obtained
at www.ICGtesting.com
Printed in the USA
LVHW110915100421
683894LV00011BA/359

9 781950 305797